AL

THE
LEGEND OF
GASPARILLA
AND HIS
TREASURE

CAROLYN ARNOLD

HIBBERT & STILES
PUBLISHING INC.

Hibbert & Stiles Publishing Inc.
www.hspubinc.com

This is a work of fiction. Names, characters, places, and incidents are the products of the author's imagination or are used fictitiously. Any resemblance to actual events, locales, or persons, living or dead, is entirely coincidental.

Names: Arnold, Carolyn, author.
Title: The Legend of Gasparilla and His Treasure / Carolyn Arnold.
Description: [Ailsa Craig, Ontario] : Hibbert & Stiles Publishing Inc., [2020] | Series: Matthew Connor Adventure series ; book 3
Identifiers: ISBN 9781989706237 (4.25 x 7 paperback) | ISBN 9781989706244 (5 x 8 paperback) | ISBN 9781989706268 (6.14 x 9.21 hardcover) | ISBN 9781988353999 (ebook)

Additional format
ISBN 9781989706251 (6 x 9 paperback large print edition)

THE
LEGEND OF
GASPARILLA
AND HIS
TREASURE

Prologue

Manhattan, New York
A Monday in January, 10:46 AM Local Time

You're telling me he's in possession of some diary that contains clues to a vast fortune?" She clucked her tongue and studied the man before her. His name was Roman. He was built like a tank and deadly—just the way she liked her men. But even better, he was loyal and submissive when it came to her. Then again, she owned him.

"That's right, ma'am. It has clues to some pirate's treasure or something."

"Pirate treasure or *something*?" She slapped him hard across the face, and he stiffened but otherwise didn't react. "What makes you think I'd be interested?"

"Could be worth tens of millions." Roman wasn't meeting her eye, and that was a wise move on his part. She couldn't tolerate insubordination.

"And you think I need the money?" The question was bait and rhetorical. Of course, she needed the money. She could never have enough. The office they were in was in her Manhattan high-rise, which was one of three such buildings she owned in the United States. She had no qualms admitting that her wealth was based on ill-gotten gains and shady deals in the antiquities market—unless she was talking to law enforcement, of course. But if a girl wanted the finer things in life, she had to be willing to take risks and create her own luck.

"I asked you if you think I need the money," she repeated with emphasis, circling around him.

"Everyone needs money." Gaze straight ahead. Back ramrod straight.

She rounded the front of him again, smirked, and put a hand on his cheek that was bright red from her assault. "You're very right, darling. And I expect you to succeed in securing this diary for me. Do we have an understanding?"

His eyes darted to meet hers briefly. "Yes, ma'am."

"Very good. Do whatever you have to do. *Kill* whoever you have to." With that, she turned and looked out over the city streets below, waving a hand over a shoulder. "You're dismissed."

One

Matthew Connor would rather be jumping out of a plane. That would actually be fun. Instead, he was looking over a crowd of easily two hundred. He'd stared death in the face many times as an archaeologist, adventurer, and treasure hunter, but he just might be brought down by a little public speaking. His heart was beating rapidly, and his hands were clammy. All those eyes on him, waiting for him to say something. He swallowed roughly and plastered on a smile. His throat felt stitched together.

He glanced at his best friends in the crowd. Cal Myers was at the back of the room taking pictures. A God-given talent he possessed and put to good use. As a professional photographer, he freelanced for some of the biggest-name magazines out there, including *National Geographic*.

Robyn Garcia, a beautiful Latina angel, was in the front row. She met his gaze and dipped her head in a show of encouragement. Her position as a curator at the Royal Ontario Museum in Toronto, Canada, often put her in situations when she needed to speak publicly. She'd been his coach and helped him practice his speech. She stressed that he needed to hook people by immersing them in a story right from the get-go.

"Good day, everyone," Matthew started and winced. He was doing it all wrong. Scratch jumping out of a plane, he'd take confinement in a tight box over this and be left to battle his claustrophobia. He gulped and gripped the podium. To hold him up. To give him support. His eyes caught his watch. He still had the full thirty minutes of speech ahead of him. He should be thankful for the opportunity—and he would be if his nerves weren't threatening to embarrass him.

He and his friends were invited to the Smithsonian National Museum of Natural History in Washington, DC, for the opening of their City of Gold exhibit. Not bad for three adults in their early thirties. He, Cal, and Robyn all played a part in discovering the Incas' lost city, but he was the one who'd netted a two-book publishing deal after returning from Egypt last July. He let his publisher, Golden Books, rope him into doing this in promotion for his upcoming book on the city, due out late fall. A book he still had to finish writing. A book he was supposed to have submitted another five chapters for two weeks ago. He should be home writing. Yet here he was, strangers staring at him. Some impatient, some mirroring his awkwardness, others smiling encouragingly.

He took a deep breath, exhaled slowly. "Imagine a city of gold, where the streets are paved with gold, the buildings are made of gold, but to get there, danger awaits you around every corner…" He paused briefly, and Robyn smiled at him and dipped her head in approval. He went on with his speech and hoped he'd pulled off what Robyn had said during a rehearsal about his words being "impactful."

Of course, it would probably be more difficult for him *not* to show the emotions he felt as he retold the journey of finding the lost city. It had been the most personal quest he'd been on. His nemesis, Veronica Vincent, had kidnapped Cal's girlfriend Sophie, and it was either find the city or risk her life. He could easily summon up the fear and the apprehension. If the threat to Sophie's life or laying eyes on a city that had been abandoned centuries ago wasn't enough pressure, tack on a tight deadline. The fact that the three of them and Sophie had all survived was a small miracle, but not everyone involved with the quest had returned home. And it had eventually taken a toll on Cal and Sophie's relationship.

Matthew would much rather leave Sophie out of the entire thing, but his publisher wanted him to delve deep into it. His editor, Riley Zimmer, had told him more than once, "People like danger, Matthew. It sells books. That's why thrillers are the number one genre out there."

Matthew mistakenly countered that maybe he should write a thriller, then. Riley told him he was, and the fact it had a basis in the real world was even better. It was never hard to miss the hunger for money in his editor's eyes. And it was quite possible his editor knew what he was talking about because as Matthew delivered his speech, everyone was silent, and most appeared motionless. One exception was a fiftysomething man with spiky, gray hair who popped into the back of the room, scanned the crowd, and left just about as quickly as he'd shown up.

Thirty minutes after Matthew had started, he closed his speech, and everyone clapped.

Robyn joined him on stage. He shuffled to the side so she could speak into the mic, but she pulled out a cordless one. "Thank you, Dr. Connor, for your exciting retelling of our discovery of the City of Gold." Robyn clapped her free hand to her forearm, and the audience followed her lead in another round of applause. She gave it a few seconds, then said, "I know everyone's eager to see the exhibit, but we have some time allocated for question-and-answer. Who wants to go first?" She smiled out at the crowd and selected a man whose hand shot up so fast it was like he'd been jabbed in the side.

He stood. Slightly potbellied, somewhere in his late forties, beady eyes. "Why did you go after a legend when there wasn't anything to truly prove its existence?"

"We knew—"

"Your friend's life was at risk," the man cut in. "From what we just heard, you didn't really 'know' anything definitive. Sounds like you took quite the gamble."

Matthew glanced at Cal, who had stepped back from his camera on the tripod. It was rare when a camera wasn't in his friend's face. Matthew had touched on Sophie's kidnapping, as much as he could stomach and to appease his publisher. Under Cal's gaze, he felt like a sellout.

Matthew tightened his grip on the podium. "I had reason to believe the City of Gold was where we ended up finding it." That's what he said, but feelings of guilt were swirling in his gut. He'd had some aerial photographs, shots from ground-penetrating radar, and a hunch. There was another alternative to getting Sophie back, but it wasn't a path he wanted to go down, and it could have landed him and his friends behind bars.

"You couldn't have known for sure. That's a gamble," the man countered with a smug tilting out of his chin.

"When you set out after a legend, nothing is for certain, but we weren't left with much choice. As the saying goes, we were between a rock and a hard place. If we didn't try, Sophie was dead." He paused there, feeling the four-letter word burrow into his chest.

"If you failed, she'd die, too."

"Then it seems luck was on our side, because as you know, we found the city." Matthew was irritated by this twit but was more cognizant of how his questions could be affecting Cal. Sophie had never been a fan of him going on expeditions, and things on that front had gotten worse after her abduction—for understandable reason.

"Anyone else have a question?" Robyn scanned the audience and numerous hands rose. She chose a woman near the back.

The man who'd first been called on was still standing. "You didn't really answer my question, Dr. Connor."

"I believe I did." He tried to tamp this man down with as much etiquette as possible, but his temper was quickly rising to the surface.

"Why did you go after a legend that by all intents and purposes never existed?"

"Again, I feel that I answered that question sufficiently, but in simpler terms, it's what we

do. Myself, my friends. We go after legends."
Matthew caught sight of the spiky-haired man
stepping into the back of the room again. He
returned his gaze to the man interrogating him.
"The world can be a hard, bitter place," he added.
"So many of us have forgotten to dream, but I'm
not wired that way. Someone says something
can't be done—or doesn't exist—and I'm about
proving it can be done or that it does exist."

"So you're naive and fickle."

The audience booed the man, and Matthew
wasn't sure why he was there if he detested him
so much.

"We have others with questions. What did
you want to ask Dr. Connor?" Robyn's tone
of voice left no room for negotiation as she
pointed to the woman she'd chosen before the
twit had interrupted.

Finally taking the hint of dismissal, the
interrogator left the room. The spiky-haired
man followed after him.

"How did you feel when you saw that giant
anaconda?" the woman asked in a Southern
accent. She held a certain charm to her that
softened everyone in the room. "I mean, I can't
imagine I'd remain upright. I hate garters."

Most people chuckled. The woman beside
her bobbed her head.

He coached himself that everything from this
point would be just fine. After all, most people
were there because they wanted to hear what he

had to say. He smiled at the woman and went on to answer her question. He fielded five more questions before Robyn turned to him.

"Dr. Connor, thank you again for being here with us today," she said.

"My pleasure."

Robyn added, "Dr. Connor's book, *City of Gold*, will be available late fall. Be sure to watch for it. In the meantime, he'll be signing posters in the gift shop, starting one hour from now." She gave them fast directions and added, "But take your time enjoying the exhibit. There's a lot to see. Matthew will be around for the next few hours. Now, what you've been waiting for..." Robyn stood back and moved to the left, and Matthew shuffled to the right. Behind them, curtains that marked the entrance to the exhibit parted.

A floor-to-ceiling remodel of the Inca pyramid had the crowd gasping. Visitors would enter a cut-out in the replica and hopefully feel an inkling of what Matthew and his friends had felt when entering the real thing. People wasted no time making their way inside.

Cal joined his friends on stage now that it wasn't the focal point of people's attention. He snapped off a couple of shots of Matthew and Robyn, then lowered his camera.

"Great job, buddy." Cal put a meaty hand on Matthew's shoulder.

"You know you had every right to be up here, too. People know all about your contribution and your..." Matthew left the rest unsaid, but he'd been thinking *sacrifice*. He'd already told Cal on a few occasions that he hated bringing Sophie into the find at all. It wasn't public knowledge that he and Sophie had broken up, but people could appreciate that Cal would have been emotionally distraught on the quest, wondering every moment if Sophie was okay and if they were going to be able to save her.

"Nah, you know me. I don't like the spotlight."

Robyn and Matthew laughed.

"What? I don't."

"Uh-huh." Robyn put her arm around Cal's shoulders. "You tell yourself what you want, but we know you better."

"Hey." Cal narrowed his eyes. He'd always been a ripe target for teasing. "Let's go meander, shall we?" He jacked a thumb over a shoulder to indicate the exhibit. "I'd like to take some candid shots of people enjoying it."

"Sure thing," Matthew said. He was happy that the topic had shifted so quickly from Sophie, but if he knew his friend at all, the guy was still hurting and trying to bury his feelings.

Two

I can't believe my publisher talked me into doing the speech and signing all those posters." Matthew rotated his right wrist. He'd scrawled his name on all five hundred handouts his publisher had provided for promotion of his upcoming book. The splash across the page of *Coming Next Fall* was there just to taunt him. *No pressure.* "I feel like I'm being pimped out."

"Poor guy." Robyn pouted, then laughed. "I think you're being a little dramatic. Maybe taking cues from Cal."

"Hey now," Cal said.

Matthew, Robyn, and Cal were set up in a booth at a restaurant not too far from where they were staying at the Colonial Hotel in the National Mall district of Washington. If the decor didn't give it away as an English pub—with its hunter-green walls and gold-framed photos of celebrities who had made their way through the place—the menu did. They'd already ordered their meals and were working on the beers in front of them.

"Am I being dramatic, though?"

"Usually when you have to ask…" Robyn took a sip of her drink.

"There weren't even five hundred at the presentation."

"You would have picked up people at the gift shop that hadn't made it to your speech," Robyn said matter-of-factly. She pointed to the framed photos at the end of their table that showcased a couple of supposedly famous people—don't ask Matthew their names. "Maybe you'll be up there one day," she added.

"Oh, pretty please." He took a drink of beer.

"As I've told you before, just remember your motivation, Matthew. It's a good one." She smiled at him and sipped her draft.

It had been Robyn's appeal to his ethical side that had swayed the pendulum in favor of accepting the book deal. She had reminded him that his motivation for unearthing legends in the first place was to bring them to the people. And what better way to extend the reach of his finds than to publish a book?

"And whether you like it or not, you better get used to being in demand," she said. "That's what it's like to be famous."

Cal took the cheap shot. "As if you'd know."

"Very funny, Cal." Robyn glared at him.

Same old performance, but Matthew wouldn't change a thing. They'd been a group of friends for the better part of four years now. While Cal and he didn't go back as far as he did with Robyn, their friendship had been solid from the start. One of those relationships where you feel you've known each other forever and the other should know everything about your past even if you haven't told them about it. Matthew was thankful that Cal and Robyn got along well, too. Everyone needed friends with whom to jest and sometimes be brutally honest.

"In all seriousness," Matthew said, "I don't know if I've got what it takes to see this through."

"What exactly?" Robyn asked.

"For starters, the book. Then the touring and public speaking. Mostly the writing." It was a toss-up, but every time he thought about putting words to the page, he started hyperventilating. As if on cue, his phone rang. Caller ID told him it was Riley, but he didn't say as much out loud. "Oh no."

"It's your editor," Robyn guessed.

It was spooky sometimes how she could read his mind—or read *him*. "Yeah."

"Well, answer."

He hesitated. He could guess quite accurately what his editor would want. He took one deep breath, then accepted the call.

"How did it go?" Riley asked. "I bet you were a hit."

"I—"

"Did you sign and give away all the posters?"

"I—"

"What am I thinking? Of course, you did."

There were times trying to have a conversation with Riley was more like listening to a monologue. Matthew waited for his editor to stop talking and would let the silence build before trying to speak again.

Matthew shook his head, and Robyn smirked. Again, like she had read his mind. Besides, she had met Riley in person and knew his tendency to talk over people.

"So? Talk to me," Riley prompted.

Satisfied that Riley was ready to listen, Matthew spoke. "It was good. Lots showed up for the exhibit."

"Your pre-order sales spiked." There was no mistaking the zeal and excitement in Riley's voice. "How do you think it went?"

Again, all about the book and the resulting influx of cash. Nothing was asked about the exhibit itself or how people responded to witnessing history with their own eyes.

"Matthew, how was it received... Good? Bad?"

"You said the sales were up, so that's good." Matthew rolled his eyes. He should probably have sought a publisher and editor more in sync with his goals and motivations.

"Everyone had good questions for you?" Riley asked. There was a twinge to his voice that hinted at frustration, like he was trying to move the conversation up a hill without help. "People showed a lot of interest?"

"All the posters went," Matthew said, finally getting out the answer to one of Riley's first questions. With reflection on the day, his interrogator flashed to mind. Not everything had been positive, but there was no sense bringing up that loser to Riley. "Yeah, everything went great."

"Great...great. So, hey, how are you making out on those chapters? You have them ready for me to look at yet?"

"I'm working on it. As they say, perfection takes time."

"No such thing as perfection in any arena, let alone literature, but I'm afraid deadlines are deadlines. Seven weeks, Matthew—that's all I can give you, and I'll need the entire thing. We need to start the editing process, and the fall will be here before you know it." He paused as if expecting Matthew to jump in and make a vow to get it all done in time—a strong-arm negotiating technique—but he wasn't going to react. Eventually, Riley offered, "But if five chapters feels like too many, why don't you just send me a few by Friday?"

"This coming Friday?" The scooped collar of his T-shirt suddenly felt tight. All of this pressure to write was taking him back to his university days and all the papers he had to produce. He must have been delusional to accept this publishing deal and then stubborn enough to think he could handle it himself. He'd never been wired for writing; he was suited to adventures and high-adrenaline sports. Out in the world, not confined to a desk. He should look into hiring a ghostwriter.

"Yes, of course this Friday."

Matthew tried to pick apart the deadline in his head. Smaller, more manageable chunks. Six days, seven if he counted what was left of a today. A couple of chapters. It really wasn't that big of a deal, was it? "I'll do my best," he said without truly committing and caught Robyn shaking her head.

"Okay, I'll follow up," Riley said, "say, Wednesday, just to see how you're coming along?"

"Sure." Panic burrowed in his chest. Why did he feel such a need to get the message about the City of Gold out there? He was cursing himself and his ideals.

"Great. Good luck. Talk soon." Riley was gone before Matthew could even think *goodbye*.

Matthew pocketed his phone and signaled their waitress. "I'll take a refill," he told her when she came over. He pointed at the beer he'd hardly touched *yet*.

She glanced at his glass and said, "I'll get that right away. Anyone else?"

Robyn and Cal shook their heads. The waitress left, and Robyn leveled a look on him.

"What's going on?" she asked.

He was too busy gulping his beer to respond.

"He'll go out into a jungle or the middle of the desert, but he's afraid of putting words to the page. Oooookkkaaay." Cal laughed and took a draw on his brew.

Matthew wiped his lips and set down his empty glass. "It's just the pressure to write. It's never come naturally to me." *Where's that other beer?*

"Stop thinking about the words and focus on why you're writing," Robyn suggested.

She always knew the right thing to say, and if anyone in their little group was "the glass is half full" sort, it was her. Nodding, he looked past her to the bar. He spotted the spiky-haired man he'd seen at the museum seated at the counter, and the man was watching him. Under Matthew's eye, the man turned to face forward, a poor attempt to conceal the fact he'd been gawking, only made worse when he glanced over a shoulder.

"Earth to Matt." Cal waved his hand in front of his face.

He caught the movement out of the corner of his eye and slowly looked at Cal. "What?"

"I asked if Riley moved up the deadline," he said.

"No, he just wants—"

"Here you go." The waitress set a new beer in front of Matthew.

"Thanks." He took a big swallow of it.

"Not a problem at all." She winked at him and sauntered off with his empty glass.

Robyn watched after the waitress, and Matthew would pay for her thoughts just then. The two of them used to be lovers—more than that, in a serious and committed relationship. He was going to ask her to marry him when they graduated university, but she'd been offered her dream job in the form of a curator at the Royal Ontario Museum, and he wasn't going to stand in the way of that. They'd agreed to remain friends, which was a tricky balance to find sometimes as the romantic feelings were still there.

Matthew's gaze went to the spiky-haired man again, and this time, he found him staring unapologetically. The man got up and headed their way.

"Dr. Connor?" The man was twitchy and awkward and had a satchel strapped across his chest, which he hugged to himself as if someone were going to steal it. He had no fashion sense and was dressed in an olive-green tweed jacket that he wore over a blue, striped collared shirt. That with his navy-blue slacks were the closest he came to a coordinating wardrobe. Even his hair wasn't so much a style, but rather a wake-up-and-*never*-brush 'do.

"That's me." The beer on his empty stomach had him feeling a little carefree, but he still didn't like lurkers. And there was no reason why this man wouldn't know who he was. Matthew's name had been on a large poster set on an A-frame at the door to the exhibit room. He would have passed it to step into the room.

Spiky's gaze darted nervously to Robyn and Cal. Back to Matthew, he said, "Could I talk with you?"

"Go ahead."

"I meant…" He gave another glance to Robyn and Cal. "Alone."

"Anything you have to say to me, you can say to them." Matthew offered a smile of encouragement. The man jittered like he'd downed a pot of coffee, but despite a little voice of caution in the back of his head, Matthew really didn't think the man presented any harm.

"Umm, could I sit down?" Spiky gestured to the half-empty bench where Matthew was seated.

"Sure." Matthew moved over to give him more room.

Spiky sat and continued to hold his satchel to his chest.

"You can put that on the floor or beside you if it's more comfortable," Robyn suggested. She must have sensed his discomfort, too, though it was hard to miss.

"No, I'm good." Spiky readjusted his satchel but retained a tight hold.

"So, I'm Robyn Garcia." She held her hand out across the table, and the man took it.

"Mel Wolf," Spiky said.

"Cal." He flailed a hand nonchalantly.

Spiky dipped his head.

Seconds ticked off in silence.

"What is it that you want to talk about?" Matthew asked.

Another adjustment to his satchel. "First of all, I'm sorry about the guy who was interrogating you during your speech."

Matthew recalled seeing his interrogator and Mel leave the room at the same time. "You knew him? That guy who put me on the spot?" The lightheartedness that came with the alcohol was fleeting quickly.

Mel's eyes darted to the table. "I guess he really did do that."

"He did, but why are *you* sorry?" Matthew wasn't sure he really liked this twitchy stranger.

"I hired him to do that." Mel slowly lifted his gaze to meet Matthew's.

"Why?" Scratch not being sure about liking him; he was definitely crossing over to not caring for the guy.

"It was necessary." Mel itched the tip of his nose. "You see, I needed to know that you're really the man you're made out to be. That you'll pursue treasure even when there's a slim possibility to none that you'll find it. Even when your life and the lives of others are on the line."

"We're not treasure hunters for hire," Cal snapped.

Robyn put a hand on his shoulder, and Cal glowered at her. She shrugged and took a drink of her beer.

"I know...I know," Mel stuttered, "that you're not for hire, but I'm hoping that I can intrigue you enough to help me. You see, I recently bought a house at auction. This house is on Marco Island, in Florida." Mel searched Matthew's eyes, almost as if he expected Matthew to piece together the point of all this from that alone, but Matthew had nada. Mel went on. "Well, I found something that I'm certain you'll be interested in."

It was probably the beer that had Matthew still hearing this guy out. "And what is that?"

"The house I bought is old. It dates back to the late eighteenth century. I happened to stumble across a hidden passageway and—"

"Lots of older homes have them," Cal cut in. "I've photographed a lot of them in my career."

"Sure, but have you photographed any in a home that belonged to John Gómez?" Mel tossed out the name, showing his first sign of spunk.

Cal groaned. "Don't tell me you mean Panther John."

"Who's that?" Matthew asked at the risk of coming across naive.

"Panther John was supposedly someone who lived in the early nineteenth century, believed to have been born in the late eighteenth century. He yapped a lot, told tall tales about his adventures in life." Cal rattled those tidbits off like he'd be more fascinated with watching paint dry. He continued. "In rumor, he's been associated with José Gaspar. Very laughable because that man's existence has never been proven. Never existed, if you ask me."

"What if I told you he did?" Mel smiled, and an expression that typically made its bearer's looks improve gave Mel the appearance of a sloth with fangs.

"Yeah, whatever." Cal picked up his glass and took a swig.

Robyn passed Cal a brief look, then said, "Okay, who is this Gaspar guy?"

"Also known by the nickname Gasparilla," Cal responded, despite her question being directed at Mel. "He's nothing more than a mythical pirate, said to have plundered the Gulf of Mexico and Spanish Main during the late eighteenth and early nineteenth centuries. Lore and something fantastical told to children. No more real than pixies."

"Yet, ask Peter Pan about pixies," Mel rebutted with a slight smile. Less fangs this time.

"See, he's nuts." Cal slumped, his body language screaming he wasn't interested in continuing the conversation.

Matthew studied his friend. "How do you know so much about Gasparilla?" Usually it was him and Robyn who educated Cal.

Cal lifted his gaze from the table where he'd started tracing a pattern on the Formica with a fingertip. "Every year, there's a festival held in Tampa, Florida, in his honor. The event organizers hired me to photograph it one year. Only reason I ever heard tell of him." Cal angled his head toward Mel. "And you said that you can prove Gaspar's existence? I'd like to see what you've got. Rumor was this Gómez character, Panther John, was Gaspar's first mate. But another guy named Rodrigo Lopez was also up for the position. Just like a typical legend, there's so many versions, it can make your head spin."

"Gómez was Gaspar's *son*." Mel adjusted his satchel again but held up his head a little higher, showing some confidence. "Not first mate."

"Sure, okay," Cal said, skeptical. Then his face screwed up. "What even makes you say that?"

"I found a diary in that passageway I mentioned, and it was written by Gómez himself. One entry says that Gaspar was his father."

"Oh," Robyn exhaled.

"Yeah, *oh*. Tell us more," Matthew said.

Cal shook his head. "You two can't be serious. We don't even know this guy." He flailed a hand in Mel's direction. "And even if you found some diary, as you say, anyone could have put it there. Someone's messing with your head."

"I don't think so, Mr.…"

"Myers," Cal said, providing his last name.

"Mr. Myers, I had this diary inspected by someone who specializes in antique documents. The paper and ink date back to the early nineteenth century."

Cal held out his hand toward Mel. "Can we see this diary?"

Mel deflated. "I don't have it."

Cal smirked and shook his head. "Uh-huh. You had it. Now you don't?"

"That's right. I put it in a safe place."

"Yep, okay." Cal looked away and took a gulp of his beer, enlarging his eyes like Mel was cuckoo.

"I swear to all of you that I'm telling you the tru—"

Plates, glasses, and cutlery smashed and clattered to the floor. A few tables away, a busboy had dropped his loaded tray.

Mel jumped, and his eyes shot to the front door as if a gunman had come in and opened fire. "Please, you must listen to me." His voice trembled. "There's a lot in the diary no one else knows about. Like in one passage, Gómez commented that his father often said that his heart will always lie with Useppa. Gómez said he never figured out what that meant."

"Ah, so we're dragging Gaspar's alleged girlfriend into this, too. Why not?" Cal set down his empty glass with a little force on the table.

Matthew and Robyn looked at their friend for an explanation.

"Fine, I'll continue to play along." Cal rolled his glass on its bottom as he spoke. "Some versions of the legend say that Gasparilla was in love with a Spanish—sometimes said to be Mexican—princess. Apparently, he named an island 'Useppa' in her honor."

"Yes," Mel began, "and some legends say she rejected his advances, and he killed her and buried her body on Useppa Island."

His heart will always lie with…

The passage Mel had quoted was kicking around in Matthew's brain. "So, was Useppa the woman's name or just the name of the island?"

"The island's name," Mel said. "As your friend alluded to, her true identity has been obscured in history books."

"One rumor says the woman was Josefa de Mayorga, the daughter of a Spanish viceroy. Other explanations are that Gaspar couldn't pronounce her name correctly—or spell it right, apparently. Hence Useppa, not Josefa, Island. Was the name Josefa in that diary of yours?" Cal asked with a little snark.

"No."

"Even if this diary was, in fact, Gómez's—and again assuming its existence—I'm not really sure how you can believe anything he wrote," Cal said. "Censuses show that Gómez changed his birth date and birth location several times."

"So, he was a real man," Robyn said.

"Don't let that distract you," Cal cautioned.

"Let it," Mel said, overriding Cal. "I have the man's diary. A man who even your friend here hasn't disputed once existed. Now, if a man can't be honest in his diary, then where?" Mel put it to Cal, who shrugged.

"I have yet to see this diary," Cal mumbled.

Mel went on. "The reason Gómez lied about his past was because he was trying to hide his lineage, all in an effort to protect the treasure."

"Let me guess. Also in the diary," Cal stated drily.

Mel nodded and carried on in a lower voice. "Gaspar's treasure is estimated to be worth over thirty million dollars in today's market."

"Rumored to be." Cal crossed his arms, but Matthew sat up straighter. His mind was starting to get carried away with thoughts of another quest. Like drugs to an addict, adventures gave Matthew a high he couldn't find elsewhere.

"Is there a treasure map in this diary or directions to Gasparilla's bounty?" He tried to keep the enthusiasm from reaching his tone; he didn't want to seem too eager.

"Not exactly, but there are clues. Well, at least one."

"A whole one. Wow," Cal said snidely.

Matthew could understand Cal's skepticism, but the dreamer in him wanted to take hold. "Maybe Gaspar hadn't meant his romantic heart when he talked about it always lying with Useppa, but rather 'heart' was symbolic of something. And there is only one thing that's of all importance to a pirate. Could his treasure be buried somewhere on Useppa Island?"

Mel smiled, the expression touching his eyes. Again, all sloth with fangs. "You are quick, Dr. Connor. I, too, believe 'heart' refers to his treasure."

"There's no treasure, Matt," Cal deadpanned. "There was no pirate."

"However, I really don't believe the treasure is somewhere on the island," Mel said, not giving indication that Cal's interruption even hit his ears.

"And all this from a diary you can't produce." Cal stopped the waitress on her way by their table and ordered another beer.

Matthew sighed with the plain truth of his friend's words. "He is right, Mr. Wolf. All that you're telling us makes for a fantastic story, but—"

"Not a story. Now, Mr. Myers, you mentioned Rodrigo Lopez. Well, according to the diary, Lopez *was* Gaspar's first mate aboard the

Floridablanca—that was Gaspar's ship," he added for Matthew and Robyn, and then turned his attention on Cal. "Have you never questioned why we know the name of Gaspar's ship, yet dismiss the existence of the man himself?"

"Can't say that I have. Thanks," Cal added for the waitress who dropped off his beer.

"Well, the name of the ship had to have come from somewhere," Mel stated pointedly. "As they say, there's always some truth to rumor. You take a little of this and a little of that, and you'll get the full story. Well, one legend says that Gaspar sent his first mate Lopez back to Spain because Lopez was in love with this woman there and sick without her. So much so that Lopez named an island after her. What we know as Sanibel Island, off Florida's southwest coast."

"Sounds like naming islands was what they used to do for the women they loved." Robyn's eyes glazed over. Either she was going all dreamy-eyed on them or she was lightly buzzed.

"It really was. Going back to Gaspar's love life," Mel started, "an entry in the diary speaks of a mutiny aboard the *Floridablanca*. It was initiated because a princess was captured from an enemy ship—likely the lady he named Useppa Island after. Well, Gaspar's crew sought to do her harm, but to protect her, apparently he sent her with Lopez to Spain."

"He saved her life." Robyn drank some more of her beer.

"There's treasure out there to be found, Dr. Connor. I feel it in my soul."

"Then by all means, we should jet off and search all of Spain." Cal laughed. No one else shared his sense of humor, and Mel was especially straight-faced.

"I could narrow it down more than that, but first I need to know you're in."

"Why us?" Matthew asked in all seriousness.

"As I said earlier, you find legends. If anyone can find Gasparilla's treasure, it's you—the three of you." Mel let his gaze take in all of them.

Matthew wanted to get caught up in the flattery, but he hadn't seen anything worth pursuing yet. "Maybe if we could see the diary…"

"But I can't show it to you."

Matthew glanced at his friends. "I'm sorry, Mr. Wolf, but without anything—"

Mel stuck his hand in his satchel and came out with a rusty skeleton key pinched between two fingers. "I found this with the diary."

Matthew took it and examined it. Definitely old. Could easily date back to the eighteenth or nineteenth century. It had an intrinsic scrollwork pattern to it. The middle almost looked like a G. "Do you know what it belongs to?"

Mel shook his head. "Not exactly, but according to the diary, it's the key to the treasure."

"Wow, it might as well say, 'Take it to a haystack and—'"

"Cal," Robyn admonished him to stop there.

Cal held up his hands. "I'm just sayin'. Really, the diary could claim anything. It's not like we can verify anything he's saying."

"As I told you, the diary's age has been confirmed. And, yes, I know you'd have to take that on faith. However, if you find it within yourself to do so and trust that it was written by Gaspar's own son's hand, then Gaspar was not only a real and active pirate, but by deduction, it would stand to reason there is a grand treasure out there to be found."

Setting out after a pirate's treasure certainly held more appeal for Matthew than slugging away at his laptop, hoping to strike literary gold, but he had a responsibility toward his publisher. Then again, he worked off a laptop—that meant he could take it with him anywhere in the world. He turned to Mel. "Can you excuse me and my friends for a minute?"

"Ah, sure…" Mel slipped off the bench and returned to the bar area where he had been seated before. Someone else had taken his spot, but he stood behind them.

"You seriously can't be considering this?" Robyn asked.

Matthew's silence was his response.

"The guy's a kook," Cal kicked out.

"I think we should take a trip," Matthew said. "It's been a while since we've had some fun."

"*Fun*?" Cal said. "Expeditions aren't so much fun as they are dangerous. And this one would be like a wild goose chase."

"You're not fooling anyone at this table, Cal. You love the rush. And yeah, maybe it's a wild goose chase, but isn't the uncertainty part of the appeal? The rush of not knowing? The rush of facing possible death—"

"That I could live without," Cal cut in.

Matthew raised his brows.

"Fine." Cal crossed his arms. "You know me too well."

"Cal has a bit of a point, though," Robyn said.

"Whoa. A whole *bit* of a point. So generous."

"We don't even know this guy," she carried on, "and this diary he claims to have could be a figment of his wild imagination."

"That doesn't explain the key," Matthew countered.

"So he went to a vintage shop," Robyn said. "You can't seriously be thinking that we'd hop on a plane in pursuit of a treasure that might not even exist."

Matthew grinned. "That statement pretty much sums up exactly what we do. And we're good at it. So what do you say? Up for a trip to Spain?"

"You are a dreamer, Matt." Robyn shook her head. "You really want to hop on a plane for Spain, on the word of a man you just met, in pursuit of a mythical pirate's treasure? We don't even know where in Spain."

Her last sentence told him she was curious. He smiled at her. "He did say he could narrow it down."

"His *one* clue." Cal pressed his lips.

"That's all it could take to set us on the right path." Matthew studied his friends' faces.

Robyn shook her head. "It really doesn't matter. I have a job I need to return to, and don't you have to write your book before you're in breach of contract with your publisher?"

"I'll get it done. And you'll be back before your museum misses you. So, what do you say? We'll just find out where in Spain and get going."

Robyn and Cal looked at each other. She sighed, and Cal shrugged.

"Excellent." Matthew looked over to the bar, but there was no sign of Mel Wolf. "Any of you see…" He got up and searched for the spiky hair and tweed jacket among the patrons.

"Easy come, easy go." Cal wiped his hands together as if ridding them of crumbs.

Their waitress came with their food orders.

"Did you happen to see where our friend went?" Matthew asked, hoping she'd tell him he'd gone to the restroom.

"He left. Just a minute ago, if that."

"Do you know why?" The question was out, and he realized how crazy he must have sounded. "Never mind."

The waitress smiled. "Yeah, I'm not in the habit of stopping customers before they leave, asking them where they're going or why."

"Makes sense." He returned her smile, but his heart sank. He'd gone and fallen in love with the idea of a new adventure.

"Enjoy your meals," the waitress said to everyone and walked off.

Robyn put a hand on Matthew's, which was wrapped around his glass. "It's probably for the best. Now I can go back to work, and you can get your book written without any more distractions."

"Wishful thinking on that," he said. "There's always something that can distract me from writing."

Three

The Colonial, Washington, DC
Saturday, 11:58 PM Local Time

Matthew stared at the blinking cursor, wishing to put an end to its misery, but nothing was coming to mind—and, therefore, nothing was flowing from his fingertips to the keyboard. It was a familiar feeling that propelled him back to university. He'd spend up until the final hour staring at a blank screen, words only coming to him in just enough time to meet a deadline. It used to drive his father nuts, and he'd try to tell Matthew if he just sat down and got it done, it would be a lot less stressful. *Ah, good advice, Dad!* It only made it that much clearer how different he and his father were.

He slumped back in his chair. He was set up at the desk in his hotel room. It had to be after midnight. A quick look at his watch confirmed it was. He could have just looked in the bottom corner of his screen, but... He put his hands on the keyboard of his laptop. That was step one. Next trick would be getting his fingers to actually strike keys and have the letters come together as words to form coherent sentences.

But a book was far different than a dissertation. Namely, the former was much longer. He'd probably do better to follow his editor's advice that was presented in a metaphor.

"How do you eat an elephant?" Riley had asked.

Matthew's first thought was he had no interest, but Riley proceeded to answer his own question. "One bite at a time. It's the same with writing. Every writing project, no matter the size, is seen through one word at a time."

Now, if Matthew could conjure the first one, he might have a place to springboard from. But his mind kept drifting to the mysterious Mel Wolf and his temptation of pirate's treasure, followed by his disappearing act. And the way he'd jumped at the busboy's spill indicated he was fearful of something or someone. Did it have to do with the diary?

He opened an internet window with the intention of googling Mel Wolf. He got as far as the browser popping up when someone pounded on his door.

"What the—" He rose from his chair and swiped his phone from the desk, tucking it into a pocket of his jeans.

The person banged again before he made it there.

"Hold on!" Matthew called out.

What the heck could be so urgent that it required knocking like the building was on fire? Hopefully the building wasn't on fire...

He looked out through the peephole and saw Mel Wolf.

Unbelievable.

He cracked the door the amount the door guard allowed.

"Please, Dr. Connor, you have to let me in." Mel was looking up the hall one way, then the other.

"Tell me what's going—"

"Please, there's no time to explain."

He wasn't about to let some crazy into his room without good reason. He was really starting to see merit in Cal's opinion of the guy.

"My life is in danger. Believe me." Mel's mouth contorted with panic.

Matthew closed the door and considered leaving it that way but ended up flipping the door guard and reopening the door. Mel stormed in past him and spun quickly, putting the security latch back in place.

"What the hell do you think you're—"

"I'm being followed."

"And you led whoever it is to my door?" Matthew was pissed and wasn't in the mood to hide it.

Mel shook his head. "They already know about you. They saw me— All of us. At the restaurant. That's why I left. I'm sorry I had to leave you like that. It's just—"

"Slow down. Who are they, and why are they following you?" Maybe it was best to play along with the delusional.

Mel met his gaze and slipped a hand inside his coat.

Matthew held out a hand toward Mel. "Stop right there." He imagined Mel pulling a gun.

Mel raised one hand in surrender but kept the other moving toward the inside of his coat.

"I mean it." Matthew's heart was thumping. He always figured he'd go out doing something he loved, a high-risk sport or on a quest for a legend.

"It's just my phone." Mel removed his hand from his coat.

Matthew let loose a long exhale.

Mel brought up a picture on his phone and extended the screen toward Matthew. It was of a man at least six four, wide and clearly muscular in his fitted jacket. He had a hardened look to him and blank eyes.

"I've seen him before," Mel said. "And when he walked into the restaurant, I knew something was off."

"It could just be your imagination getting to you. Could have been a familiar face from the museum." Matthew shrugged.

"No," Mel snapped. "He's after the diary and the key." Fear saturated Mel's eyes, and it caused the skin to tighten on the back of Matthew's neck.

"Maybe you should leave." That was the wise decision and what he'd said, but he was intrigued. Even though he had no right to be. He'd offered up the City of Gold in exchange for his friend's life, and they'd gotten lucky. Luck had a way of running out.

"Leave? No, I can't… I need your help."

"Listen, I don't even know who you are—"

"Mel Wolf, I told you."

"That's not what I mean, and you know—"

The door handle jangled.

"They're here!" Mel's eyes widened and watered.

"Let's just step back a moment, think logically. It could just be that someone has the wrong room."

The handle was being attacked with fervor, and Matthew's gaze shot to the door.

"You really believe that?" Mel's eyes bugged out. "We have to go."

"Where?" Matthew looked around the room, landed on that blasted blinking cursor. He scooped his laptop into a bag and threw the strap of his carry-on over a shoulder. They had to get out of there, but how? He spun and faced the window, but breaking it and jumping out wasn't an option. He was on the tenth floor. There was only one possible solution. His eyes shot to the door that adjoined his room to Robyn's. He opened his side and knocked urgently, calling out to her. No response, but she could be a sound sleeper, and given the hour, she'd be in dreamland.

The doorframe to Matthew's room cracked loudly. Whoever was on the other side was definitely determined to get inside.

"Robyn!" he hissed loudly against the door, but nothing.

"We've got to—" Mel stopped talking when Matthew took a run at the door and thrust a heel to the part near the handle. The lock busted, and he pushed into Robyn's room. Mel was right at his back.

Robyn bolted upright, let out an ear-piercing wail, and flicked on the bedside light. "What the— Matthew?" She was squinting.

"Grab your stuff. We've got go." Matthew beelined for the sitting area in the corner of her room and grabbed a chair. He hauled it over to the adjoining room door and braced it against the handle. He could hear another *thwack* against his door. One more strike and they'd likely be in. He was surprised it was taking them this long.

"I'm not going anywhere until you explain—" Robyn stopped talking.

There was a loud crack, and the intruders gained entry to his room.

"What's going on?" she asked.

"Just move it!" Matthew stressed, and motioned for Mel to help him hold the door shut. The handle was being shaken, and it was already sitting loose in its slot from Matthew's inflicted damage.

Robyn jumped out of bed in a pair of red, silk pajamas, and she stuffed her laptop from the desk and other things in the room into her carry-on bag.

Matthew braced his shoulders against the door, pulled out his phone, and called Cal's cell phone. He didn't answer until the third ring. "No time to explain, but grab your stuff. Use the stairwell and meet us in the parking garage. P1. Go now."

"Why?"

"Cal, just do it. Use the stairwell," he emphasized. "Trust me." Matthew wanted to avoid the lobby just in case there were more waiting down there to apprehend them.

"My God, Matt," Cal mumbled. "What the hell—"

"Just do it."

"Fine."

Cal hung up, and Matthew prayed that he would just do as he'd directed him. His life might depend on it.

Four

Sophie always told Cal that one day treasure hunting would kill him. It was never the high-risk sports he liked to take part in, but the quests for legends that spelled true danger. And that edge to Matthew's voice told him danger was there, tonight, at this hotel, in this moment.

He got out of bed, changed quickly, threw his stuff into his wheeled hard-shell suitcase, and headed for the door. But he took some precaution and popped his head out first, looking both ways. The place was empty. Probably because everyone in their right mind was sleeping at this time of night, not gathering their things and slipping out like a wanted fugitive.

He headed toward the stairwell at the end of the hall and tucked inside. There he froze. He'd watched too many action movies where the killer hid out in a stairwell, ready to attack, either armed with a gun or a knife.

He picked up his suitcase and took each step with caution and awareness of his surroundings. He walked down flight after flight, tentatively holding his breath, and focused on getting to the parking garage in one piece.

He opened the door that had a sign next to it that read *P1*. The smell of rubber, car exhaust, and concrete filled his nose. Screeching tires rounded a bend somewhere in the distance. The noise of sirens filtered in from outside. The latter formed the soundtrack of his life in Toronto, and he normally paid it no attention, but he was on high alert. He wondered if the sirens had anything to do with why he had to rush down to the parking garage in the middle of the night.

Cal looked around for Matthew and Robyn, but he saw no sign of them.

A car headed toward him, its roaring engine amplifying off the concrete like a megaphone. Cal ducked behind an SUV and peeked out as the vehicle drove past. The driver didn't seem to notice him.

Then came voices, and he peeked around the other side of the SUV. It was Matthew, Robyn, and that Mel Wolf guy coming from the stairwell area.

Cal came out from his hiding spot, beelined straight for Mel, and thrust a pointed finger his way. "Does this have something to do with you?"

Mel gripped his satchel to his chest. "I'm afraid it does. I have some men following me who are after the diary and the key. Dangerous men."

"'Dangerous men,'" Cal repeated. "Just great." He snarled and looked at Matthew. His friend never should have entertained this whack job. All that garbage about a mythical pirate and a diary—one he conveniently couldn't produce. "And they're after a make-believe dia—"

A thunderous bang stopped Cal instantly.

A bullet had whizzed over their heads, and chunks of concrete flew from an abutment in front of them.

"Move!" Matthew yelled.

No need to say that twice!

Cal set into a run, suitcase still in hand. Matthew took the lead, Robyn followed, and Cal was neck and neck with Mel for the rear.

More bullets pinged metal as they struck cars. Footsteps smacked against the concrete and were getting closer.

"In here." Matthew held a door that had a sign next to it that read *Exit to Street Level.* The four of them entered and bounded up two flights of stairs.

They stepped out onto the sidewalk. The city street was surprisingly quiet, but the reverberation of footsteps still clambering up the stairwell behind them boomed like thunder.

"We've got to move," Matthew urged, and they all resumed running.

The January air was brisk and reminded Cal he'd forgotten his coat. Robyn must be freezing in her silk pajamas. Matthew was wearing a long-sleeved tee, and Mel was still in that ugly jacket of his.

They hadn't made it too far down the street when the garage exit door sprung open and slammed against the wall. Their pursuers were still on their tail.

They passed shops that were closed and others with glowing LED signs advertising they were open for business. They moved past one coffee shop that advertised "Donuts to die for."

Cal didn't care for the irony, given their situation.

"Stop! Police!" one of their pursuers yelled out.

"They're no effin cops!" Cal screamed.

"No shit." Robyn nudged him to take a sharp right to follow Matthew, who'd ducked down an alley.

"Are you sure we should…" The question died on Cal's lips, but they had no idea where they were going, and he wasn't blessed with a good sense of direction. He followed but imagined them picking a dead-end. Then what? The four of them shot and their bodies tossed into a dumpster. He rounded the corner and was relieved this alley was open-ended, but it didn't provide them a way to shake the gun-toting lunatics behind them.

A gun report sounded into the night, and all of them picked up speed.

No witnesses in an alley, Cal thought and gulped.

Matthew juked right, and everyone followed. Cal's steps came up short when his nightmare was realized. A six-foot-high chain-link fence blocked their path. He was six-foot-five, and it shouldn't be a big deal, but it was. His legs were melded to the ground.

Matthew sprung up the side like he had rockets on the soles of his shoes, toting his carry-on bag as if it were no big deal. So much for "white men can't jump." Robyn and Mel reached it at the same time. Robyn tossed her bag over and climbed quickly. Matthew helped her stick her landing on the other side. Even Mel, for all his awkwardness, made it up and over the fence as if he did it every day.

"Come on, Cal. It's just a little fence!" Robyn urged with wild gestures.

He couldn't get himself to move.

Another shot fired and had them all ducking. It hit something metal—and close! Cal turned around to see two shadows had just rounded the corner, heading their way. Both figures unmistakably men. One of them was huge, and the other lithe but a good few inches shorter.

"Cal!" Robyn screamed. "Get your ass over that fence!"

Cal looked back at it. He could do this, if only he put his mind to it. He'd have to forget his bad history with climbing if he wanted to live. He tossed his suitcase over, and the hard shell cracked against the concrete. He backed up, ran at the fence, and jumped on it about two feet above the ground. But the tip of his right shoe didn't find purchase, and he slid down. His chest pressed against the chain link.

The pursuers cried out for him to stay where he was.

To hell with that!

He refused to go down all because of a little fence. He didn't even want to think about that ludicrous obit.

He took another try and, this time, got a good hold on the fence with both his hands and feet. He was almost to the top when one of the men grabbed one of his pant legs and pulled back. Cal kicked, and the sole of his shoe met the big man's nose. The man let go and fell back.

"Cal!" Robyn cried out, shaking him from his shock.

He rolled over the top of the fence and let himself fall to the other side. He tucked and rolled and, with surprising grace, got to his feet in one fluid motion. He collected his suitcase and tucked into the side alley where his friends were. He just got around the corner when another shot fired.

"You can run all you like, but we'll get you, Wolf!" one of the men shouted. Given his deep baritone and bitter rage, Cal would guess it was the big one he'd hit.

Matthew peeked his head around the corner. "They're leaving."

"Ha, so a little fence climbing scared them." Cal was feeling a little more validated.

Matthew made eye contact. "They know they'll catch up with us later."

A sick feeling tossed Cal's stomach. He was probably spot-on. Men like that didn't just give up unless they had a plan B. He leveled a hot glare on Mel. "This is all because of you," he hissed and lunged forward.

Robyn stepped between them. "Not right now."

Cal heaved and scanned her eyes. To him, right now seemed as good a time as any to kick this guy's ass.

Five

Matthew's first reaction was to throttle Mel Wolf, but he acted on his second one. The pursuers' footsteps were headed back the way they'd come. He jogged down to the end of the alley, confident that it returned to the main street that they'd started out on. He ducked his head around the corner. A block away, the thugs were emerging and approaching a waiting black SUV.

He pulled out his phone and went to get into position, but Robyn yanked back on his arm. He shrugged free. "Just getting a picture of the license plate." He took the photo just before the vehicle pulled away. The image was a little out of focus, but nothing that couldn't be worked with. He turned to confront Mel, but there was no sign of him. "Where's Mel?"

Robyn spun and looked around. "He was right here. He…"

"He's right here." Cal was standing next to a dumpster. "The coward took to hiding."

Matthew found Mel huddled on the ground, hugging his satchel. "You've got to be kidding me."

"Matt, he's been through a lot," Robyn empathized, shivering and rubbing her arms.

"And we haven't? We just took fire, and we're lucky to be alive." It was only by the grace of God or the thugs' bad aim. "It's time you start talking, Mr. Wolf."

Mel was trembling and kneading his satchel like a huge wad of clay.

"Who the hell are those guys?" Lord help the man if he came back with "I don't know."

Mel said, "They're after the diary. They have to be. Maybe treasure hunters?" He went stark white and stared into space.

"They know your name. How?" Matthew took another step toward Mel. "Start talking to us now or so help—"

Robyn moved closer to Mel. "He's right. You got us involved with a mess. You owe us an explanation."

She might have been in the mood for manners, but Matthew was all for screwing the "more bees with honey" bullshit. "You said you saw the one man before. Where?"

"He…" Mel clamped a hand over his mouth, composed himself. "They murdered him… I watched him die."

Robyn glanced at Matthew and pressed her brow.

"Nope. No. No way." Cal held up both hands and backed away. "No blasted treasure is worth this risk. And…" Cal spun. "They're probably not even after you because of some stupid diary; probably has more to do with the murder you witnessed."

Mel kicked the toe of his shoe at the ground.

"Who did they murder?" Robyn asked, seeming far calmer than the rest of them. She was hugging herself and bouncing, likely to warm herself.

Mel slowly lifted his gaze. "Professor Edwin."

Matthew jumped on that. "And who—"

Robyn glanced at him to take a back seat. "Who was he?"

"He was the document specialist who verified the age of the diary. I work with him at Hodges University in Naples, Florida. I'm a professor there of American history." Mel hefted his satchel like it was starting to weigh heavy in his hands, but its bulk would have been supported by the strap he had slung over a shoulder. "I'd left the diary with him, but then changed my mind. Something that valuable I had to keep with me. So, I went back for it later that same day. I texted him to let him know I'd taken it, though, so he wasn't worried if he went back to reexamine it and didn't find it." Mel swallowed roughly and licked his lips. "He called me that evening and asked that I bring it back to him."

"Why?" Robyn asked.

Mel met her gaze. "He said that he wanted another look at it. He thought he might have missed something the first time around."

"And you believed that?" Cal slapped out.

"I had no reason not to."

"What happened after that?" Robyn asked.

"They murdered Edwin. I'm only alive because when I went into the office, I didn't call out his name like I so often do. I heard men's voices and didn't like the sound of them. Very menacing. So, I hid behind one of Edwin's cluttered bookshelves and watched through the bric-a-brac. I saw that…" Mel swallowed roughly. "*That* big guy—the one who was following us—shoot him like it was nothing."

"Did they know you saw them?" Matthew asked.

"I don't know about that, but they must have found out about the diary. They're probably behind Edwin telling me to return with it. When I didn't show, they must have decided to shoot him."

Robyn angled her head, sympathy in the set of her mouth. "When did this happen?"

"Six days ago."

"I'd like to know how they even came to know about the diary," Matthew began. "Were they keeping some sort of tabs on Professor Edwin? Or was anyone there when you showed up with the diary originally?"

"Just Edwin, I believe… Oh, actually, his student was around."

"His student?" A shiver visibly tore through Robyn, but she said to Matthew, "I'll be fine."

Mel went on. "He mentors one lad, a student by the name of Brent Gibbons. He was tinkering with something when I showed up. I remember now that he said 'Hi' to me."

"He could have easily known that you dropped off something to Edwin, but would he know your suspicions about what the diary contained?" Matthew narrowed his eyes on Mel, trying to read the man's facial expression and body language, but there was nothing to draw on other than Mel's slumped posture and doughy eyes.

"Unfortunately, I didn't make it much of a secret at the time. I was excited. I've had a personal interest in pirates all my life, a fascination, really, bordering on an obsession."

"So you flaunted a book that spoke of treasure? Not too smart, *Professor*," Cal lamented and crossed his arms.

The professor turned to Cal. "Now you believe that what I've been saying is the truth?"

"Never said that."

"How much do you know about this Brent Gibbons?" Matthew was determined to piece together who was after Mel and how they'd come to know about the diary. There had to be a leak somewhere.

"Not too much, really," Mel said. "I know that he respected Edwin, looked up to him as a mentor. He was an honor student, too, if that helps."

"Not at all," Matthew said. "Nor does it mean his nose is clean. We've got to poke into this kid's background, maybe even go pay him a visit."

"Whoa, hold up," Cal said. "We're not detectives, and we just met this guy—" he thrust a pointed finger in the professor's face "—and people are chasing us with guns. I say we cut and run. Now."

Matthew shook his head. "We figure out who's after us—"

"Nope," Cal stated. "And they're not after us; they're after *him*." He glared at Mel.

"Do you have any idea how these thugs found out about the diary?" Matthew asked, again finding it hard to believe Mel had no clue.

"No. Maybe Edwin was excited and let knowledge of the diary slip to the wrong person? But I told him to keep it to himself. I can't imagine him breaking that confidence."

"Sadly, we never know anyone as well as we think we do," Matthew reasoned. "This Professor Edwin, he was a good friend of yours?"

"I'd worked with him for years, decades. Twenty-eight years. Most of my career. He was a good man. Certainly didn't deserve what happened to him. Sometimes I wish that I never found the diary." Mel met Matthew's gaze, but there was a flicker in them that belied that claim. The thought of treasure and a mythical pirate making his way into reality had infused life into the professor.

"I don't think the diary itself is the problem. Bad people tend to come out when there's the possibility of treasure. It's as if it's a trigger word they're listening for."

Mel slowly nodded.

Matthew thought more about what he'd just said. "And you're certain you didn't call anyone about the diary? Friends, family? Let them know?"

"I lead a rather isolated life." He shuffled his bag. "And my family is all dead, that I know of."

"Well, we're going to need our hands on that diary."

Cal stepped in front of Matthew. "Why?"

"Because we need to find the treasure." Those idiots had made this personal when they chased them down and fired on them.

"You've got to be kidding me." Cal's eyes bugged out.

"Where's your sense of adventure?"

"My sense…of…" Cal choked. "This side of the grass! Those guys have guns, Matt. They could have killed us."

"We've survived such scrapes before."

"How much do you want to press your luck?"

That was a good question, and one Matthew had recently asked himself, but he figured his answer would always be "at least once more."

"Let's go somewhere warm to talk," Matthew suggested, eyeing Robyn in her silk pj's and chattering teeth. "And not that I don't like the look, but you might want to change."

Six

The four of them tucked into an all-night diner named Clancy's. Robyn took her bag into the restroom to change. The rest of them slipped into a corner booth. There were a few other customers, a small group of ladies who, given their scanty clothing, could have been strippers getting off shift. They were eating stacks of pancakes loaded with butter and syrup and talking animatedly.

"No setting up camp in here." A big man with a stained apron came over and dropped four menus on the table. "You order something, or you leave. You don't leave…well, I've got a shotgun behind the counter. I'll give you a minute to look over the menu." He walked off but left a stench of vat grease and armpit odor in his wake that made Matthew want to retch.

"Just get us coffees all around," Matthew called out to the man's back. There was no way he was eating anything here. He was certain, given the looks of disgust on Cal's and the professor's faces that they felt the same way.

Robyn returned, wearing a white T-shirt and fitted jeans with a jacket and sat across from Matthew, next to Mel. "What did I miss?"

"You don't want to know." Cal waved a hand in front of his nose.

Matthew set his gaze on the professor. "First thing we need to do is get that diary. Where is it?"

Mel gripped his bag tighter, just like he always seemed to in response to the topic of the diary.

"Is it in your bag?" Matthew pointed to it.

Mel shook his head. "No. I told you it's someplace safe."

"Why do you keep hugging your bag? You must have something important in there."

"It's where I have the key and my research notes."

"Where's the diary?" Matthew's patience was starting to run dry. "We'll go wherever we have to in order to get—"

"I told you. I put it in a safe place."

"Sure, and where is that?" Exasperated and again ready to throttle the good professor.

Mel bit his bottom lip, his gaze darting around the diner and then settling on Robyn. He tapped his head.

"Here ya go." The big man was back and set down the coffees with enough gusto the brew spilled over the edge of each cup. "Cream and sugar are on the table. You want milk or sweetener, I'll tell you how to live without it." He took his leave.

Robyn turned away from where the man had stood, her eyes watering.

Matthew opened a creamer, and it *plopped* into the coffee. Soured. He pushed his cup away. He probably didn't want to drink it anyway. "You were about to tell us where the diary is." He laser-focused on Mel, and the professor's cheeks paled.

He went through the same show of awkwardness, his eyes darting all over. He eventually tapped his head again.

"Why do you keep— *Oh*," Matthew said.

"You've got to be shitting me!" Cal exclaimed, putting it together.

"I'm not *shitting* you. I have an eidetic memory. I recall it perfectly."

"Okay," Cal dragged out, "but where is the actual physical diary?"

"I burned it." Stated quick and punchy with no room for misinterpretation.

"You... *what*?" Cal had his hands on the collar of Mel's shirt in a hot second, and Matthew worked to restrain his friend. It took a lot of effort, but eventually Cal let Mel go.

"Why did you burn it?" Robyn's voice was soft but contained true curiosity mingled with some disbelief. For someone who valued antiquities, no doubt the thought of an ancient document becoming ash both angered her and made her sad.

"It's already to blame for the death of Professor Edwin, and there's no way they deserve to put their hands on it or the treasure." Stated as if his decision had made perfect sense.

"Blooming effin treasure ain't worth it. I'm telling you," Cal seethed.

Matthew studied the professor's face. "You said you have an eidetic memory?"

"Yeah, but—"

"You're going to recreate the diary."

Mel's eyes snapped to Matthew's. "And why would I do that?"

"Because we never know when it might come in handy." Matthew was thinking that they'd have something to bargain with if it came down to that. It seemed if they set out on this quest, they'd have company along for the ride.

"You're thinking to use as leverage?" Robyn asked, pulling from his brain.

"Yeah."

"Well, even if he could write out the contents of the diary, Matt, where is he going to get an old journal that could pass as being from the late eighteenth century?"

Matthew hated that she'd made a valid point. "I think it should be written out anyway, just for us even. Robyn, you read Spanish and could take a look at it."

"I won't do it." Mel shook his head in protest.

"You will, if you want our help."

"Matt, are you sure we even want to get involved?" This was from Robyn.

Cal jabbed a finger at Robyn. "I'm with her."

Matthew looked at his watch. It was just after two in the morning.

"I'm just terrified to transcribe the diary," Mel offered up. "If they get their hands on it, Edwin really would have died for nothing. *And* they'll have the first clue to finding the treasure."

"Which is?" Matthew asked.

"Earlier I think you hit the mark more than you know. You brought up the possibility Gaspar hadn't been referring to his romantic heart, but rather his bounty, that would always lie with Useppa. I strongly agree and believe his treasure is in Spain."

"Connected with Lopez?" Matthew asked, taking a gamble.

"Yes."

"Spain's a big country," Robyn said, shaking her head. "Where do we begin?"

"El Acebuchal."

"I'm guessing that's a town?" Cal asked. "Would be nice if that was narrowed down some."

"It's a village actually, and it's not too big. I believe finding where Lopez lived is our next step in finding Gaspar's treasure."

"There's a few before that," Matthew said, "and speaking of one, I need to make a phone call."

Seven

Matthew excused himself from the group and went to a corner of the diner out of earshot. Before he'd left the table, Robyn had made eye contact with him. She'd know who he was calling, and so would Cal, but there was a pleading in her eyes that asked that he let this quest go.

And maybe he was making a mistake even considering taking this one on, but the entire thing felt like it had become personal after being shot at. It could have been a point of pride, but he just wanted to see it through—at least a little longer.

He selected Daniel Iverson from the list of contacts on his phone. Daniel was his father's house manager by his official title, but he also aided Matthew in previous expeditions. He helped gather research and sometimes even suggested legends to pursue. It had actually been Daniel's insights that set them out after the City of Gold.

"Sir?" Daniel answered, sounding proper and slightly groggy.

Matthew had told him many times to address him by first name, but he wasn't about to correct him right now. "I need you to do something for me."

"I will do whatever you ask."

Matthew believed Daniel's claim. While he didn't know Daniel's history, it felt like he had contacts for everything—and he probably did. That would have made him valuable to his father. But as mysterious as Daniel seemed to be, in person he was a rather unassuming fiftysomething-year-old man. At the moment, Matthew could imagine him perched on the edge of his mattress, slipping his feet into slippers, and heading for his rolltop desk.

"I've run into a situation in DC." Matthew paused there, tempting Daniel to jump in and say something, but he remained silent. Then again, it wasn't Daniel's place to question him, and Matthew often found himself in "a situation." Matthew went on. "I need your help with a few things. We've met a professor here by the name of Mel Wolf. He teaches American history at Hodges University in Naples, Florida. I need you to look into him and see what information you can gather on the man. It seems he's come into possession of an ancient diary that is the basis for our next quest, and it's attracted the interest of a third party."

There were a few seconds of silence on Daniel's end of the line as he would have processed the implication of Matthew's words, then, "May I ask, sir, what the quest is?"

Matthew smiled. "You may ask."

"When will you be leaving for this quest and for how long? I can arrange everything with Blue Skies."

Blue Skies was an airline charter service they often used. "No, I'll take care of this one myself." If Daniel was trying to worm out their destination, he'd hit a brick wall. "There are some other things I do need you to handle, however. Mel told us he witnessed the murder of a Professor Edwin, a colleague of his at Hodges. Supposedly, it had to do with this diary. But according to Mel, there were only a limited number of people who knew of the diary's existence. Professor Edwin—"

"The murdered man?"

"Yes. And also a student at the university by the name of Brent Gibbons."

"And, it would seem, this third party you mentioned also knows of its existence."

"Correct. I need you to find out whatever you can about the student and Edwin's murder. I also need you to figure out who is after us."

"How do you propose I do that?"

"I have a photograph of a license plate I'm going to send you. You'll need to do some tweaking to it. Unfortunately, it didn't come out very clear. I need you to find out who the plate is registered to. I know you have contacts for everything."

"I don't know about *for everything*, but I'll do my best. And you're sure you're all right?"

"Yes," Matthew assured him.

"Very well. What should I tell your father?"

Matthew still lived under his father's roof, but it was a *huge* roof. A palace of 26,000 square feet located in Toronto's affluent Bridle Path neighborhood, father and son had their own wings in the house and rarely had a need to run into each other. And as a grown man of thirty, Matthew didn't really have to keep his father apprised of his schedule, but he did his best, especially after the situation on their quest for the City of Gold had escalated and put his father at risk.

"Sir?" Daniel prompted.

"I'll text him before I head out." His father slept with his cell phone by the bed and lived his life on-call as Toronto's mayor. Matthew didn't relish the thought of waking him.

"Okay."

"Oh, and if someone calls looking for me, field those calls as best you can." Matthew wasn't going to say that someone could be calling from the Metropolitan Police Department in Washington. "No matter who it is, don't let them get through to my father to the extent of your ability. Tell them you'll take a message for me, but all you know at this time is I've left the country."

"Sounds like that's going to be the truth."

"On second thought, if you need to tell anyone anything, just say that I'm currently unreachable."

"And for how long will that be?" Daniel repeated one of his earlier inquiries that had gone unanswered.

"Say a week." Though it probably wasn't anywhere near enough time to search the Spanish countryside—village or not—for a house that belonged to the supposed first mate of a mythical pirate.

"I'll get on everything you've asked of me, but how should I reach you with what I find out?"

"Use my Google email account. You still have it?" It had been a while since they'd communicated that way, but it would work out in this situation. He certainly wasn't going to leave his cell phone on while he traveled, especially with the police likely being interested in questioning him about what had taken place at the Colonial. He wouldn't put it past them to trace it if they were desperate enough for answers.

"I do."

Trace it…

"Daniel, I've got to go." Matthew hung up and hurried back to the table. "Where's your phone?" he asked Mel.

Mel snaked a hand into his satchel and came out with one. "It's here."

Matthew took it and turned it off, removed the SIM card. "This is how they're tracking you."

"Wait, you can't just—"

"We don't have a choice here, Mel. Not if we want to live. You understand." It wasn't up for debate. He looked at his friends. "We all need to turn off our phones and extract the SIM cards, just as further prevention from being tracked."

"I mean, all of this is…" Robyn's words petered out as she got her phone from her jacket pocket and did as Matthew said. "If your suspicion is true, these men are sophisticated and have access to technology."

"More than that." Matthew plucked the SIM card from his phone. "They have connections and money backing them. It should have occurred to me before. Mel, you came from Florida, and they caught up with you here. They either have associates they can get guns from or they brought them with them from Florida. And if they brought them from Florida, they—"

"Took a private plane," Robyn finished.

"What…what are you saying exactly?" Mel asked.

"The men who are after the treasure have both the money and means to make this a healthy competition."

"Competition?" Cal balked. "We could die."

"You could die drinking that coffee." Matthew gestured to the mug in front of his friend.

Cal shoved the drink toward the middle of the table. "But we should be good now, though, right? I mean, we all turned off our phones. There's no way of tracking us."

"Let's just hope all they had was a tracker on the phone," Matthew said.

"What aren't you saying?" Robyn asked.

Matthew met her gaze, glanced at Cal and the professor, and shook his head. There was no sense bringing up the possibility that the bad guys could have also been listening in through Mel's phone, too. And if that was the case, they'd know their next stop was El Acebuchal, Spain.

Eight

The Connor Residence, Toronto, Canada
Sunday, 4:07 AM Local Time

Daniel could fall asleep anytime, anywhere, under any circumstances, but it only took a little provocation to stir his mind awake. Matthew had provided a lot more than a little. A situation in Washington involving an ancient diary, a new quest, and a murder. Not to mention the people after said diary were probably behind the murder. He'd tried to doze back to sleep, but his thoughts were rapid and plentiful. Matthew's father, William, would never forgive Daniel if he let anything happen to his son. And Daniel cared about Matthew too much to ever let it come to that.

Matthew seemed aware Daniel had contacts, but the kid didn't know the scope, and he'd never tell him. For the most part, Daniel liked to bury his past and his outreach, but he did have it to pull on if need be. And it would seem like this was one of those times.

The clock read just after four in the morning, and Daniel had resigned himself about twenty minutes ago that he would be up for the day. He'd showered and dressed, got himself a coffee, and was now positioned in front of his computer.

He had Matthew's message open and clicked on the attached image. It was the back of an SUV, and as Matthew had noted, the plate was out of focus. He used to have to send things like this to one of his contacts, but his skills with technology had improved over the years— mostly out of necessity.

He brought the image into Photoshop and worked the various tools until he'd tweaked it enough. The plate was issued in the state of New York, and he wrote down the license number on the notepad on his desk.

He had two contacts he could ask to track it down. One was a private investigator, Justin Scott, the son of an old friend he'd lost years ago. The other was Wes Hansen, a childhood friend from Norway. Justin's reach was somewhat limited, whereas Wes was more international as an agent with the Norwegian Intelligence Service, or NIS. Essentially Norway's equivalent of the Central Intelligence Agency in the United States. He could never keep up with his friend's advancements through the agency and was pretty sure he'd make it to the top position at some point. Even more appealing was Wes would be awake and well started into his day. It would be going on ten thirty in the morning there.

Daniel was one of few who had Wes's cell phone and home numbers. He tried the former, and the call rang to voicemail.

"Wes, it's Danny," he said, still that small kid at heart when he and Wes used to get into all sorts of trouble—and usually at Wes's prompting. Wes was one of few permitted to call him Danny. "Hope you're doing well, but I need a favor, friend. If you could call me the first chance you get." Daniel ended the call and, while he was waiting on Wes, figured he should get on some of the other things Matthew had asked him for.

Based on the list, he must admit the murder intrigued him, but then again, so did this Mel Wolf character who seemed to have shown up in Matthew's life relatively out of the blue. And if Daniel surmised correctly, Matthew was planning to hop on a plane with him for who knows where.

Daniel brought up an internet browser window and keyed in *Mel Wolf, Professor, Hodges University*. The fact Matthew had asked Daniel to look into Mel and the others and had brought up Daniel's contacts told him Matthew was seeking far more information than could be gathered from a simple Google search, but it was a place to start.

The search results were plentiful. Mel had profiles on several professional forums and platforms, but he didn't appear to have any accounts with popular social media sites. There were also links to articles he'd written for prestigious university magazines.

Daniel clicked on one of the platforms and read the brief bio. It told him nothing more than Matthew had. Wolf was an American history professor at Hodges University and the associated headshot showed a distinguished-looking gentleman. Probably in his sixties. Graying at the temples, groomed hair, smooth face. The collar of his silver dress shirt was undone. It seemed a little too relaxed and casual for a university professor.

Daniel would get far more information on Mel through one of his contacts, but for now, he opened another tab for his Google email and composed the message for Matthew with the photo. It would at least give Matthew verification of the professor's looks. A place to start—assuming that Matthew hadn't gotten that far for himself already.

The covert email accounts had started years ago when Matthew operated under the secret identity of Gideon Barnes. It was an alias Matthew had invented to hide the fact he was more treasure hunter than run-of-the-mill archaeologist from his father. Daniel had been happy to see the double life become exposed; it made it easier than being wedged between father and son.

Next, Daniel did an internet search on Brent Gibbons, the student at Hodges University. He quickly found that Brent was on several social media sites, but he appeared to be a socially awkward person, given the nature of his status updates. His profile picture showed a college-age young man, but he was still fighting the battle of acne. Red dots flamed across his forehead, nose, and chin—the T-zone.

Looking closer at Brent's Facebook account, he had just over a hundred friends. He posted status updates almost daily. However, in the last six days, there was nothing. His last entry was vague, only offering, "Had an exciting day today!"

Daniel had a feeling… He opened another tab and looked up Professor Edwin's murder. A news article disclosed his full name as Ralph Edwin and the date of his murder as six days ago. The same day that Brent had claimed to have had an "exciting day" and then disappeared.

What makes a student consider the murder of his professor an exciting *day?* Unexpected, certainly, but "exciting" seemed too upbeat given the circumstances.

Daniel continued reading about the murder, not that there was much in the way of details. Just that he was found dead at the university.

An accompanying photograph of Edwin showed a man who appeared arrogant. His nose was turned up and he looked down it, as if he viewed everyone else as beneath him. Like Mel Wolf, Edwin had a full head of gray hair but appeared far more formal. He was dressed in a suit jacket, shirt, and bowtie. His smile for the camera was a pressed-lip one, bordering on a grimace.

It wasn't until the third article covering the murder that the reporter included the tidbit that Edwin was found by one of the university's students. The student was left unnamed, but Daniel had to wonder if it was Brent Gibbons. And if it was, how did that tie in with an "exciting day" he'd posted online? Was it just the awkward wording of someone socially inept, or had Brent been happy to find Edwin dead?

None of the articles shed any light on suspects or leads, not that Daniel was too surprised. He scribbled down, *Ask Justin about the murder investigation.*

Justin's accreditation as a PI might give him some leverage with the Florida detectives working the case, maybe a pull on professional courtesy. Maybe. Though police detectives probably didn't consider private investigators their equals.

Daniel's phone rang, and caller ID told him it was Wes.

"Hello, my friend," he answered.

"Ah, how nice to hear your voice. Hope all is well."

"So do I," Daniel replied, no doubt inciting Wes's curiosity.

"You need my help with something? You didn't kill anyone, did you? I can't aid and abet murder." Wes chuckled.

"As if I'd tell you." Daniel smiled. Every time they spoke, it pulled him back to a time when life seemed less complicated. "I have a license plate, and I need to hunt down the owner."

"I suppose you don't want to tell me why you need that information."

"You'd suppose correctly."

Wes was quiet for a few beats, then said, "What's the number?"

Daniel rattled it off for him. "It was issued in the state of New York."

"Okay, you're just looking for registration ownership?"

"Correct."

"You do know that I shouldn't be doing this, and I'm sure you have other people you could call about this, so why me?"

"May need more from there. How to reach them, etcetera, but one step at a time." It was the *etcetera* that had Daniel asking Wes, not Justin, about the plate. Depending on the direction this took, it would be advantageous having Wes already on board. He just had this sinking feeling in his gut that Matthew's "situation" was going to become a lot worse before it was over, and having someone like Wes in his corner wouldn't hurt. "Besides I know you're still a rebel," Daniel offered up, hoping that it would pull on Wes's inner child who couldn't turn down a dare.

"You know me far too well, my friend."

"How are Ella and the kids?"

"Growing up too fast, the kids anyway. Ella's refusing to grow up." Wes laughed. "And the kids aren't so much kids anymore. You know that, Danny Boy."

Danny Boy. Talk about nostalgia.

"Yeah, suppose I do," Daniel said. "The kids have kids." Not that he could relate completely as he'd never had any, or at least none that he knew about.

"Don't remind me. With every one that pops out, I swear a few more gray hairs show up, too. Anyway, I better get going. I'll call as soon as I can get to this. I guess it's rather urgent to you, given that it's—what?—four in the morning or so there?"

"It's important, yes."

"I'll call. *Ciao*." Wes hung up before Daniel could say goodbye.

Now it was just a waiting game. The license part, anyhow. He'd go downstairs, grab another coffee and some breakfast, and wait until a more reasonable hour to call Justin Scott and tell him to expect some company this morning.

Nine

Matthew had pulled out his laptop and hopped onto the diner's free Wi-Fi. He found the number for another air charter service he'd used in the past and had a credit account with. If he was going to keep his destination from Daniel, he'd have to boycott Blue Skies Charters. The diner owner had given him the stink eye when he brought up the internet browser. And Matthew wouldn't have done it at all, but with their cell phones out of commission and no way to access his contact list, he'd had no choice. Asking to use the business's phone line cost Matthew breakfast for everyone, but it was a small price to pay, even if the plates of food would go untouched.

He'd made the call to the charter service and told the lady who answered everything he needed and how many would be traveling with him. The closest airport to El Acebuchal was Costa del Sol Airport in Málaga, Spain. He'd requested that they take off from Dulles International as soon as possible. They'd asked for time to arrange things and said they'd call him back.

That had been the better part of two hours ago.

They all ended up pecking at the meals, somewhat out of desperation and partially out of something to do. Surprisingly, the food was delicious, and most of them cleaned their plates. Yet the dishes still remained in front of them. The big, stinky man in an apron glared at Matthew, and he imagined him pulling out that shotgun he'd mentioned when they'd first arrived.

"I think we've overstayed our welcome." Matthew sank into the booth, frustrated and wondering if the charter service was ever going to call him back. Then the phone in the diner's kitchen rang. The diner owner's face contorted into a bunched-up snarl.

"It's for you."

Matthew got up and said to his friends, "Wish me luck."

"If you don't come back in five minutes, we'll send a search party," Cal teased, but Matthew hoped his friend would hold true to his word.

Thankfully, it wasn't necessary. Matthew returned about two minutes later, if that.

"It's all set up," he announced, remaining standing at the end of the table. "Flight doesn't leave until nine—"

"So five more hours?" Robyn asked.

"Yeah, not too happy about it either, but it is what it is. Commercial flights won't get us there any sooner, and the charter pilots have logged too many hours and need some rest."

"Rested pilots are a bonus." Cal smirked.

Matthew nodded. "Very true. I was just hoping to get on with this."

Robyn smiled.

"What?" he asked her.

"It's just you." She glanced at Cal and smiled again, let it carry back to Matthew. "Once you make your mind up, it's full speed ahead."

"It's how I've always worked."

"Oh, I know, but that impulsiveness might not always work out."

"It has so far." It might hold true of expeditions, but it didn't cross over to his relationships. Especially the ones that started hot and quick. They always fizzled out just as fast as they began. His thoughts briefly went to Alex in Egypt. Long-distance relationships were brutal, and he wasn't sure how anyone salvaged them.

"You've been luck—" She yawned and shook her head. "Let's take this time to get some rest."

"The flight to Spain is twelve hours nonstop. There will be plenty of time to sleep on the plane," he countered.

"Maybe you can wait, but I need some shut-eye now."

"I could use some, too," Cal interjected.

Matthew looked at Mel who had been quiet all this time. He was still hugging his satchel like a security blanket. "And what about you, Professor?"

He slowly lifted his gaze to meet Matthew's. "I could handle some sleep. At least my body could. My mind is awake."

"That makes at least two of us." Thoughts of how quickly life changed direction weighed heavily. He'd just been giving a speech, signing some posters, and now he and his friends were going to set off across the world in search of a mythical pirate's treasure. He was aware that pirates had existed, and still did, but that was about the extent of his knowledge. It's not something that ever touched his world before now.

Robyn yawned again, and Cal followed.

"Okay, we'll get a room," Matthew said. "You guys can get some sleep while Mel and I take care of some things."

"Sounds good to me," Robyn said.

He'd get her and Cal set up, and then he and Mel would talk.

Ten

Detective Colin Doyle stepped into the master bedroom. The woman, Judy Finch, was curled up on her husband's side of the bed, hugging a pillow against her chest. She'd died in her sleep—typically a peaceful way to go, and while she wouldn't have known what hit her, Doyle did. There was no exit wound, and except for the top of her head and the blood spilled on the bedding, Judy's face was unmarked by the tragedy. She even looked peaceful, like she was still sleeping and having pleasant dreams.

This case wouldn't bring with it the same procedure a normal homicide would. He and his partner, Detective White, would still go through the process of questioning friends and relatives. They'd speak with the husband at length, too—a thing called due process. But it was most likely the person responsible for killing Judy Finch hadn't even met her. Her death—her murder—was simply the result of being in the wrong place at the wrong time. Taken out by a stray bullet that had traveled through the exterior wall of her ground-level apartment and found purchase in her skull.

Doyle would do all he could to find out who'd fired the bullet, but he'd seen such investigations go cold.

As he looked at her serene expression, her dark chestnut hair, images of his wife filtered in. He'd been too late to save her, and he was too late to save Judy.

"Husband's a mess." Detective James White entered the room behind him.

Colin turned to look at his much younger partner. "Imagine that."

"No need for the sarcasm."

Colin kept his gaze on James, willing him to continue as it was obvious he had something more to say.

"David, that's the husband, said he and his wife planned to sleep separate tonight."

"Troubles in the marriage?"

James shook his head. "I wouldn't say so from first impression. Married twenty-four years. Their silver anniversary was coming up next month. Only reason I know is because he kept blurting it out between bouts of crying. Guess they had a 'shindig' planned. His word, not mine."

Colin didn't get excited about long-lasting couples with their alleged happily-ever-afters, because he'd learned a long time ago those stories just weren't finished yet. Exhibit one was his own marriage. Flash forward several "exhibits," and it brought him to there with Judy Finch's lifeless body. "Why were they sleeping separate?"

"Guess the wife's been having a problem with her allergies lately and snores like a freight train. He just wanted to get a solid night's sleep."

"No one can blame him for that." Not that Colin slept. His body simply passed out when it needed a reboot. "But it's below freezing. What can she be allergic to?"

"Dust."

"No getting away from that." And Judy certainly hadn't lived in the right place. The apartment was in an older building that probably wasn't set up with a proper ventilation system. He walked around the end of the bed, his gaze going to an air cleaner that was humming at the end of the room. He pointed at it. "She was doing what she could."

"The husband feels like he should be the one who's lying there."

Colin didn't need to say anything to that. He knew the feeling all too well. The guilt that would eat him alive if he didn't pour himself into his work to drown it out. He should have been home when Nancy had perished. They'd promised to go out of this world together, an ideal of the young and in love, as if such a vow could be fulfilled intentionally short of a suicide pact.

"Let's go talk to him." Colin led the way out. "See if he heard or saw anything that might help."

Colin went into the living room, where the sofa bed remained pulled out, the sheets tousled. David was sitting in a chair that matched the couch, his head cradled in his hands. A uniformed officer was standing behind him.

"David Finch," Colin said.

Slowly the man lifted his face from his hands, his cheeks tear-streaked, his eyes bloodshot. "Our silver was coming up next month." He blinked, and fresh tears fell.

There was a tug on Colin's heart, but he shut it down. This wasn't about him and his loss; this was about David's. "You and your wife always sleep separate?"

"No…rarely… Sometimes, when her allergies get acting up. I love my wife, Detective. But she snores so loud, all night long. I need sleep sometimes. What is really killing me is I should be the one who's dead. She was sleeping on my side of the bed." That admission started him on a crying jag so intense his entire body heaved. Colin let him get it out.

"How did you come to find your wife?"

"Judy, please, *please* say her name."

"How did you come to find *Judy*?" Colin played along, thinking maybe somehow hearing her name would bring her back, but if that's what David had hoped, it backfired. His face contorted as more tears fell.

He sniffled and took a deep, stuttering breath. "I heard a thump." He met Colin's gaze. "I'm a light sleeper. This is all my fault."

Colin knew it wouldn't do any good to point out how self-sacrificing David had been by leaving the master bedroom for his wife, and that he'd have had no way of knowing that act would backfire. "The only person who is at fault, Mr. Finch, is the man who fired the bullet that killed your wife."

David's eyes blanked over, as if he were processing the "killed-your-wife" part. It would take a long time for the horror of that reality to sink in—if it ever did.

"Now, there's some questions we need to ask you," Colin started. "They won't be easy to hear."

David nodded. "I guess you're going to ask if I had any reason to want Judy... I can't say the word." He cupped his mouth, and Colin glanced at his partner.

Colin had been a detective for twenty-five years—but was ten years past his silver with the badge—and no matter the number of murder cases or death investigations, it never got easier to work with the loved ones left behind. Selfishly, he was grateful his time with them was brief before victim services or grief counselors stepped in. "I do need to ask. Were you and your wife having any problems?"

David squeezed his eyes shut a moment. "No, as I told that detective." He gestured toward James, who was standing next to Colin. "This is like a nightmare," David muttered between sobs.

"It *is* a nightmare," Colin told him with such starkness it had David meeting his eyes again. "You suffered a great loss, Mr. Finch, and I'm truly sorry." He wished his words could soothe, but he knew personally that sentiments did little to excise grief.

A uniformed officer, who was posted in the hall, opened the apartment door. "Detective Doyle?"

Colin walked over to him, James in tow. The officer's name badge read *Kennedy*.

"What is it?" Colin asked.

"A canvassing officer found someone who saw armed assailants running down the back alley."

"The one in back of this building?" Hope blossomed in his chest.

"Yes."

"What apartment?"

"Number 302. Her name's Rita Smith."

"You and Officer Buikema are in charge of the scene." Colin was already on his way to the stairwell and spoke over a shoulder to his partner. "This could be the break we need to get this closed up quick."

Eleven

A Hotel Restaurant, Washington, DC
Sunday, 6:05 AM Local Time

While Robyn and Cal tried to get some sleep, Matthew and Mel had gone down to the hotel restaurant, but not before Matthew tucked away and checked his email to see if Daniel had sent anything over. All that was there was a photo of Mel Wolf, one Matthew could have found for himself on the internet if he'd had a chance. Daniel promised to get more information as soon as he could.

There was a sense of a peace that washed over Matthew, though, because the picture was a match for the man in front of him. It was there in the facial structure and eyes, but that was where the resemblance stopped. The image of a composed and fashionable professor didn't line up with the man in front of him. Of course, he had recently suffered the loss of a friend—and witnessed his murder, no less.

"Refill?" Their server came back around with a steaming carafe of coffee.

"Sure," Matthew told him. "Thanks," he added after his cup was refilled.

Mel took a top-up, added another creamer and a sugar packet. "I'm sorry I got you roped into all of this." Mel slowly turned his mug by the handle in one direction, then the other.

Matthew took a long, cautious sip on the brew. The mug was hot against his palms and fingers. He wanted to reply in kindness to the professor. Something along the lines of "I know you are," but apprehension swirled in his gut. It could be as simple as excitement and anxiety about the trip. His heart often fluttered rapidly at the onset of a new quest. But there was a niggling inside him that told him to exercise extra caution. It didn't hurt to admit that Robyn had been right about him making up his mind quickly and seeing things through—"full speed ahead," as she had said. But did he really have the right to drag his friends along with him? And was all this a writer's procrastination tactic to avoid *butt in chair, fingers on keyboard*?

But as he looked at the man across from him, he wasn't too sure he had a basis to mistrust him. Well, besides the fact he'd shown up out of the blue. But he had a find he wanted Matthew's help with, so it wasn't really "out of the blue," was it?

"There are a lot of archaeologists and adventurers out there," Matthew began. "Why me specifically?"

Mel stiffened and hugged his mug with both hands. He had yet to take a sip of his refreshed cup. His satchel was still in his lap and never out of his sight. "You pursue treasures and legends that don't have any real basis in reality. Most people aren't dreamers, but you are, Dr. Connor. Even many of my students have lost their ability to dream by the time they reach me. They haven't even entered the real world yet. Such a tragedy."

"I like to entertain possibilities," Matthew admitted.

"I see that, and look at what you've accomplished. Finding the Incas' lost City of Gold, uncovering the tomb of a lost pharaoh, and so much more than I'm aware of, I'm sure."

Matthew listed off a few more artifacts and finds in his head. The foremost being one he had been obsessed with for years, only to finally lay his hands on it and, for the good of the world, had to keep it secret.

"You are certain this diary is the real deal?" Matthew asked, feeling as if it was too late to be entertaining doubts. The flight was booked, and he'd also called the charter service back and asked that they arrange lodging.

"With my entire being, or I wouldn't be here. Unlike you, Dr. Connor—"

"Matthew, please…just my first name is fine."
He gave him a pressed smile.

Mel dipped his head in acknowledgment and carried on. "I'm more a man of fact and science. Not frivolity or daydreaming."

"Hmm. I find that interesting given what you just said a moment ago."

"About the state of the world?"

"Yes."

"Well, it's much easier to see that which you can relate to. A weakness in oneself is much easier to spot in another."

Matthew supposed that was true. "You've also admitted the reason you want our help is because we've been in the field. You said something like that when we first met. I assume by that you haven't been?"

"Not really the outdoorsy type."

"This quest could take us who knows where."

The professor's eyes sparked. "Another reason I'm so looking forward to it. For the most part, my life is rather dull and uneventful."

It had certainly taken a turn when he found the diary. "You said you've had a fascination with pirates for a long time?"

"My entire life."

"And you had no idea that the house you bought at auction belonged to Panther… What was that nickname again?"

"Panther John. And, no, I didn't. Such a lovely surprise."

"This hidden passageway you found. Do you have any pictures?" Matthew was surprised he hadn't thought to ask that before now.

"No."

"Tell me about it."

"I was in the study one day, and the toe of my shoe caught on a loose board. The corner was sticking up just a bit. Enough. I bent over, cussing the bloody thing, and found the nail was also loose; the wood had pulled out from around it. This is where I suppose I am a bit of a dreamer, after all. You've heard tell of people finding money in their homes in hidden boxes, under floorboards, in the wall, the attic. Well, I couldn't turn that voice off. I went and got a hammer, returned, and pried the board loose. What I found was that it was one of several that formed a hatch or a lid, as it were. I lifted them and found there was an opening beneath the floor with an old ladder standing there. As you can imagine, my heart was racing, but I fetched a flashlight and down I went."

Matthew was inching forward on his seat and hadn't noticed how much until his chest touched the table. He moved back. "Go on." He had to admit that he was beyond intrigued.

"Well, I went down the ladder. My heart was in my throat, I tell you."

"I bet."

A smile crossed Mel's expression briefly. "At the base of the ladder, which was about five steps equaling a distance of about eight feet beneath the study, was a small space. There was a short tunnel, and at the end of it, there was a square-shaped room."

"How big?"

"Say twenty feet square."

"That is rather big. It would have taken a lot of effort and manpower to make it."

"Yes," Mel said with an animated bob of his head. "And that room was empty except for a wooden desk and chair in a back corner."

"And that's where you found the diary and the key?"

"That's right. In one of the desk drawers."

"It sounds like he'd used the room as his private escape."

"Yes, but I think also something more."

Matthew angled his head.

"That's an awful big room for a desk, don't you think? I mean some people like big offices but during that time period? It seems unlikely," Mel said.

"Right. So what do you think he used it for?"

"You have this room, hidden beneath the floorboards of the home. Whatever was down there had to have been something he wanted to keep secret."

"You said before that he wanted to keep his relationship with Gasparilla unknown. Maybe it was just a place he went to be alone with his thoughts. Was he married?" The question tumbled out.

"He was."

Matthew smiled. "His man den."

Mel chuckled. "Could be." The professor's expression soured and turned serious. "But I think the room may have been used for something else. Gómez talked of his father visiting once and storing something of great value. He didn't come out and say it was treasure."

"But you think it was?"

"Sure, why not?"

"Where is it now?"

"Isn't that question of the hour?"

Indeed it was. Matthew hoped that once they got to Spain, between entries from the diary and good Karma, they'd find the treasure with rather ease. But he wasn't naive. It had never worked out that way in the past, and he didn't expect that to change for this go-around. He wanted to pepper Mel with questions, including what else he might have in the way of clues that could help them once in El Acebuchal, but then he'd be going over all of them again with Robyn and Cal. No, they'd discuss all of that on the plane together. But he was putting his life and those of his friends in the hands of a stranger. He hoped the anticipated payoff would be worth the risk.

Twelve

National Mall District, Washington, DC
Sunday, 5:00 AM Local Time

Colin had learned from experience that no matter how helpful an eyewitness, the sooner you could get to them, the better chance of getting the real story. Wait too long, and memories merged with imagination. Colin knocked on Rita Smith's door, and it opened the amount the chain would allow. A woman peered out at them. Even with cops all over the building, she apparently didn't feel safe.

Colin and James held up their badges. "Detectives Doyle and White with the Metropolitan PD," Colin said, "Are you Rita Smith?"

The door was closed, the chain slid, and the door reopened. "I am."

"We understand you saw something?" Colin said. "Can we come in?"

Rita stepped back, letting them inside. She was a big woman, carrying at least a couple extra hundred pounds on her small five-foot-six frame. She closed the door behind them.

"I saw more than something." She hugged herself. "I understand that Judy was shot?" Her tone and posture was one of empathy, but she wasn't falling apart like she might if Judy were a close friend.

"She was," James confirmed.

Rita's gaze shifted to him. "And she's dead?"

"She is," Colin replied this time.

She pressed her lips and shook her head. "None of us ever know when our time's gonna be up."

Cheerful thought.

"Is there someplace we could sit and talk?" Colin looked at the couch in the small living room that was just inside the door. It was always best to get witnesses off their feet and comfortable. It set them at ease and loosened lips.

"Sure." She went to the couch, and Colin and James sat on chairs.

Colin wanted to get right into asking about what she saw in the back alley, but due diligence had him needing to inquire about her relationship with the victim and from there if she might know of someone who'd want to harm Judy. "Did you know Judy very well?"

"No, I didn't, but I feel for her husband. They both seemed like nice people. Whenever I ran into them getting my mail downstairs they'd always say 'hi' to me."

"So they seemed like a happy couple to you?" Colin asked.

"Uh-huh."

Satisfied that part of the procedural checklist was marked off, Colin nodded and said, "Tell us what you saw."

"It's what I heard that first got my attention. Gunshots. I know what they sound like because my father and brother are hunters. Sort of like the Fourth of July, but it's January."

"How many gunshots did you hear?" James asked, leaning forward.

"Two?"

Colin didn't like that answer. They only knew where one had ended up.

"I guess I shouldn't have been too surprised. I do live in a city, but this has hit a little too close to home."

Very much so for Judy Finch.

"Where were you when you heard the shots?" Colin asked.

"Right here, watching TV. I listen to it low."

"What did you see?" Colin glanced toward the window at the side of the living room.

"Yeah, that's where I was looking out," Rita said.

Colin pointed across the room. "Do you mind?"

"Not at all."

Colin got up, and so did James, and they walked to the window. There was a clear view of the back alley.

Rita came up behind them. "There were six of them."

"Six?" That word felt tight coming out.

"Yeah. Only two had guns, though. At least that I could see."

"Both were firing?"

"I didn't see the gunfire. I heard it, then went to the window and saw them chasing four people."

Colin's ears perked up. There was a running pursuit, which he'd get to, but one thing at a time. "So two of them were carrying guns?"

"Uh-huh. Two men. One big guy. Had to be over six foot, and the other was rather small, reaching for five-five."

Colin wasn't sure how Rita would have been able to make an accurate estimation from her third-story apartment window.

"Could you describe the men who had the guns in any more detail?" James asked.

Rita put a hand on her right hip and bit her bottom lip. "Not really. The alley is rather dark and shadowed at night."

"So any idea what they were wearing?" Colin asked, hoping a more pointed question might net them some description.

"Both were wearing dark jackets and blue jeans."

Nothing real distinguishable...

"And the four who were being chased, were they men, too?" James asked.

She shook her head. "One was a woman."

That surprised Colin. He'd been thinking maybe a gang turf war, but it was quickly losing that feel. "Get a good look at them?"

"She was wearing red pj's."

"You're sure?" Colin had heard a lot in his life as a cop. A woman being pursued through the streets wearing pajamas was a first.

"Positive. I got a pair just like 'em. Bigger, though. She was trim."

"Okay, and the other ones. Men?" James prompted.

"Uh-huh. One was about six foot, I'd say, a white guy. Another white guy, but older than the other three being chased, also about six foot. The third man was over six foot, black."

Colin studied Rita. "How old would you say they were?"

"The lady and two of the guys were in their early thirties—that's just a guess. The other man I mentioned, I'd say he was probably in his fifties. Again, a guess. But what was really strange…"

Colin couldn't even begin to imagine what was *really* strange after red pj's.

Rita finished, "…was they were carrying luggage with them."

"Luggage? You sure?"

"Yeah. See that chain-link fence?"

Colin did and nodded.

"The black guy threw a hard-shell suitcase over the fence before eventually going over himself. I thought they were going to kill him, but he managed to kick the bigger guy in the face."

"So the four being pursued went over the fence," Colin said, "and then what?"

"They went out of my view, but the guys who were after them turned back around to the way they'd come from."

Colin found that interesting. Why pursue the four of them only to retreat at a fence that was easily scalable? "And the age of the gunmen?"

"I'd guess the bigger guy was in his forties, the smaller one maybe thirty."

"And for the record, Ms. Smith, what time was this?" The chances of what she saw and heard not being connected with Judy's death was a million to one, but it was good to have the time of death on record. The medical examiner would make the final ruling on that, but this account would help.

"Between midnight and one in the morning."

Definitely connected. Now what did three thirtysomethings and a fiftysomething have to do with two armed men?

Thirteen

Somewhere over the Atlantic Ocean
12:05 PM Eastern Time, Sunday

Robyn leaned against the headrest on the airplane and closed her eyes. She might have gotten some shut-eye before leaving Washington, but it wasn't near enough. She was what people call a long sleeper, operating best on ten to twelve hours a night. She hadn't racked up anywhere close to that in the last twenty-four hours, and her body and mind were letting her know. The former sagging from exhaustion, and the latter groggy.

She didn't expect to catch much sleep on the plane either, as she wasn't one to just tap out anywhere. Not something that served her too well on expeditions, but that's when her stubbornness and determination took over.

At least her boss had taken the news of her leave from work better than she'd anticipated. She'd called from the airport before they boarded the plane. All she told him was she'd be taking some vacation days to enjoy Washington while she was there. He'd told her to have fun. She didn't feel good about lying to him but thought it might go over better than bringing up pirate's treasure. She just hoped if the police got involved with what had taken place at the Colonial Hotel, they wouldn't call her boss in an effort to reach her.

"When we land, it'll be the equivalent of nine tonight Eastern time," Matthew said. "Local time, it'll be tomorrow at three in the morning. There's a six-hour time difference."

"Okay, that's screwed up," Cal lamented.

Robyn opened her eyes and sat up straight. It was too much to wish she could just lose herself in a REM cycle. "What did you expect? We're crossing the Atlantic Ocean." She pressed the call button for the steward, eager to order a hot coffee.

Cal leveled a look on her. "I guess I'll sleep when I'm dead."

"Works for me." She snickered and winked.

"Ha-ha." Cal didn't manage sleep deprivation well, either. His brow was knotted up, and even in a resting state, his mouth sat in a scowl and his gaze was intent on the professor.

The steward came, and Robyn asked for a coffee. When he left to fulfill her request, she made eye contact with Matthew. He might be able to read her mind, as she often felt she could his. If so, then he'd know how she was going over everything they'd been through up until this point. The two gun-wielding maniacs who chased them through the streets of Washington foremost on her mind. She hated guns—and for good reason. She'd been shot before and was lucky enough to survive.

She touched her left shoulder. It had been almost two years ago, but she could recall the searing pain on command.

Not far behind were suspicions about this Mel Wolf character. As much as she was lured by talk of pirate's treasure, she'd opted to come along to keep an eye on her friends. She was sure that Matthew had asked Daniel about their travel companion and to look into Professor Edwin's murder, the student, and the license plate he'd photographed. Knowing Matthew like she did, she could imagine he'd been a talented gumshoe in another life, and that's why he found it so hard to leave learned habits behind. Even now, given what he dedicated his life to, he was a detective of sorts. He poked and prodded, looked at things from different angles to find legends that the rest of the world had either forgotten about or long ago written off as the thing of fairy tales and folklore. She just hoped that he wasn't using this quest as an excuse not to write his book.

The steward returned with her coffee, made just the way Robyn had asked for it, and she took an eager sip. With just a smidgen of caffeine, it felt like her synapses were firing again. She glanced at Mel. Even on the plane, he kept his satchel hugged to his chest. There were only brief moments in time when he relaxed his hold on it.

"Tell us about El Acebuchal," she said, adjusting the papers on her lap, which were Mel's transcription of the diary thus far. She'd been reading them before leaning back to rest her eyes.

"Have you heard of Almijara and Alhama Natural Park?" Mel asked.

She shook her head, as did Matthew and Cal.

"It's between Málaga and Granada provinces. The park acts like a natural borderline. La Maroma, also known as Tejeda, is a mountain there. Its peak is 2,069 meters."

"Fascinating," Cal mumbled, the single word drenched with sarcasm. "Wait, does this mean we need to climb a mountain?"

"No." There was a twitch to Mel's lips that told Robyn he found Cal's fear amusing, which got her back up a little, as if only she and Matthew had the right to tease Cal. "Well, not mountain climbing as such. Anyway, El Acebuchal is a small village in the heart of the park. It used to be popular with traders back in the seventeenth century. It was wiped out during the Spanish Civil War, and it only started to turn around in 1998."

"The war lasted from 1936 until 1939," Robyn said, mostly for Cal. History she had a handle on; pirates not so much. She crossed her legs and took a long draw on her coffee. "And you truly believe we might find Gasparilla's treasure there…in El Acebuchal?"

"Hopefully. That or a clue to its whereabouts."

"Hopefully?" Cal blurted out.

Robyn felt the same way. They were on a plane to Spain because of Mel. "I see," was all she said.

"So let me get this straight—" Cal shifted in his chair, leaned forward, propping his elbows on his knees "—we're on a twelve-hour flight on nothing more than a 'hopefully'? This entire thing is a joke, Matt."

"The guys who shot at us weren't," Matthew tossed back.

"Please, let's not turn on each other," she intercepted. "We're here now. We'll do what we can to see this through. We'll take a look and see what we see. We can cut and run at any time." She didn't call out Cal, but surely, he didn't expect there'd be any guarantees with this. Besides, if getting the treasure was going to be easy, Mel could have made the trip himself.

"Getting to the village shouldn't be too difficult," Mel said. "It's become a tourist destination. But if we need to branch out into the park, we'll need to take precautions as the terrain isn't necessarily the most easily traversed. But let's take things one step at a time."

Cal crossed his arms. Matthew glanced at Robyn, possibly to say something, but she was out of encouraging words. They were in a situation that was hard to paint with rose-colored glasses, and they'd rushed in, spurred on by the armed men. She didn't love setting out unprepared at the best of times, but this was the least ready any of them had been. And as she thought about that now, she realized she'd left her perfume, makeup, and shampoo at the Colonial Hotel.

"I think we could all use some sleep," she eventually said, offering up an excuse for the frayed nerves and short tempers. "Then from there, regroup and figure out what comes next. I know we'll need to do some shopping once we get to Spain." Her mind wasn't solely on hygienic products, but also on what they'd need for their hike and travel into the countryside.

"Sounds logical," Matthew agreed. "But it will have to wait until sunrise. Remember, when we land, it will be three in the morning tomorrow local time."

She nodded solemnly. Lack of sleep while in one time zone was enough. Tag on jet lag, and it became that much worse.

"We should probably get what sleep we can." Matthew's gaze went to her coffee, and he raised his brows.

She lifted what pages the professor had already transcribed as if to explain she wanted to read more. She was beyond exhausted but getting a second wind.

"Well, everyone do as you wish, but I'm catching some Zs." Matthew reclined his chair.

She watched him nod off. Cal, too. Mel gave her a tight smile, then took out a notebook and started scribbling away.

"More of the diary," he said needlessly, and she put her attention on what was in her hands.

She read the words, but her mind drifted. She just hoped that Matthew's impulsiveness hadn't gotten them into real trouble this time.

Fourteen

First District Police Station, Washington, DC
Sunday, 12:15 PM Local Time

By the time noon rolled around, Detective Doyle had some answers and some forensic evidence. Captain Richards had called in that there was a disturbance at the Colonial that resulted in property damage to a couple of rooms. The complaint had been placed to the backburner, where it had stayed for hours. That was until it was discovered the vandalism was connected to an armed pursuit through the hotel's underground garage, which the hotel's security firm had on camera.

As Colin and James watched the videos— one from the hallway outside the rooms, and one from the underground garage—it seemed unmistakable that the people on screen matched the general descriptions provided by their eyewitness Rita Smith. He had the security guy play the videos a few times to see if he could get anything new, and he was able to get a couple of screenshots of the armed men. Hopefully, their faces would pop up in facial recognition software.

Identification was easier for the three thirtysomethings: Matthew Connor, Cal Myers, and Robyn Garcia. All from Toronto, Canada, and there to mark the opening of an exhibit at the Smithsonian. Apparently, Connor was an archaeologist, and he and his two friends had found the Incas' lost City of Gold. Colin had sent James on a fishing expedition with clear instructions to reach out to the three friends and pull their backgrounds.

Colin had returned to the police station a bit ago and handed over the stills to Andy in Tech for running through the system. He'd also requested footage from the city for the streets in front of the hotel and the ones surrounding the Finches' neighborhood.

Forensics had reported back that blood was recovered from the back alley near the chain-link fence. The DNA might come back, but Colin would probably be a ripe old man by that point. If only the process worked as fast as it did on TV.

There still wasn't any sign of bullet number two, but the good news was no more calls of fatalities had filtered in. Hopefully, it had just lodged into brick or concrete. And speaking of, forensics had pulled a bullet from an abutment in the hotel's garage. Colin was pretty sure it would match the one that would be extracted from Judy Finch.

James walked in with an extra-large coffee and a self-satisfied smirk on his face.

"'Bout time you showed up. Where have you been?"

"While you've been sitting around with your feet up, I've been working."

"Don't push me, White."

"Hey, I did what you asked and more."

Colin leaned back in his chair and clasped his hands in his lap. "Okay, impress me."

"I made a bunch of calls. None of the Canadian Trio, as you'd tagged them, are answering their phones. I did reach out to Garcia's work and Connor's father—who happens to be the mayor of Toronto, by the way."

This case just kept getting better and better.

James continued. "I didn't know who to reach out to for Myers. Tried a Sophie Jones. Thought she was his girlfriend, but it turns out they broke up almost seven months ago. She hasn't heard from him." James sat in his chair and put his feet up on his desk.

"What do their backgrounds show?"

"Nothing of interest criminally."

"Okay, so you got nowhere."

"Wouldn't say nowhere. Why are you riding me so hard? Hit a wall? Taking out your frustrations on me?"

"Just tell me what else you got."

"I tracked Connor's phone and—"

"You got the subpoena for that signed off?"

"You must really think I'm a rookie. Yeah, Judge Anderson did it."

There was something new he learned about his partner every day. He'd found out a few months ago that James was a trust-fund baby, the son of a tech tycoon. The discovery only made Colin respect him more. James could have been sitting up in an ivory tower, but he was on the streets, making a difference. And, apparently, he had solid connections. "Okay, what did you find out?" He'd suppress his excitement until he heard the results.

"Connor—his phone, anyway—went offline at Clancy's. It's a diner not far from where the friends hit the chain-link fence. Talked to a big, fat, smelly son of a bitch who owns the place. He confirmed the trio had been there, along with that older dude in the tweed jacket."

Colin leaned forward. "Did he have anything else to say?"

"Sure did. He overheard them saying something about pirates and treasure."

"Pirates and treasure?" Just when he didn't think life as a cop could serve up any more surprises.

"Uh-huh. Well, we know this Matthew Connor is an archaeologist, but supposedly he really keeps himself busy hunting treasure. So, I did some more digging. I found some online articles that dub him as the Legend Hunter. Connor signed a two-book deal, too. Apparently, his first book comes out this fall. It's on the City of Gold."

His partner had done good work. Maybe next time he wouldn't doubt him so much.

"Think this pursuit has anything to do with what the fat guy told me at the diner?" James asked. "Some treasure?"

"You've got an archaeologist known as the Legend Hunter, his two best friends who go on these expeditions with him, and some cockeyed guy who looks like a crazy professor. Tag on some goons? Yeah, I'd say it very well could have something to do with treasure."

"I was sort of hoping it wouldn't come to that."

"And why's that?"

"The fat guy seemed to think they were headed to Spain."

"Spain?" he asked, wondering why James had held that tidbit back for so long.

James shrugged. "Just the messenger here."

"What the heck could be in Spain?"

"Guess that's what Matthew and his friends plan to find out. Mr. Tweed Jacket, too, likely."

Colin narrowed his eyes at his partner and thought, *Smart-ass.*

"So, what have you been doing while I've been working?" James clasped his hands on the back of his head, getting really comfortable.

"Got the security videos and some stills to Andy in Tech. Watched them more times than I care to count."

"Any word on facial rec?"

"Nothing yet." Colin told him about where the case was from a forensic standpoint.

"Hopefully, between the bullet striations, the facial images, and the blood, we'll be able to get the man who shot Finch."

"That's the goal." Colin was also intrigued—whether he wanted to be or not—by the treasure-hunter angle. "One thing that bothers me is that older man, the one in the tweed jacket." He could easily call to mind how awkward the man was and how attached he was to his satchel. "He doesn't exactly look like he'd be the trio's friend, so how does he fit in?"

"I'll tell you what's weighing on me," James started, and Colin was surprised to hear that anything weighed on his partner. He always seemed to take everything in stride. James went on. "They were shooting at the Canadian Trio, but never hit any of them. I'd say bad aim, but they had Myers cornered at the fence. Why try to haul him back? Why not shoot him right then and there?"

His partner raised a hell of a good question, but it wasn't one that Colin hadn't thought of before. "Don't know." The admission deflated him. Like anyone, he supposed, he'd much rather have the answers.

Fifteen

Daniel entered the Starbucks and spotted Justin Scott at a table in the back next to a fireplace. He waved at the young man, always happy to see him, even though the situations that brought them together usually involved Matthew being in some sort of trouble.

Justin already had a cup in hand and an opened laptop on the table in front of him. Daniel ordered himself a double espresso and headed over.

"Thank you for meeting me on such short notice," Daniel said.

"Anytime. Sorry I couldn't meet any earlier, Mr. Iverson."

He'd told Justin to call him by first name more times than he could count, but the kid kept reverting to old habits. Sort of like Daniel did with Matthew, always addressing him as "sir," against Matthew's wishes.

Daniel settled in and made himself as comfortable as possible in a wood chair. He crossed his legs and smoothed his trousers with his hand. "How have you been?" There really wasn't time for small talk, yet there always was time for small talk. He didn't see Justin often but felt some sort of a responsibility toward him, like he owed it to his deceased friend to keep an eye on him.

"I've been good. I met a girl." Justin drank some of his drink, which was in a clear plastic cup with a straw. Looked like some berries were floating around in it.

Daniel would stick to caffeine. "Someone special, I see," he concluded. The young man was all bright, sparkling eyes.

Justin nodded, flushed a little. "She is. Her name's Maria, and she's a tech nut like me. Very smart. Pretty."

"Wonderful. I'm happy for you." News of this would have made Justin's father proud, as the man had expressed his wishes, not long before his death, that Justin would fall in love and settle down. Justin had been seventeen at the time. He was turning twenty-eight this year.

"Thank you." Justin dipped his head and glanced down at his laptop, closed the lid. "You said you needed my help but didn't give any details over the phone."

Daniel would rather there be no trails to anything he said or did. "I need you to pull a few backgrounds."

"Okay, easy peasy."

Daniel handed him a piece of paper on which he had written the names of Mel Wolf, Ralph Edwin, and Brent Gibbons. "Now, not sure if this makes it trickier for you, but they are all American."

"Shouldn't be a problem, but why am I looking into them?"

Daniel hesitated. This was the only problem with getting Justin involved with investigations; it potentially placed him in danger. By a stretch surely, but still. Whoever had killed Edwin might find out about Justin's prying and view it as a threat. He leaned in closer to Justin and disclosed, "It involves a murder."

"A mur—" Justin didn't finish the word. "And these people?" He held out the piece of paper almost like he wanted to give it back.

"Just people of interest. Except for Ralph Edwin. He was the unfortunate victim."

"I see."

"It took place in Naples, Florida, at Hodges University six days ago. Regarding all of them, I need to know if their backgrounds show anything worth noting. Criminal activity, if anything pops regarding their associations… You know, in your search." Daniel could trust that Justin wouldn't be satisfied with simply generating a report. When Justin was asked to look into someone, that's what did; he dug deep and utilized several resources.

"There is more." This next part he didn't relish asking Justin, but the kid was likely in the best position to do it. "I need you to find out as much as you can about the murder."

"Sure. I'll look into it—"

"I'll need you to contact the Florida police and see if you can call upon some professional courtesy to get information they're not sharing with the papers. The internet isn't saying anything useful."

"I can see what I can do, but professional courtesy? Not sure any exists between cops and PIs."

Something that Daniel had suspected. "Just do what you can."

Justin nodded.

He hoped Justin would have more luck getting details about the murder than he'd had. And he prayed that his fear about Matthew being tied up with killers wasn't justified.

"How fast do you need all of this?" Justin asked.

"As fast as you can." Daniel didn't need to add *without sacrificing details*.

"Understood." Justin put the piece of paper into his laptop bag, put his computer in after it, and got up. "I'll get started right away."

"Thank you." Daniel rose and shook his hand. Justin's grip was firm like his father's had been.

After Justin left the coffee shop, Daniel lingered. He dropped back into his chair, gazed into the fireplace, and thought about Matthew and what sort of trouble he'd gotten himself into this time.

His phone rang, and he flinched. He'd been so deep in thought and intent on watching the flames dance, the brilliant orange, the red flicker...

"Hel—"

"Daniel, why is a Detective White with the Metropolitan Police Department of the District of Columbia interested in Matthew?" It was William Connor, and he was in a mood.

"I'm not sure, sir," Daniel replied calmly, even if that was the furthest thing from the way he felt. Matthew hadn't said anything about his "situation" involving the police.

"To hell you're not, and why can't I reach him? His phone goes straight to voicemail."

Daniel could imagine William's face was a brilliant red from his chin to his hairline. The man had already survived two heart attacks, and given his line of work and the pressure that came with it, he was queued for another one—without the worry of his son's welfare.

"Daniel, are you there? Hello?" William tapped his phone against something hard.

"I'm here, sir."

"I need some answers."

Again, Daniel was being placed between father and son. Rock, meet hard place. But what bothered him more was that Matthew was supposed to text his father to let him know he was going to be unreachable for the next while. Why hadn't he? Daniel didn't really want to consider the worst-case scenarios that his mind was serving up.

"Did the police tell you why they want to speak to Matthew?" Daniel tiptoed.

"That was my question for you," William spat. "That detective I mentioned left a message with my assistant. Said he was concerned with Matthew's safety."

A tight knot formed in Daniel's gut.

William added, "But I'm not buying that. My son has proven he can get through scrapes. What I want to know is, what's going on?"

What his employer didn't have to stress was that he didn't need any scandals. "I'll find out what I can."

"Be sure you do."

"I won't let you down."

"See that you don't." William hung up.

Daniel gripped the phone tightly in his palm. He felt so powerless. And even though William could come across like his priority in life was his reputation and status, Daniel knew it was where the man was comfortable, barricaded behind the impenetrable wall of his career, as if his vulnerabilities couldn't be found there. But Matthew was the only family William had left, and he was the product of a love that many would envy.

Daniel had the means to track Matthew down, if it really came to it, but he didn't want to go that route unless absolutely necessary. Still, his number-one responsibility was to protect the Connors. With Matthew's chosen lifestyle, he attracted more enemies than his father did in politics, and that was saying something.

Step one, Daniel wanted to find out exactly what happened in Washington so he could better gauge the situation that Matthew now found himself in. Step two, find out where Matthew was, and possibly step three, call in another favor from a contact. But one step at a time.

Sixteen

Matthew **had woken with a start** when the plane's wheels had touched down, and he stayed in a state of somewhere between awake and asleep as they made their way to Hotel Málaga. Sort of like he was sleepwalking through his life. He still couldn't help but take in the beauty of the country around him—half comatose and the darkness of early morning aside.

There was a chill in the air, and he recalled looking up what they could expect weather-wise on the plane. There wasn't any call for precipitation in the next few days, but it wasn't exactly a warm and balmy destination in January. Though it was a lot friendlier than DC's or Ontario's forecast. They'd get away with a light jacket here, unlike the parka and gloves back home.

As the taxi driver took him and the others to the hotel, Matthew noticed how there were flowers everywhere. The splashes of color they offered up would be spectacular in daylight. While taking in his surroundings, he also found himself looking over a shoulder in case they'd been followed.

The taxi driver stopped in front of a quaint boutique hotel, and Matthew wouldn't believe they were at the right place if it hadn't been for the sign out front.

"You're very lucky to stay here," the driver said as he popped the trunk and took out everyone's bags, except for Mel's, of course—he hadn't parted with his satchel. "This is a beautiful place. Enjoy your stay in my beautiful country."

"Thank you," Matthew said. The four of them looked like zombies walking. Jet lag wasn't for the faint of heart and neither was leaping "the pond." Europe, where he had been before, had a different feel than North America. It was more relaxed, laid back. People here enjoyed life and had found the secret of happiness was to do what one loved.

The taxi drove off into the night, and Matthew led the way inside the hotel, curious about the place the charter had reserved for them. He'd told them money wasn't an issue, to just charge it to his account and he'd settle up later. Maybe he should have given them a budget.

"Welcome to Hotel Málaga." A man greeted them from behind a waterfall countertop that boasted a small card letting guests know they offered free Wi-Fi with every room. He was bright-eyed with a pleasant smile. "I assume you are Gideon Barnes and guests."

Robyn shook her head and rolled her eyes. "Really?" she said quietly to Matthew.

He wasn't getting into it here, but he was trying to cover their tracks as much as possible. "That's us," he told the man with a smile.

"Wonderful. I have three rooms for you." The man went about doling out the keys and room assignments. Another man came to help with the bags. Mel wouldn't hand his satchel over.

"It should have been four rooms." Matthew found his gaze going to Robyn and remembering how they used to share a bed, but those days were long over.

"Oh, my apologies. I only have three rooms available."

Robyn put her hand on his arm. "I'll share with Cal." She didn't say it, but somehow he also heard, *I know you like your space.*

"No, that's fine," Matthew said. "Us guys will share a room."

Robyn smiled. "Sold, but you're going to be sorry. The guy snores like a tank."

"Hey." Cal narrowed his eyes and glared at Robyn.

She hitched her shoulders. "I'm just telling you the truth."

The staff went about showing them to their rooms, and after seeing Mel dropped off at his, Matthew wondered if he shouldn't have had Mel with him. At least that way he could keep his eye on the professor. He didn't need him to go missing when they were "this" close to the treasure.

"And last but not least, as they say..." The man who'd hauled Matthew's carry-on and Cal's suitcase up the hallways of the establishment gestured into a modestly appointed room. Definitely old Spanish charm with its stucco walls, arched doorways and columns.

"Thank you." Matthew handed him ten American dollars, and the man retreated into the hall with a dip of his head.

"If you need anything at all, don't hesitate."

"I won't." Matthew smiled and closed the door.

"I could sleep for the rest of the year." Cal walked out of his shoes and dropped onto the bed, sprawling over the entire surface.

Matthew scanned the room. There was a teak dresser, two nightstands, a double bed, a coffee table, and a couch. He checked under the couch cushions to see if it was a pullout. "Looks like it's going to be a little cozier than we thought. There's only one bed."

Cal wormed up to sitting position. "You've got to be kidding me. We're sharing a room *and* a bed?"

"Yep. Come on, move over. We both need our sleep tonight." Matthew nudged his friend's legs, and they were as heavy as dead weight.

"Don't you mean *this morning*?" Cal grumbled but complied, shifting his body to one half of the bed. Matthew assessed the situation. He preferred to sleep in his boxers, but that wasn't happening tonight, next to his friend. He shucked his jacket and kicked off his shoes, but otherwise stayed fully dressed and got into bed.

His eyes were closed for two seconds before they shot open. New place. New smells. New sounds. He kept telling himself he had a long day ahead and that he needed his rest, but the more he repeated it, the more alert he seemed to become.

He rolled from one side to the other, back again. Cal was oblivious and snoring like the tank that Robyn had warned him about. Matthew kicked his head into his pillow, continued to stare at the ceiling.

His thoughts went deep as he considered how fast life could change. Just over twenty-four literal hours ago, he'd been in Washington at the opening of the exhibit with no plans but a return trip back home to Toronto. Now he was in Spain, the other side of the world, after a mythical pirate's treasure.

It both excited and filled him with apprehension. He wished he knew who those men were and who they were working for.

Knowing your enemy was advantageous. That's why the adage about keeping one's enemies close was wise counsel.

One thing seemed for certain, though, and that was those men had money and connections. They knew right where to find Mel Wolf, and he'd come to Washington from Florida. So either they had tapped Mel's phone as Matthew had suspected or they were informed another way. It was "another way" that made Matthew go cold.

Matthew just hoped that they'd left the gun-toting men behind and wouldn't need to give them any more thought, but his experience with treasure hunting taught him that was likely wishful thinking. It was rarely an endeavor one did without attracting unwanted tagalongs. He just hoped that in the end the risk would be well worth it, and he and his friends would prove the existence of an otherwise mythical pirate. Finding the treasure wouldn't be a bad payoff, either.

Maybe Daniel had some luck tracking down the owner of the SUV. He dragged himself from bed and fired up his laptop, remembering the advertisement from the front desk about free Wi-Fi. He squinted in the light from his laptop screen in the otherwise dark room and logged onto his email. There was a message from Daniel, and as he read it, his gut tightened into a knot.

*Did you text your father? He doesn't
seem to know you are out of the
country. I'm a little worried about
you myself. The MPD is looking for
you. Please let me know you're okay.*

Shit! He'd forgotten to text his father. It made
sense, as seconds after promising Daniel he
would, he'd had the epiphany that their phones
could be tracked, and they all got taken offline.

He clicked Reply and watched the blinking
cursor, trying to formulate how to respond *and*
trying not to succumb to the cursor's hypnotic
powers.

Everyone's fine, he typed. *Arrived
safely at our destination. Sorry about
not texting father. Please let him
know that I'm fine but out of the
country for a last-minute getaway
with Robyn and Cal.*

He stopped there, watching the cursor blink
again. He hadn't even touched on the police but
wasn't sure exactly what to say to Daniel.

*Situation with the police is a
misunderstanding. All will be fine.*

He closed the lid on his laptop. Daniel
wouldn't like that answer, but it would have to
suffice.

He dragged his body back to bed. Cal had ducked under the covers, so Matthew opted to stay on top of them. He closed his burning eyes, and he could feel his mind drifting away and his body become limp. Within a few minutes, if that, Cal's snoring faded into obscurity.

Seventeen

The Connor Residence, Toronto, Canada
Sunday, 10:30 PM Local Time

Daniel was in his room and had just seen Matthew's response. *Situation with the police is a misunderstanding. All will be fine.* Easy for him to say; he wasn't there in Toronto with his father. William was a man who was accustomed to getting answers… and on *his* timetable. The fact that Daniel had been able to push him off for as long as he had was a blooming miracle.

Daniel had considered calling this Detective White himself to field what he'd wanted from William and why the interest in Matthew, but he didn't want to poke his head up for that and make himself a target, too. Still, if he didn't present some answers to William soon, it was likely his employer would rip him a new one.

He'd googled for news in Washington throughout the day, but the headlines gravitated toward politics. Maybe he should look it from the local-news perspective.

He brought up the *Washington Post* and scanned the site. After seconds of searching, he spotted a band along the top of the page that showed a button labeled *Sections*. There he found *D.C., Md., & Va.* and a subpage called *Crime & Public Safety*. He took a deep breath, very much hoping he'd be wrong to look there, and clicked. He scrolled down until a headline had him stopping cold.

> *Shots Fired in National Mall District, Metropolitan Police Department Investigating.*

He opened the article and skimmed it.

> *Shooting…one dead…believed to be stray bullet…chase through city… police suspect it originated at the Colonial Hotel.*

Daniel sank in his chair. Now, this, *this* had Matthew's signature all over it and would definitely constitute a "situation." The Colonial was where Matthew had been staying, and he'd told Daniel that people were interested in a diary they had. That could justify a chase. Then there was the ominous black SUV, synonymous with bad guys the world 'round.

"What have you gotten yourself caught up in now?" Daniel murmured, then revisited the article.

The victim was a forty-three-year-old married woman, shot in her bed. The bullet had come in through the exterior wall. Death would have been quick. Of course, that didn't make it easier for the husband she left behind.

There was a quote from a Detective Doyle saying, "No comment." Doyle wasn't the one who had left a message for William, but White could have been his partner. It wasn't uncommon for homicide detectives to work in pairs.

How was he ever going to explain all of this to William? The second the question came, Daniel knew he never could and never *would*. There were some things William was best kept in the dark about, and this was certainly one of them. Though he wasn't quite sure how he was going to juggle the deception just yet.

His phone rang, and he was quick to answer.

"I looked into that license plate," Wes began, "and it's registered to a numbered company."

It wasn't just a couple people after Matthew, but rather an organization. It was now confirmed. "Who's behind the company?"

"That is proving to be a little more elusive. It's like every string I pull leads to another string."

"So you have nothing?"

"I have a post office box."

"In what city?" Daniel asked, knowing that it wouldn't necessarily point him to the actual physical location of the company.

"Manhattan."

Daniel went cold. He knew of someone who lived there, but her involvement was impossible. He'd been able to dismiss her when all he had was a plate registered in New York state, but not now that it tracked back to Manhattan of New York *City*.

"Danny Boy?" Wes prompted.

"Yeah, I'm here."

"I take it Manhattan means something to you?"

"You could say that."

"And it's not good?"

"It's not good," Daniel affirmed.

"Is there anything I can do to help?"

"I'll let you know."

"Okay," Wes said, but he didn't sound like he felt too certain about that. "Did you want to know the company names I found, the strings I mentioned?"

"Ah, yeah, that would be good." Daniel shook his head; his mind was clouded with thoughts. If she were involved, whatever secrets this diary held had to be substantial enough to draw her out. After all, she was already on the line for criminal charges.

Daniel grabbed a pen and was at the ready over a fresh sheet of paper. "Hit me."

Wes gave him two company names. Neither was familiar.

"I looked them up, and they deal with antiquities and art," Wes added.

That cinched it. Matthew was in a lot of danger. "Not good."

"I mean it. If I can help any more…"

"It's probably best I don't get you involved further."

"Okay, but know I'm only a phone call away." Wes disconnected the call.

There was something Daniel needed to do, a line he needed to cross, even if he wished not to. But this moment called for him to pull on his background. As they say, life gives us challenges to prepare us for our future. Well, growing up in Norway had come with its challenges. The country had undergone a period of civil unrest, and its effect had rippled down to the civilians and everyday life. His father had done his best to provide, but it wasn't without struggle. He had four mouths to feed, not counting himself or his wife's. The poverty Daniel experienced growing up was one thing that had led him to North America. First to the United States, where he got involved with the wrong crowd. He'd done things he wasn't proud of, things he'd rather forget. It was why he had a very low threshold for violence nowadays; he'd simply seen too much of it, had bloodied his hands personally.

He met William Connor through a mutual American associate and when William offered Daniel employment, it had been attractive. He'd have to move to Canada, but he wouldn't need to hurt, maim, or kill anyone. He'd be able to use his learned means of gathering intel to achieve desired results instead. He also believed in William and his son, the way both men lived their lives—no matter how vastly different. William streamlined, focused, efficient, and Matthew wild, carefree, without a schedule. After all, the world needed both types of people.

Even though his first commission was with William, he'd become roped in by Matthew's charms. He wasn't like most people, but what he did mattered and changed history. It's why Daniel had helped him line up expeditions in the past and why he felt an unwavering loyalty to father and son.

But now Matthew had taken things too far. He'd ventured to God-knew-where with trouble undoubtedly following him. Especially if Daniel was right about the person behind the numbered corporation, he had no choice but to cross a line.

Daniel brought up a special software on his computer. Justin had helped him set it up and was sworn to secrecy about its existence. Legally, it broke numerous privacy laws, but he considered it his duty to do whatever necessary to keep Matthew safe. And with the person he suspected on Matthew's tail, the sooner Daniel found Matthew, the better.

Even as the program loaded, he tried to ease his conscience with William's request of Daniel after the City-of-Gold fiasco. William had told him to "do whatever you need to in order to keep my son safe."

Daniel had simply been obeying his boss and would continue to do so. He'd installed a small GPS chip in Matthew's watch so that no matter where it was in the world, Daniel could pinpoint its location and, by extension, one would assume Matthew's.

The program opened, and Daniel clicked a button labeled *Locate*. Within minutes, Daniel had him.

Málaga, Spain. *Málaga, Spain!*

What the heck is Matthew doing there, and how does it tie in with some ancient diary found by a Florida university professor?

There were, needless to say, many things the program couldn't answer. But he wasn't out of information just yet. The GPS gave him a little more detail than just the city; it gave him the location within a few blocks' radius.

Daniel grabbed that address and entered it into an internet search. There were several hotels and bed & breakfasts in the area. He'd start with the hotels.

He called each one and asked to be connected to the room for Matthew Connor and then he'd repeat the request for the name of Gideon Barnes—just in case. He only had three more left on his list when he met with success at Hotel Málaga when using Matthew's alias.

Daniel shook his head, slightly amused that Matthew had pulled out the pseudonym. At least he was trying to cover his trail and using some precautions—even if it did nothing more than delay people from finding him. It had become public that Gideon and Matthew were one in the same after the discovery of the City of Gold, and it really wouldn't stop the woman Daniel suspected.

"Is Mr. Barnes expecting your call?" the hotel clerk asked.

"I'm not sure what business that is of yours."

"It's five o'clock in the morning here, and I don't want to disturb Mr. Barnes unless—"

"What if I told you it was a family emergency?"

"Is it?"

"It kind of is, yes."

"I'm sorry, *señor*, but it either is or it isn't."

"Very well. I'll leave a message for him, but see that he gets it first thing when he wakes up."

"Certainly."

Daniel left a message for Matthew to call him and left his burner number. There'd be hell to pay when Matthew found out he'd tracked him down and how he'd done so, but there really was no getting around it.

While he hoped he was wrong about the person behind the numbered company, he really couldn't take any chances. He had to take advantage of all at his disposal. He called Wes again, and his friend answered right away.

In Norway, it would be about four the next morning, but Wes answered like he was up.

Daniel said, "I have a job for you, and it's life or death."

Hotel Málaga, Málaga, Spain
Monday, 5:03 AM Local Time

Carlos scribbled down the message on a tiny piece of paper and hung up the phone. He was so tired, exhaustion made his bones weep. It was his second time working the night shift, and he hated it, but he'd do what was needed to provide for his beautiful wife and their beautiful newborn daughter.

Juan came to relieve him, and Carlos couldn't have been any happier. In his haste to leave, he didn't notice the tiny piece of paper had been swept off the desk and disappeared between two grates in a floor vent.

Eighteen

Matthew woke up to Cal shaking him and shouting his name. "What the—"

He could barely open his eyes, and the little he did, sunlight filtered in, blinding him. He shielded himself and turned away from the window.

"Matt, wake up."

"I'm…awake," he mumbled. It was the best Matthew could produce at the moment.

Cal gave him one more hard shake, and it was enough to rouse him. "What is it?" Matthew sat up and looked at his friend's face.

"Mel's gone."

"He's— What?" Matthew got up so fast, his head swooned. "What do you mean he's gone?"

Cal angled his head. "What does that normally mean?"

"He could have just gone on a morning stroll or something?"

"Hello? Are you still asleep?"

"Ah, yeah, I kind of am. What time is it?" Matthew searched the room for a clock and didn't see one. He thought of his cell phone, but remembered it was out of commission for now, then went to look at his watch that was still on his wrist.

"It's almost ten local time," Robyn, whom he hadn't even noticed was standing there until now, told him before he had a chance to read his watch.

"Man, my head hurts." Matthew put a hand to his forehead. It felt like he'd had a few too many cocktails. Too bad he hadn't. At least then he would have had a good time. "Anyone talk to the front desk?"

"I doubt a piece of furniture would have anything to say," Cal countered.

"Very funny."

"We've talked to the clerk, Matt," Robyn said. "He saw Mel somewhere around seven, and he left in a taxi."

"Did he say where he was going?" he asked.

Robyn shook his head. "Not to the clerk."

"It could be all innocent. He might have just wanted to see some of the town and didn't want to wake us." Matthew was trying to give the professor the benefit of the doubt, but it didn't mean he bought into it.

"The guy just abandoned us in Spain," Cal spat.

Matthew shook his head. "That doesn't make any sense. There'd be no reason for him to bring us here and take off."

"Did someone make him leave?" Cal mused. "Maybe those people from Washington followed us here and lured or coerced Mel out. I just knew this guy was bad news from the first time he mentioned Gasparilla. The pirate's mythical. Meaning not real, never was." He paced in a circle and kicked up the edge of the carpet as he moved past.

Matthew flattened the carpet back out with his foot. "Let's go talk to the clerk."

"He's just going to tell you what he told us," Cal said but was the first to the door. He held it open for Matthew and Robyn.

"Same clerk." Cal gestured toward the thirtysomething at the front desk.

"Good morning. I hope that you found your accommodations most comfortable."

"Everything was lovely." The clerk's inquiry took him back for a few seconds. "We're just concerned about our friend," Matthew added.

"Yes, I told your friends that he left in a taxi this morning about seven."

"Do you know where he was going?"

"Not my business, sir."

Matthew nodded. "And he was alone?"

"Yes."

"Did he happen to say when he'd be back or ask that a message be passed along to us?"

"No. I'm sorry."

Matthew scanned the clerk's face, and he could see the man was being genuine. Then again, what motive would he have to lie? That was the downside to Matthew's line of work; he tended to look at most people like they had something to hide. "Thank you."

"No problem."

No problem. That was yet to be determined. Why would Mel have them take him to Spain only to ditch them? "He used me," Matthew said to his cohorts. "All his talk about needing our help? It wasn't to help find the treasure; he needed the money to get here."

"Bastard," Cal muttered.

"No, I don't think that's it." Robyn tilted her head. "He hasn't gotten his hands on the treasure yet."

"As far as we know, it's really close by. We've never seen the diary," Matthew said.

"I read part of it, and nothing too noteworthy stood out to me. At least no directions to the treasure."

"Because he didn't record those parts so he could claim it for himself." Cal enlarged his eyes. "We don't even know this guy is who he says he is."

"Actually, he is a professor at Hodges University, as he says." Both of his friends regarded him incredulously. "I should have said something before now, but Daniel sent me his picture."

"That's all?" Robyn asked.

"All I have so far."

"Okay, but just because he's a professor doesn't mean he's not a crook or a con man, too," Cal said.

"Look." Robyn nudged Matthew's elbow and pointed.

Matthew followed the direction of her finger, and Mel Wolf was getting out of a taxi, his satchel held tightly. Matthew led the way over to him.

"Where were you?" he asked.

Mel tucked in his chin, seemingly surprised by the question. "I was getting a head start on the day."

The taxi driver got out of the vehicle, made his way to the trunk, and began to unload a couple of shopping bags. Lastly, he set a white confection box in Mel's hands, collected his fare, and left.

"Looks to me like you did a little shopping." Matthew pointed to Mel's loaded arms.

"All of you have clothes with you. I had none. Everything is back in my hotel room in Washington."

Anxiety tightened Matthew's chest. He'd done what he could to stay off the grid, and Mel could have just messed it all up. "Did you charge all this?"

Mel shook his head, and Matthew resumed breathing. "I had some cash," Mel said.

"We're a team in this, and as a team, we talk before we act. Do you understand?" Matthew said through gritted teeth.

"Yes… I… I didn't think this would hurt anything or anyone."

"You could have left us a note," Robyn interjected.

"I could have, and from the looks of all of you, I probably should have. For that, I apologize."

Matthew studied the man for any tell of deception, but all he saw was the awkward professor fidgeting with the packages in his hands and toeing the ground with the tip of his shoe.

"I also managed to scout out where we can rent a vehicle…for later, when everyone's awake." Mel smiled at Matthew and held out the confection box to Matthew. "Turrón. Supposedly, they are divine. Nougat, honey, toasted almonds—can't go wrong. Shall we enjoy while we sip on coffee? Oh, assuming none of you have nut allergies?"

"None of us do." Matthew regarded him. Sugary treats and coffee? He was all in, but this wasn't a pleasure stop; they were here on business. Then again, what did a little down time hurt anyone? Besides, he did need to shake his sleepy head awake, and willpower alone wasn't going to do it.

From a practical standpoint, they did need to discuss their next steps, and they might as well take a minute or two to do so. He also wanted to find out how far Mel had gotten with transcribing the diary. He recommended that they seek out a private part of the terrace, and no one raised any objections.

As they sat there, Matthew inhaled the fragrant salty air that carried the smells of flowers. A heady concoction to say the least, and if Matthew didn't know any better, he could let himself slip into the daydream that he was there on a getaway, not on a treasure hunt.

Nineteen

Hotel Málaga, Málaga, Spain
Monday, 10:15 AM Local Time

The stakes were always high when it came to treasure hunting. It was part of the reason Robyn had taken a break from it a while ago. Going after the City of Gold was what had gotten her back into it. Just the resulting rush that came with discovering the ancient city was exhilarating. She wished for a similar experience in Spain, but she was still suspicious of Mel. Why the need to set out on his own before any of them was awake? What he told them could have been the truth, but she had a sick feeling it wasn't the *complete* truth.

"You said that Lopez lived in the village of El Acebuchal," Robyn started, "and you're pretty certain that's the best place to start?" She didn't have many pages of the transcribed diary yet, but there had been no word about El Acebuchal.

"I absolutely do."

"You seem to be holding out a lot of hope," she said. "What if our efforts meet with a dead end?"

"What if?" Mel's lips twitched. "But *what if* we do find what we seek?"

"So, all we have is El Acebuchal?" Matthew asked it in such a way that Robyn found a touch of amusement in it. He'd carted them all the way to Spain on a hunch and was now doubting the move. Typical Matthew. She had a bad feeling all along, but she could tell there was no talking him out of this, and she wasn't going to bail on her friends.

Mel looked at the garden next to where they sat on the terrace.

"Mel?" Matthew prompted.

"The diary may not have said El Acebuchal in so many words." He winced.

"You lied to us?" Cal exclaimed.

"I didn't lie... Okay, I may have lied. I just know the clues led me to the village."

"What clues?" Robyn sat back and crossed her arms.

"There's mention of a road that winds like a snake and hugs the sky."

"Yes, okay, I do recall reading that." She straightened up.

"I don't like the sound of that," Cal said, and Robyn shook her head. He loved the risk that came with adventures but could jump at his own shadow. Or freeze at a fence.

"'A road that winds like a snake and hugs the sky.'" Matthew repeated Mel's words.

"I looked into El Acebuchal, and there's a dirt road that hugs a mountainside," Mel explained.

"Could be what was meant easily enough," Robyn said. "But surely there's more that made you zero in on El Acebuchal."

"There's mention that the village was a popular stop for passing traders."

"There's also talk of traversing water," Robyn said, recalling a portion of what she'd read.

"Yes, and mountains. As I told you before, El Acebuchal is in the heart of a natural park. There are many mountains."

Robyn glanced at Matthew. She wasn't one for scaling mountains, but she was aware Matthew hadn't minded doing it in more recent months. Probably because Daniel had told him that he was no mountain climber, and Matthew took it as a personal challenge.

Mel went on. "Mention is made that Lopez lived nestled in the mountains with vistas overlooking the Mediterranean Sea."

"Surely that could be numerous places in Spain," Matthew said.

"It could be, but it's the age of the village that really strikes me. It was flourishing during the lifetime of Lopez. And those traders I mentioned would have been plentiful at that time."

Robyn wasn't sure if she was ready to accept El Acebuchal as their go-to for the treasure, but Mel certainly did. His gestures got more animated as he spoke, and his eyes were sparkling with excitement.

"You can drive up the base of some of the mountains," he said, "but we'd definitely benefit from getting an all-terrain vehicle. There will be a point from which we need to walk, of course. As I told you, I sourced out a place to rent a vehicle when I was out this morning. They're expecting us."

"You're just a busy beaver, aren't you?" Cal said. "You got yourself a wardrobe, lined up a car…"

"A truck, actually, but I like to be prepared." Mel smiled at the group, and Robyn found herself smiling in return.

Cal tore off a bite of Turrón. "So, what? We're just supposed to go running around mountaintops in the hopes of finding something?"

"He has a point, Professor," Robyn said with such seriousness that all three men looked at her. "You lured us here by telling us you had a place to start, when really all you had was a hunch."

Mel met her gaze and held up his hands. "I never meant to deceive—"

"But that's exactly what you've done." She sat back, crossing her arms in front of her chest again. "You know more than you're telling us, and it's time for you to be honest with us. What's in that bag of yours?"

Mel shifted it in his arms.

"I mean it, Professor Wolf. My friends and I are on the first plane back to Canada—"

"Fine." Mel put his hand into his bag and pulled out a few pieces of paper. "They're scans from the diary. As you can see, I only have a few pages."

"You told us you burned the diary," Cal said.

"And I did. This is all I have left."

"Let me see it." Matthew held out a hand.

As the pages were passed across the table, Robyn saw the handwriting was tight and heavily angled to the right.

"It's very hard to read," Matthew said.

"Let me see it," Robyn requested, and Matthew consented. She read the pages, and it was a painstaking process. They were snippets pulled from different entries, and they seemed to capsulize the landmarks Mel had mentioned. There was also the section where Gómez declared himself the son of José Gaspar, "the last of the great buccaneers."

"So?" Matthew prompted her.

She slowly looked up. "I'd say these are legitimate scans of an ancient diary. Whether or not it was written by Gómez's hand, I'd have no way of knowing." She handed the pages back to Mel. "These pages cover a lot of what you told us."

"Yes."

"But why the scans?" she asked. He'd expressed his concern about holding on to the diary for fear it would end up in the hands of someone who'd secure the treasure, yet he carried key pieces around with him. He'd also said that he had an eidetic memory. None of this lined up.

"I wanted to have something in case you insisted on seeing proof."

"Yet you held off until now."

"I like to live my life on the side of caution. I always have."

Robyn preferred living that way, too, and Mel's actions were setting off all sorts of alarms, but when she scrutinized the man in front of her, it was hard to see the awkward professor as dangerous.

Twenty

Matthew had taken whatever precautions he could to stay off the grid. That's why when it came to renting the four-wheel-drive pickup, he had to pay cash. And that had required a stop at a local bank and a withdrawal from a foreign, untraceable account he had in the Caymans. If they were going to do some trekking today, they would need to hit a store for supplies, too, but they'd agreed this was just going to be a look-and-see mission.

They all loaded into the truck that had enough seating for the four of them and headed out in the direction of Almijara and Alhama Natural Park. A brochure on El Acebuchal, found in the lobby of Hotel Málaga, provided them with rather detailed instructions on how to reach the village.

Matthew did the driving. It wasn't long before they found themselves on a narrow dirt road that headed up the side of a small mountain. It made him think of the entry from the diary that spoke of a road winding like a snake and hugging the sky. They were literally in the clouds and out the passenger door would be a sudden drop.

"I don't like this." Cal's face was hidden behind his camera, and he was taking shots out the passenger's-side window, but he scrunched toward the middle as if that would affect the point of balance and keep them from toppling over the ridge.

"I've got it," Matthew assured him, but his hands were getting a little greasy on the steering wheel. He didn't exactly want to take a plunge to his death any more than Cal.

Eventually, they reached a junction—just as laid out in the brochure—and they proceeded right, following signs for El Acebuchal. The road nosed down, and ahead of them was the spread of the village. Twisty cobblestone streets and a cluster of small white, stucco buildings.

The sign at the entrance announced it as El Acebuchal.

"Looks like we found the village," he said, stating the obvious.

"Now let's find the treasure." Cal kept his camera in front of his face as he spoke, but Matthew caught the smile on his lips.

Matthew found a parking spot, and the four of them got out and looked around. A definite

Spain attraction, but it wasn't overloaded with tourists. Then again, it wasn't a hot-spot destination such as Barcelona or Madrid. The average vacationer's loss, as this place was incredible. Gorgeous panoramic views of the countryside and the Mediterranean Sea stole one's breath. The winding streets were picturesque, and the architecture of the buildings was very similar on the hillsides of Greece. White stucco, cut-outs for windows with no glass and benched by colorfully painted shutters in purples, blues, and reds. Most with safety bars or barriers made of clay tile and brick that came up less than a third of the height of the opening. Small porches and walkways made of red clay tile. Vibrant doors and potted plants and flowers added more color to the landscape.

"It is absolutely stunning here," Robyn cooed, adjusting the strap of a small bag she'd brought along.

"Say that again," Matthew seconded.

"It is beautiful, I give it that." Still behind his camera, Cal pivoted and took shots from every possible angle.

Matthew smiled at his friend, though it would be lost on Cal, who had disappeared into the world of his photography. Cal had once told him that he felt the most alive when looking at the world through a camera lens. From this point, it would be a miracle if they saw his face clear of his camera at all.

Mel was looking around, squinting in the bright sun.

"Do you recognize something from the diary?" Matthew asked. Something seemed to be weighing on the professor's mind.

Mel slowly met Matthew's gaze and shook his head. "It's just…being here… It's magnificent. Have you ever been to Spain before?"

"No," Matthew admitted. "One of a few places I haven't been."

"This trip will be very educational for you, too, then."

There was no need to reply to that. Every time Matthew set out into the world, it was "educational."

Robyn wrapped her sweater more tightly to her body. The sun was doing its best to warm the air, but there was a cool breeze.

"I say that we start with the chapel. Assuming they have one." She looked at Mel. "We could find books there that mention Lopez."

"That's if they are any books left," Mel said somberly.

Due to the ravages of the Spanish Civil War, Matthew thought.

Robyn glanced at Matthew. "We have to start somewhere. Maybe when they started to rebuild the city, artifacts and books made their way back here."

"It's possible," Matthew admitted and hoped it was true. "Okay, the chapel it is, but where to find it…"

A woman in her twenties approached them, grinning. "Welcome to El Acebuchal, known to us locals as the Village of the Ghosts."

Cal slowly lowered his camera. "This could be where I change my mind."

Matthew snickered. His best friend, the reluctant adventure junkie.

"I'm Salma." She pointed to the name badge on her chest, which also announced her as a guide. "What brings you to El Acebuchal?" She looked right at Matthew, her eyes piercing him.

"Just seeing all we can of this beautiful country," he said.

"It is a beautiful country. Do you know the history of El Acebuchal?"

Matthew gestured to the professor. "We do. We're actually looking for the chapel, assuming there is one?"

"Excuse me." A tall, lean woman with a tanned complexion and long, dark, wavy hair inserted herself into the group. She swept some of her hair over her shoulder as she matched her gaze with Matthew's. "Please, excuse me for interrupting and overhearing." She paused there and smiled at him.

Beautiful country. Beautiful women.

"No problem at all," Matthew said.

"You're looking for the chapel?"

"Lady, are you a guide?" Salma said, jutting her hips to the right. "I don't think so."

"She's right. I'm not a guide, but I grew up in the area, and I won't charge you a dime or ask for a tip." She never took her eyes off Matthew.

"Hmph." Salma crossed her arms and stuck out her chin at Matthew. "Your call."

"Thank you for your hospitality and welcome, but—"

"Uh-huh." Salma walked off in a snit.

"That chapel, did you want to see it?" the beautiful stranger asked.

"I'd like your name first. You know, before we follow you around the village." Matthew smiled at her. He'd like a lot of things from her, but first things first. Though he didn't need a name to know the woman had legs that went on forever. Sultry, full lips. The kind he'd love to nibble—

"Angelica." She held out her hand to him first, then the others. After all the introductions were made, Angelica asked, "Why are you interested in seeing the chapel?"

Robyn stepped beside Matthew, the fabric of her sweater brushing against his long-sleeve T-shirt. "We're die-hard history buffs with a particular interest in old manuscripts. Are there any here from before the Spanish Civil War? Say the late eighteenth and early nineteenth centuries?"

"Oh, yes. I can help you with that. Would you like me to take you to them?" Her attention was on Matthew, even though Robyn had made the request.

"Yes, we'd like that." Matthew glanced at Robyn.

"Very well, follow me." Angelica set out, heading east.

"After you." Robyn rolled her eyes and gestured for him to lead their group behind the guide.

Angelica either naturally swayed her hips a lot or she was putting in an extra effort for him. Regardless, Matthew enjoyed the view. She was wearing a white shirt and a white skirt that came mid-thigh and fluttered in the breeze created by her steps.

Angelica took them to a small building with an engraved and hand-painted sign that told them it was the El Acebuchal Museum. "This place houses recovered artifacts dating back to the time of the original settlement. We're grateful that they found their way home in recent years. You know that the Spanish Civil War had destroyed the village?"

"Yes, thanks to this guy." Matthew nudged his head toward Mel, who actually waved at Angelica when she glanced at him. The professor needed to work on his charisma.

"Let's go take a look, shall we?" She gestured for them to go inside.

Glass cabinets, like the ones in jewelry stores, displayed household items and trinkets, coins, and crosses. There were also books. Some were opened, and others closed. Matthew, Robyn,

Cal, and the professor gravitated to a case with the former.

"Ah, yes, you were most interested in books." Angelica slinked up beside Matthew. Her hip brushed against his, but she didn't move to put any space between them.

Robyn was leaning over the case, her nose pretty much pressed against the glass. Mel was next to her, looking at another opened book, his satchel gripped to his chest.

Cal was taking pictures of everything the light hit—and probably of the shadows where it missed, too.

"This is great," Matthew admitted to Angelica. "But it would be even better if we could get a closer look."

"I'm not sure what you're saying."

"Would there be any way we could hold these books for ourselves, flip through the pages?"

"I don't see how." She bit her bottom lip, but a flicker in her eyes betrayed her. Matthew would press that.

"What if we came back after hours? I'm sure a place like this isn't open to the public all the time?"

"Even if you came back after they closed, I don't see how such a thing could be permitted."

"Huh, that's too bad. It would mean a lot. Oh well." Matthew turned from her, feigning disinterest.

She put a hand on his shoulder and drew him back to her. "I might know someone who can help. But he's not the most reliable person on the planet, so I don't know if he will."

"Whatever you could to do to help us would be appreciated," he said.

She locked eyes with him and licked her lips. Something devilish and carnal stirred inside him.

"Give me a few minutes," she said.

He dipped his head. "Take your time."

Angelica sauntered off, and Matthew watched her hips sway all the way to the exit.

Robyn smacked him on the arm.

"What?" He rubbed where she'd struck him.

"Focus on why we're here, or is that too much to ask?"

"It might be too much," he teased, and she narrowed her eyes at him briefly but ended up shaking her head. "Besides, she's going to help us."

"So I overheard, and I'm sure she'd be more than happy to accommodate you."

"Someone's sounding a little jealous."

"You wish." She shoved him playfully and smiled, but the expression didn't touch her eyes.

"We're better off as friends," he felt the need to remind her. "That's what we agreed to."

There were a few seconds of awkward silence before Robyn said, "Well, if she can help us get our hands on these books, I might kiss her myself."

Matthew tried to squeeze that image out of his head. If he didn't need a cold shower before, he needed one now.

Angelica returned and came over to him and Robyn. "I have good news. Come back here after midnight, but don't tell anyone else. Just the four of you are to know anything about it." She traced her gaze over them, settled it on Matthew.

"Consider it done. Thank you," he said.

"Don't thank me quite yet. Pablo isn't known for keeping his word." Her body tensed and her jaw clenched—just enough to notice—then relaxed. "In the meantime, I'd be happy to give you a tour of the village. It seems you have plenty of time."

"Sounds lovely," Matthew replied. In his head, he was doing the math. It was about one in the afternoon now. They had eleven hours to pass. Sleep didn't seem like part of the plan for this expedition.

Twenty-One

I n Colin's twenty-five years on the force, he was certain of one thing. For the most part, people were predictable. At least when it came to the hunger for money. It was at the root of most crimes, most murders, most atrocities. The admonition to follow the money was spot-on. It just usually didn't take him to actual treasure.

Yet treasure hunting was exactly what Matthew Connor did. And it would seem whatever was in Spain held the motivation for a running pursuit through Colin's jurisdiction.

They were still waiting on the video from the city. It didn't surprise him, though. Any time bureaucratic offices were involved, time seemed to come to a halt. In the meantime, the fate of Matthew, his friends, and the mysterious geeky-looking man were in the air. It would seem one of the armed men shot and killed Judy Finch.

Hopefully, they hadn't caught up with the Canadian Trio or Mr. Tweed Jacket.

He'd called into U.S. Customs and Border Protection to see if there was any record of the trio boarding a plane and had yet to hear. He also submitted an inquiry on one of the armed men they were able to identify. They still had none on the other armed man or Mr. Tweed Jacket.

The large perp was Roman Murphy from Connecticut, and he had a rap sheet a mile long. He'd served time for murder and armed robbery and had gotten out of prison two years ago. Apparently, he hadn't been rehabilitated or learned any lessons. But some habits die hard.

Colin leaned his elbow on the arm of his chair and rested his forehead in his hand. He was at the police station behind his desk, staring at Roman's ugly mug. If he didn't know any better, he'd say the man was challenging him. But that was something that was instinctual in Colin himself. Life itself or other people weren't the competition; he was his own. Probably one reason why he was at work early while James was still asleep at home.

He rolled his chair forward, planning to run Roman's name through some databases. Maybe he could see if anything would click for him. Namely, how did a murderer and an armed robber go from that to treasure hunting? He keyed in a search, and the results brought up the man's known associates. A fairly lengthy list, but one name stood out.

Oscar Vincent.

It was the last name that was familiar. A Veronica Vincent was the woman behind the abduction and ransom of Matthew Connor's friend in exchange for the City of Gold. Veronica was a chilling psychopath with a love for three things: herself, money, and power. Any of those—or *all* of them—could serve as motivation for going after Matthew in Washington. But was Oscar a relative?

Colin opened another database and entered Oscar's name. Looking back at him was a handsome, yet young face. Colin read the statistics. Oscar's last known address was in Albany, New York. He was twenty-seven and only five foot six. Short.

He brought up the still taken from the video in the hotel's underground garage. It showed the thugs as they ran by an import sedan. He googled how tall that vehicle was and focused in on the small man. Vincent's height lined up.

Colin returned to the background on Vincent. No criminal record, but he was under surveillance by the FBI a few years ago in connection with their interest in Veronica. The world wasn't that big; they had to be related. But under Oscar's and Veronica's backgrounds, there were no notes to indicate that. Still, it was worth considering that if the FBI suspected

Oscar was working with Veronica in the past, it was very possible he was again.

The system showed Veronica was facing criminal charges and out on bail. To achieve that she had to have powerful people in her corner. The judge, however, did order that she was to surrender her passport and remain in the United States.

But if life had taught Colin anything, people like Veronica couldn't be strong-armed, and they carried on and lived whatever way they saw fit.

And if the nonsense about pirate treasure was true, he'd bet his next paycheck she was already somewhere in Spain. She'd just have assumed another identity with a fake passport. Regardless, there would be no way of tracking her down that he could think of right now. He'd submit an inquiry with U.S. Customs and Border Protection on Oscar.

He could feel the headache moving in and grabbed a couple pills from his top drawer, popped them in his mouth, and dry swallowed.

He hated feeling powerless. He walked himself over to the bullpen and made himself a coffee, hoping the brew would somehow stimulate some good ideas.

He didn't do well with waiting, and if he wasn't getting anywhere with the thugs, maybe he'd get somewhere with Mr. Tweed Jacket. His identity was still a mystery. They'd asked around the hotel, but no one recognized him, and the manager adamantly concluded he hadn't been their guest.

So, how does he know Matthew Connor, and where did the two meet? The opening of the City of Gold exhibit?

Colin wasn't really brushed up on exhibit-opening etiquette. Was it by invitation only or open to the public? He'd have to find out. It might lead to an ID on Mr. Tweed Jacket.

He got up and grabbed his coat, but when his eyes went to the clock on the wall, his entire body sagged. It was only approaching seven in the morning. There wouldn't be a soul at the museum. He might as well go home and catch whatever sleep he could. If this possible lead paid off, he might not be sleeping again for a while.

Twenty-Two

Frigiliana, Spain
Monday, 5:12 PM Local Time

Angelica had provided them with a slow-paced and thorough tour of El Acebuchal. Matthew enjoyed learning more about the history and the people who had lived there and passed through. As an archaeologist, he was enthralled by the past, but as his passion for that grew, it had morphed organically into a desire to unearth legends. He blamed his first assignment—a dig in Egypt after completing his doctorate—as something that made him hungry for such adventures.

Once they'd seen all of El Acebuchal, Angelica had suggested they take a twenty-minute drive to the nearby town of Frigiliana. It was there that they settled into a local bar and restaurant, Angelica with them. They all had ordered food but were currently nursing drinks. Matthew, Robyn, and Cal, beers; Angelica a fruity non-alcoholic cocktail; Mel an herbal tea.

Cal had finally put his camera down, but only after taking shots from every angle in the restaurant. He'd been so thorough that the owner had asked him what he was doing. When Cal explained he was a freelance photographer and dropped a couple of names for magazines he'd done work for, the owner had smiled and told him to take as many pictures as he liked. He also encouraged Cal to share them online.

Now, Cal's head kept dipping as if he might fall asleep at the table.

"Wakey, wakey." Matthew waved a hand in front of his friend's face.

"How can you be so awake?"

"Good question." By all accounts, the jet lag should have him knocked out, but between the day's excursion, the promise of treasure, and Angelica, he was rather alert. Robyn and the professor appeared to be hanging on, too. But would they all be able to say the same thing by the time midnight rolled around?

"I think you should just leave me here to die." Cal slurped some of his beer.

"We're all tired, but we should probably lay off the booze and caffeinate instead," Matthew said, glancing at Mel and Angelica. "They're the smart ones."

"Why are all of you so tired?" Angelica asked. Through their travels that afternoon, they'd told her they were from Canada and Mel from the United States, but they hadn't gotten into when they'd arrived.

"Jet lag is part of the problem." Matthew didn't think he should tell her about the chase in Washington which had prevented sleep. He certainly didn't want to tell her what brought them to Spain and El Acebuchal. The fewer people who knew, the better. "We just got in this morning, about three thirty your time."

"Ouch." Angelica pursed her lips. "Yeah, that's rough. Could you get some rest before returning for midnight?"

"That's probably not a bad idea," Matthew replied, looking at Robyn, Cal, and Mel. "We could go back to Hotel Málaga and get some, come back later."

"Please, no," Cal said. "I didn't like the drive in during the day. That narrow road on the mountainside… Just imagine driving that at night."

Matthew had to admit the prospect didn't sound pleasant. "There must be rooms we could rent in El Acebuchal or here in Frigiliana." He looked to Angelica as if what he'd said was a question, but he'd seen a few places where they may be able to crash for a few hours.

"Luck would need to be on your side," Angelica said. "Resorts around here are often booked months in advance. You could stay with me, though." The way she'd latched her gaze with Matthew, he wondered if her proposal was for him only. "*All of* you could," she added and took in the rest of them.

"How kind of you," Robyn mumbled.

"Well, it's the Spanish way. We are a hospitable people." She grinned and put an arm around Matthew.

He'd love to find out just *how* hospitable…

"I take it you live close to El Acebuchal, then?" he asked her.

"I grew up right here in Frigiliana."

"You never said that before now."

She hitched her shoulders. "Had no reason to."

The server came over and delivered their food. It included these delicious baked potatoes in a tomato sauce.

"I don't know what these are called, but we don't have potatoes like this back home." Matthew pointed his fork at his plate.

"That dish is called Patatas Bravas. Like home fries you'd have back home."

"Nothing like I've eaten in Canada," Matthew repeated.

"Then you'll just have to come here more often."

He didn't say anything back or even smile, but he held her gaze. This afternoon had been a nice detour, and peering into her eyes, it was easy to forget why he was even in Spain. But she said she'd grown up in this area. Maybe she'd heard rumor or talk about Lopez and pirate's treasure. She could have knowledge that would help them, but he reverted to his earlier thinking that it was probably best to leave her in the dark as to their purpose there. Treasure hunting attracted enemies. He didn't need her becoming a target, and he didn't need their ally to become an enemy.

They all ate in relative silence, and Matthew settled up the bill. Angelica thanked him for covering her portion, and he dismissed it with, "That's the least I can do."

After eating, Angelica gave them directions to her *casa*, which was only a block from the restaurant. The place was expansive and lavishly decorated with priceless artwork and statues. She showed them to different rooms.

She took Matthew to his room last. "I'm going to turn in for a bit, too. I'll be next door if you need me." She paused at the door, her words and her body language enclosing an invitation—one he was greatly tempted to accept. But he had to keep his mind about him. Angelica was new to them, and she'd just shown up, really. That alone should have made him suspicious from the start, but he'd been blinded by her beauty. It was time to redeem himself. "You do quite well for yourself. What is it you do again?"

"I never said." She smiled at him and left the room. "Pleasant dreams."

Matthew got into bed and stared at the ceiling. There was a niggling in his gut telling him to exercise a little more caution with Angelica. He'd sadly fallen into the web of a beautiful woman before, and she'd been his kryptonite, almost costing him the lives of those he held most dear. He had to squeeze Angelica's gorgeous face out of his consciousness and focus like Robyn had reminded him to do. He stared at the ceiling, looking for the strength to do just that. His gaze followed the cracks in the plaster until his eyes became heavy and closed.

Twenty-Three

Frigiliana, Spain
Monday, 10:05 PM Local Time

Matthew woke to raised voices and excitement for the second time in one day. At first, he thought the commotion was part of his dream, but he opened his eyes only to realize that it was really happening. He dragged his sleepy limbs from bed and headed in the direction of the commotion.

"What's going on?" He could barely get his eyes to open all the way, given the light in the living area of the house.

"I'll tell you what's going on." Mel's eyes were bugging out. "She—" he pointed a finger at Angelica "—is bad news. She tried to take my bag."

Matthew turned to the woman.

She held up her hands. "It was just a misunderstanding."

"Clear it up for us." He was determined not to be a sucker to a pretty face again.

"I just happened to notice that he was sleeping with his bag against him. I thought he'd be much more comfortable without—"

"See?" Mel burst out. "She admits to trying to take my bag."

"And why would I take it?" she spat.

"Why would you want to move it?" Matthew volleyed back. "He's a grown man. If he was comfortable the way he was, why not just leave him alone?"

Angelica squinted, studying his face. "Obviously it was wrong of me. I see that now, but I didn't mean anything by it."

He wanted to believe her and for this all to be smoothed over with gracious words and a pretty face, but her reasoning for touching Mel's bag was somewhat unsettling. "You weren't trying to look inside his bag?"

"Hey, Matt, we're all curious about what he's toting around in there," Cal inserted.

Matthew never took his gaze off Angelica. "He's right, but we've come to a truce, respecting it as his property." It was still a matter that gnawed at him, but he'd learned to tolerate it for the time being.

"You're a far more trusting sort than I am," Angelica admitted.

Her rebuttal struck him as contradictory to what he'd seen of her. "You welcomed us into your home. You just met us today."

"Maybe that's why I…" She stopped talking.

"You *were* trying to see in his bag," Matthew said.

Angelica eventually nodded. "You could say that I'm curious about it—about all of you, really. What brought you to Spain, and why are you interested in ancient books?" Her gaze danced over all of them, but again settled on Matthew.

Seconds ticked off in silence.

"If you want to get into the museum tonight, I need you to start talking. All it would take is a phone call and—" she snapped her fingers "—the offer goes away."

Matthew detested ultimatums, but if they had any hope of finding anything on Lopez in the old manuscripts, it would start with Angelica's assistance.

"We're legend hunters, treasure hunters, whatever you'd like to call us." Matthew gestured to himself and closest friends. "That man over there is a university professor. He teaches American history in Florida. He sought us out to help him with something."

Angelica's eyes were calculating. "To find a treasure?"

Matthew glanced at Robyn, Cal, then the professor.

"You think there's something to be found in El Acebuchal?" Angelica pressed.

"Yes and no," Matthew replied.

"What?"

A single word that if left unanswered had the potential of blowing everything up. He didn't want to bring Angelica into this, but now it seemed he had no other choice. "Clues to a pirate's treasure."

Angelica's lips twitched, and then she gave birth to a full-fledged laugh that had her shoulders heaving. "You…you can't be serious?"

Matthew didn't say anything, figuring that would be the strongest response of all.

Angelica's lips set in a straight line. "You *are* serious." Her eyes darted to Mel. "What led you here?"

"Dumb luck. It doesn't really matter," Matthew answered on behalf of the professor.

"I see. You're wanting to hold some back."

"Just following your lead," he snapped. "Who are you?"

Angelica regarded him with serious expression. "You know my name—"

"First name anyway," Matthew countered.

"My last name is Pérez, but I assume you're wanting to know what *I do*. Well, I'm the woman who's going to help you get what you want."

Again, a deflection, a non-answer, and it didn't help endear her to him, but it reminded him of the place in which he was stuck.

"Go ahead and tell her," he directed Mel.

The professor filled her in about the diary. She dropped into a chair at the mention of Rodrigo Lopez.

"Rodrigo…" Her tone nested surprise at the name—and possible recognition?

"You've heard of Lopez?" Matthew asked.

Angelica met his eyes and nodded. "You could say that."

"Oh." Matthew pulled out a chair next to her, swung it around and sat, straddling it.

"My great-great-great-grandmother was fascinated by pirates, the lives they lived, the adventures they had. Family scuttlebutt is the older she got, the more stories she told." Her gaze drifted to a curio cabinet in the corner of the room.

"What sort of stories?" Robyn asked.

"She loved a pirate. Apparently, she told everyone she could that no woman knows love unless she's been loved by a pirate. She said that he accepted her for who she was and that he commanded any room he entered. She was like a moth to a flame." She paused and smiled. "That's what my grandmother told me from the stories she'd heard passed on."

"You're the descendent of a pirate?" Mel gulped and squirmed like he needed to pee.

"No. Probably why most of my family dismissed her stories as ramblings. My mother among them, dismissing the entire thing as nonsense. But I always liked to believe that my great-great-great-grandmother actually loved a pirate." Angelica glanced at Robyn. "You can probably understand the allure to a wild heart."

Robyn's cheeks flushed. "There is something about bad boys," she admitted, her voice a little gruff.

"What happened to the pirate, then?" Matthew asked. "You said you're not a descendent of one."

"He died before they had a chance to marry."

"Any word on how?"

Angelica shook her head. "That was one thing my great-great-great-grandmother wouldn't discuss. Part of why the family dismissed her story of a pirate. But I do have something that you might like to see." She got up and went to the cabinet, opened a drawer, and returned with a gold brooch.

"Can I see that?" Mel crossed the room to her.

Angelica's jaw tightened, then relaxed as she handed the item to Mel. "Please be careful with it."

"Of course." Mel let go of his satchel, though it still hung around his neck, both hands turning the brooch. "The engravings on this are definitely Spanish. Could easily date back to the late eighteenth or nineteenth centuries." Mel kept on examining the artifact.

"It was all she had left of him, she said, and she passed it on to her daughters, and it made its way to—"

"Lopez," Mel burst out and held up the brooch. "His name is on here."

Angelica was grinning. "It's why I recognized the name."

"It's inscribed with 'To my love Sanibella. R. Lopez.'" Mel stared at Angelica.

"Sanibella was my great-great-great-grandmother, and I recalled the pirate's name being Lopez."

"No shit." Cal came over, bumping against the professor and causing him to stagger to keep his balance.

"Bull in a china shop," Mel grumbled, his eyebrows pointed down in a V-shape.

"Sanibella," Robyn began, "that's the supposed woman who Lopez returned to Spain for."

Matthew's suspicions about Angelica muted to the background, but they were still there. She'd shown up at the right time and just happened to be related to *the* Sanibella? It was almost hard to accept. But stranger things had happened. "You said that your grandmother gave you this brooch?"

"Yes," Angelica responded. "Mom never had it in her possession because she didn't believe in the stories. My grandmother said because of that she wasn't worthy to have it."

"Is your grandmother still alive?" Matthew asked. "I'm thinking maybe she has journals or diaries that your grandmother Sanibella may have kept."

"She died five years ago, but I never heard mention of any journals or diaries."

Matthew slowly nodded. It had been a reach and a wish.

"Do you know where she met Lopez?" Mel asked.

"At a market. The story passed down was they just saw each other and were drawn together. She said she couldn't resist his charms."

Mel swatted away her last statement. "Yes, she was smitten. Did he—Lopez, the pirate she fell for—ever say where he got the brooch?"

Angelica paled under the professor's intense glare, and she snatched the brooch from his hand and returned it to the cabinet. "He was a pirate. How do you think he got his hands on it?"

Now Mel dropped onto a chair. "He likely plundered it while serving aboard the *Floridablanca.*"

Matthew wasn't sure why Angelica had reacted so strongly to Mel's question, but it seemed to cement one thing: this had become personal to her. And given the authentic response, their meeting and her connection to Lopez was entirely a coincidence.

Angelica squinted and angled her head. "Is the *Floridablanca* a ship?"

"Yes, but not just any ship," Mel replied.

"Okay," she dragged out.

"It's a ship said to have been captained by a pirate by the name of José Gaspar," Matthew jumped in, and received a glare from the professor for the intrusion.

"The pirate whose treasure you seek?"

"That's right," Matthew confirmed.

Angelica sat there, silent, her dark eyes skimming over all of them. "Well, I'm in."

"Wait," Matthew said, "what do you mean you're in?"

"Just that. You can't shut me out now. Not when it's connected in a roundabout way to my grandmother Sanibella. Besides, you told me what you're after. I could start telling everyone."

"You wouldn't do that," Matthew said.

"Why wouldn't I?"

"As you essentially said, it's personal to you."

"Fine, you have me. But this sounds like a grand adventure, the kind my great-great-great-grandmother would have loved, would have wanted for me. If for nothing more, I'd love to tag along in honor of her. I'm not in it for any monetary reward."

Her motivation was attractive, but he had to warn her. "Treasure hunting's not for the faint of heart."

"I'm hardly a delicate flower." She held out her hand to him. "Partners?"

Matthew looked at her extended hand. "And you're sure you don't want anything in return?"

"Nope, all for Grandmother Sanibella's memory."

"Very well." Matthew shook her hand, hoping he hadn't just made a deal with the devil. "Just remember what I told you about treasure hunt—"

"Yadda-yadda. It's not for the faint of heart." She grinned and let out a loud, "Whoot!"

Matthew shared in her excitement, but Robyn wore a serious expression.

"You shouldn't make light of his warning," she said. "I've been shot before while looking for a legend, and in this particular case, the professor here has attracted some unwanted attention."

Angelica's gaze flicked to Mel. "Such as?"

"Men with guns," Cal butted in. "They were shooting at us, chasing after us through the streets of Washington, DC."

"I see. And you don't think I can handle myself?" She raised her brows at Matthew.

"Hey, no one's saying that. No one would dare."

"What I like to hear." She narrowed her eyes seductively, and he felt himself grow warm. But that was him getting distracted again. Truth was that while there hadn't been any sign of Mel's stalkers in Spain, Matthew hoped she wouldn't need to defend herself against them.

Twenty-Four

El Acebuchal Museum, El Acebuchal, Spain
Monday, 11:50 PM Local Time

Robyn had been mentally preoccupied with the books beneath the glass in the museum—until Angelica dropped the news her great-great-great-grandmother had loved the pirate Lopez. Small world. Huge coincidence. But incredible, nonetheless. Sometimes life saved up and served a huge surprise. She just hoped that it was a good one. Matthew certainly didn't seem to have any reservations about Angelica, but Robyn wished she were more forthcoming with what she did for work. Hopefully, her secrecy wouldn't end up hurting them.

They were outside the El Acebuchal Museum waiting on Angelica's friend to let them inside. Pablo was his name, if Robyn remembered right. She'd built him up in her mind to be some gorgeous Spaniard with salsa hips and a sinner's smile. Boy, had she created a fantasy. The real Pablo was a pale-skinned white man and scraggly like he hadn't eaten in a few months. There was a crazed quality that danced in his eyes like he was a wild animal.

"It's about time you got here." Angelica padded up next to Pablo as he worked the key in the lock.

"Just be happy I'm here."

"True enough. Your word usually is unreliable."

Their interaction made Robyn question the nature of their relationship, and their history, but neither was her business.

Pablo held the door for everyone, and Robyn filtered inside last. The way Pablo smiled at her made her crave a shower.

"Not sure why you guys want a private audience with a bunch of dusty trinkets," he said, unlocking one display case after another, "and I don't care. Just don't hurt anything, or it will be my ass on the line."

Robyn collected the book she'd read two pages of earlier in the day—or technically yesterday, as it was a bit after midnight. She sat on the floor in a corner and started reading.

She appreciated the nuance of the language, the style of the author, though she or he was unnamed. Everything seemed to be painted with the brush of an artist, the words chosen colorful and poetic. But with the more pages she read, the tone of the passages changed.

There were some dated entries that placed them around the time of the Spanish Civil War. There was comment about the people of El Acebuchal's fears. There was no mention of treasure or Lopez or pirates.

She picked out another book and started to read. She was sure the hours were ticking off as she, Mel, and Angelica worked their way through the tomes. Pablo kept ducking outside for a cigarette and returned reeking of smoke. Cal and Matthew had made conversation on the other side of the room for the first while, but by this point, Cal had his knees bent to his chest and his head leaning against a wall, eyes shut. He wasn't full-out snoring yet, but given the sound of his deep breathing, it wasn't far off.

She got up and went to the cabinets for another book, and a kink bit in her lower back. She stopped walking and stretched, rubbing her back as she did so. Her gaze tripped to a small chest about ten inches long, ten inches deep, and five inches wide. It had intricate scrollwork in its design that looked familiar.

"I need to see that key again," she said to Mel. She didn't have an eidetic memory, but she had strong recall, and she was pretty sure the scrollwork on the chest and the key were a match.

Mel didn't respond, and when she looked at him, he had his nose buried in a book and was muttering as he read, his lips moving at a rapid pace.

"Professor Wolf?" she jabbed out.

"Ah…yeah?" He sounded like she'd wrested him from a deep sleep. His mind and imagination no doubt on a trip with the words he consumed.

"The key?" She went over to him and held out her hand.

"Ah, yeah. Sure." He rooted in his satchel, which remained strapped across his chest even as he sat on the floor. "Here it is." He handed her the key.

She hurried to the case and made the comparison. "Is it just me or does—"

Pablo entered the museum with his arms in the air. Behind him were two men she'd recognize anywhere. The thugs who fired on them in Washington. The large one sported a rainbow-colored nose thanks to Cal's kick to his face and was holding a gun to Pablo's back.

She palmed the key and tucked it into a front pocket of her jeans and, at the same time, noticed Angelica lower herself behind a cabinet across the room.

"Move it." The large one nudged Pablo hard enough that he fell forward to the floor.

Hands still up, submissive and compliant, Pablo was shaking, and tears streaked down his face. The large man walked up to him and pulled the trigger.

Robyn screamed, and it came back to her ears as if it had come from someone else. She shuddered and ran into a corner, putting space between her and the cabinet with the chest as well as the men.

Footsteps hurried after her. She spun, expecting one of the thugs to take hold of her. But Matthew intercepted.

Her insides turned to liquid. "Please! Don't do any—" Her pleas were interrupted when Cal threw a book at the large one's head and it struck the side of his brow.

"You're going to die!" The giant barreled toward Cal, thankfully not fulfilling his vow with a pull of his trigger.

Matthew and Cal tackled the large one. Matthew kicked the gun out of his hands, and it fell to the floor. Cal stuck his thumbs into the man's eye sockets, and the large guy gripped Cal's sides and squeezed so hard that Cal cried out. The man lifted Cal and tossed him aside like a six-foot-five rag doll.

Matthew hammered punches into the man's chest and fenced off blows to his head.

Robyn felt wiry fingers dig into her arm.

"Stop or I'll shoot her." The smaller thug had a tight hold on her, and he nudged the unforgiving steel muzzle of his gun against her forehead.

She went cold with terror, and her legs lost strength. Her captor's hold was the only thing keeping her upright. "Matthew!" she shrieked.

He stopped his struggle immediately, stepped back from the large man, and held up his hands.

The large man kicked Matthew's legs out from under him, and Matthew fell hard to the floor.

"Son of a bitch!" the large man roared and cupped his eyes.

Cal was on the floor, as still as a manikin. He was about six feet from where the large man's gun had fallen. Robyn prayed he would make a move for the weapon, because she couldn't. The man who held her strengthened his grip, digging his fingernails farther into her flesh. Warm blood trickled down her arm.

"Just let her go," Matthew pleaded. "We'll do anything you want."

"Sounding better all the time," the small man said.

Robyn closed her eyes and tried to put her mind elsewhere, but when she opened them, her gaze was on Pablo's dead body. His face was toward her, and his dark eyes were fixed in a stare. She lifted her gaze and had a small line of sight to Angelica, who had her left index finger to her lips. As if Robyn would disclose her.

"Now if anyone else thinks about doing something stupid, think again," the large one said, reclaiming his gun.

Mel spoke up. "I won't surrender the diary."

"Oh, we don't want your stupid diary. Not anymore," the small one stated with authority. "We want the whole damn treasure."

"Once you find it, enjoy. It's all yours," Matthew said.

The large one clicked back on his gun and held it on Matthew. "Smart-asses get themselves killed."

"If you value her life at all, you'll get us Gasparilla's treasure." The small one pressed the gun harder to Robyn's skull.

She could hardly breathe. It felt like…like… The room spun.

"Robyn, stay strong. We'll get out of this." It was Matthew encouraging her.

"Don't make promises you can't keep." The thug ratcheted his hold on her arm, something she didn't even think possible.

More piercing of her skin and more warmth. Glancing down, she saw the blood trickling out from the cuff of her sweater and over her hand.

"We'll cooperate. Do whatever you want. Just let her go." Matthew was beseeching both men, his hands in the air.

"Sounds more like what I want to hear," the small one said. "Tell us where the treasure is."

Matthew's eyes flicked to Robyn's, and she blinked slowly.

"We don't know where the treasure is," he admitted softly and regrettably.

"Ah, but we think you do." The large one paced a few steps but kept vigilant of the three men in the room. But none of them would make a move and risk her life. At least Robyn hoped none of them would. The unknown variable was the professor. Well, him and Angelica, who so far had gone unnoticed by the two thugs.

"We don't know," the words squeaked out of Robyn, backing up Matthew's claim.

The small one jerked the gun muzzle into her brow. "Pow."

She flinched, certain the metal had cut her forehead. No treasure was worth dying over. "There's a key," she burst out through gritted teeth.

"Whoopie." The large man lassoed his arm above his head to indicate *big deal*.

"It's important. I…I have it in my pocket." She squirmed, praying that the guy would loosen his hold on her.

"No funny business."

"Wouldn't dream of it." Smug and delivered with far more courage than she felt.

He let go of her, and she slipped a hand into her pocket. Movement across the room caught her eye. Angelica had just pulled a handgun from inside her jacket with one hand, while her other hand went into an outside pocket.

Robyn slowly held up the key.

The small man snatched it from her and looked at it closely, then grimaced. "What's it for?"

In her head, she screamed, *The chest!* Out loud, she said, "I don't know… We don't know yet."

"Bullshit! Start talking."

"You know all we know," she slapped out, her newfound bravado buoyed by hope that

Angelica would salvage the situation and save them.

"What if I said I don't believe you?" The large one moved to within a foot of Robyn and lowered his face to within mere inches of hers.

Her heart throbbed, keeping a constant rhythm and a pulse she could hear and feel beneath her left ear. For the briefest of seconds, her eyes locked with Angelica's, and in that finite amount of time, Robyn received her message and lowered to the floor.

Angelica rose from behind the counter, gun held high, and with two *pfts*, both men dropped to the floor. Dead. Bullets nested between their eyes.

The large man had fallen backward into a cabinet. The glass had shattered and made a horrendous noise far louder than the suppressed gunfire.

"Holy shit! What the hell was—" Cal was the first to stand and was gripping his head. He spun to look at the fallen thugs.

Robyn expelled a deep breath, but she was afraid to give herself over to success just yet. Where there were two thugs, there'd be more. Someone had to be behind the wheel of that SUV in Washington.

She looked at the man who'd gripped her arm, the one she'd been so threatened and intimidated by. The man who would have happily pulled the trigger of his gun and ended her life. He was harmless now, sprawled out on the floor.

"We've got to go." Angelica was the epitome of calm as her pistol literally smoked in her hand.

"Thank you." Robyn's throat felt stitched together, but she managed to get out the expression of gratitude.

Matthew hurried over to Robyn and handled her arm as if it were the broken wing of a bird.

"I'm fine. Really." She smiled at him, and eventually he nodded.

"We need to leave." Angelica unscrewed the silencer from her gun, stuffed it into her pocket again, and slipped the gun back under her jacket. She must have been wearing a holster.

"We need to talk," Matthew said.

"It's going to have to be somewhere else." Angelica proceeded to collect the men's guns. She ensured the chambers were clear and handed one to Matthew. She offered the other to Cal, but he didn't take it, and neither would Robyn. Angelica never even asked Mel and put it in her jacket pocket. "Let's go."

"Wait." Robyn reclaimed the key from the large one's hand and stuffed it into her pocket, then rushed to the cabinet with the small chest. She retrieved it and left the building with the rest of them. Outside, she took a good look around but didn't see any other thugs.

The five of them managed to squeeze into the rental truck meant to accommodate four adults.

Matthew asked, "Where to?"

"We can go back to my place," Angelica said. "It should be safe. I can't say the same for the hotel where you were staying."

Robyn's entire body was quaking, and she looked down at the chest in her lap. With everything that had just happened, no one had even asked her about it yet. She stared at its keyhole but held off trying the skeleton key. They'd almost been killed, but three men hadn't been so lucky. One of them Angelica had known. Robyn didn't have the heart to ask who Pablo had been to her right now, but she offered her condolences.

"He never kept his word," Angelica tossed back nonchalantly.

"He did tonight," Robyn said softly.

"Yeah, the one time he kept his word…" Angelica left the rest unsaid, and they drove for some time in reverent silence for Pablo.

Twenty-Five

Smithsonian National Museum of Natural History,
Washington, DC
Monday, 10:02 AM Local Time

Colin woke up feeling more tired than he had before he'd lain down and instantly regretted the catnap. He would have been better to simply have caffeinated and carried on. His shrink was always telling him he needed to get more sleep. What his shrink didn't seem to appreciate was the fact that every time Colin closed his eyes, he was back at the house on Bernard Street, watching from the sidewalk, being held back by firemen and his fellow officers. Being told there was nothing he could do and that it was "too late."

He'd grown to despise those words as they repeated relentlessly in his mind, like a cruel taunting, only to remind him that he'd failed. Failed at the one thing that was the most important responsibility he had. He visited Nancy's grave every month on the day of her death and apologized through tears for the fact he'd been *too late*.

They were two words that spurred him forward with all his investigations. Like he was in a race he hadn't registered for but was determined to win, nonetheless. It was one reason why he and James were outside the Smithsonian waiting for its doors to open.

"So, you really think finding out who Mr. Tweed Jacket is will unravel the puzzle for us?" James asked.

"He might get us closer to where our killer is. One thing's for certain: we have a better chance of getting somewhere with him than we do tucked into our thousand-thread-count sheets." As if Colin had thousand-thread-count sheets.

The museum's doors were unlocked, and the two of them shuffled inside. At the front counter, Colin asked a young woman if he could speak with the museum's manager. She went off to fetch him.

"They're actually eighteen hundred," James said.

"Eighteen— Oh, the thread count." Colin shook his head.

"Yep. And you should really get yourself some. They're worth the investment."

If a person sleeps, and eating isn't *important...*

A man of just over six foot came toward them, still on the backside of the counter. He was regarding them with marked curiosity. Slightly pursed lips but friendly eyes.

Colin held up his badge. "Detective Doyle, and this is Detective White."

"How'd you do?" James said, likely thinking he was amusing.

"I'm fine," the manager said slowly.

"And your name is?" Colin prompted.

"Lester Peterman."

"Well, Mr. Peterman, we think you might be able to help us with an open investigation. Do you have a minute?" Colin posed his request as a question, but he articulated it in such a way that he figured the manager would pick up on the fact that not speaking to them wasn't really an option.

"Sure." Peterman waved for them to follow him and guided them around the side of the counter to a back hallway that housed a few offices. He stood next to the door of one and gestured for Colin and James to go inside.

Colin went first, followed by James, then Peterman.

It was a cozy office and decorated with the touch of a man who loved history and Africa. Large wooden giraffes stood sentinel in two corners behind Peterman's desk. There was a zebra-striped area rug and bamboo shoots sticking out of a vase.

There were two chairs that faced the desk, but neither Colin, James, nor Peterman sat down. Colin, for one, was hoping for a short but worthwhile visit.

"We'd like to ask you about this man?" Colin brought out a colored print of Mr. Tweed Jacket, which had been extracted from one of the hotel's videos. "Do you recognize him?"

Peterman took the photo and studied it closely. "I do not."

"Huh. That's too bad." Spoken like the manager had disappointed him beyond measure—which wasn't far from the truth.

"I'd tell you if I did." Peterman straightened his posture and adjusted his tie.

"We understand that you recently opened an exhibit here. The City of Gold," Colin said.

"That's right."

"Was it open to the public or by invitation only?"

Peterman smiled at the latter, likely pulling from a place of pride. "That would have been a lovely idea, and we have done that in the past, but the specific opening you mentioned was available to the public. At the request of Dr. Connor and his publisher."

A promotional opportunity, Colin thought.

"We have reason to believe that this man—" Colin held up the photo "—was at the event, but we're trying to establish his identity. Is there anything you could do to help us in that regard?"

"I'm sorry. As I said, I never saw him. You could always ask the staff. Tiffany and Otto stood at the entrance of the auditorium and handed out brochures about the exhibit. One of them might remember his face."

Colin perked up. It wasn't a name, but it could lead them closer to one and, by extension, possibly net them a lead to the location of the shooter who killed Judy Finch. "Could we speak with Tiffany and Otto?"

"Sure. They're both in. One minute." Peterman rounded his desk and made a brief call. "They'll be here very soon. In the meantime, would either of you like a coffee, tea, water? I could get one rustled up for you."

"No, we're fine," Colin answered for him and James. "Thank you."

Colin paced the man's office, feeling restless and impatient.

About fifteen minutes after the call, Tiffany and Otto entered Peterman's office. Both of them seemed to stop short at the sight of Colin and James.

"Please," Peterman began, "these are detectives with the Metropolitan Police Department, and they have a question for you."

Tiffany was twenty—if that—and Otto was only a few years older. Both of them had wide eyes and nervous energy.

"It's okay," Colin assured them. "We're not interested in the two of you." He swore both their shoulders raised in unison as a sigh of relief. "We just need to know if you've seen this man." Colin showed them the picture of Mr. Tweed Jacket.

Otto looked first, his eyes squinting at the photo as if he could will it to produce a result. Eventually, he shook his head.

Tiffany's turn, and at the sight of Mr. Tweed Jacket, her jaw went slack. Her gaze darted to meet Colin's. "Yes…yes, I saw him." Her admission came out in a rush, carried on a single breath.

"Where did you see him?" James interjected, and Colin shot him a subtle glare for pushing his nose into the conversation at this point.

Tiffany's eyes went to him briefly but returned to Colin. "At the City of Gold exhibit…well, at the speech. We were supposed to hand out brochures to everyone who entered, and he wouldn't take one."

The skin tightened on the back of Colin's neck. "Did he say why?"

"He just insisted he didn't need one and that he knew the story."

So, Mr. Tweed Jacket had come to the opening to seek out Matthew. For his help in finding a pirate's treasure? Colin should start drinking. Life might start to make more sense.

"He was rude to you, then?" Colin asked, trying to get a feel for the man's state of mind.

"No, I wouldn't say rude. More like…" Her eyebrows shot down. "Distracted…yeah, that's the word."

Mr. Tweed Jacket had shown up to introduce himself into Matthew's world, then. But obviously something had taken place between the museum and him winding up at Matthew's door with two gunmen in tow.

"Why are you interested in him?" Tiffany's voice was small, almost so quiet it could have simply been imagined.

"We'd just like to ask him some questions about an open case we're working on." Colin butted a head toward James.

She followed the direction of the gesture but said to Colin, her bright blue eyes piercing right into his, "He visited the gift shop. I don't know his name, but I love crime shows on TV, love reading mysteries and thrillers, too, but isn't there a way—assuming he bought something—you could track down his name somehow?" She worried her bottom lip, but her eyes were glistening with some latent excitement.

"The gift shop, you said?" Colin asked.

"Uh-huh. There is a way, isn't there?"

"There could be. You've been a big help. Thank you, Tiffany." Colin held out his hand to shake hers, and the young woman stared at his hand oddly at first, but then took it. Chalk it up to a generational difference.

"Oh, there's one more thing," she said. "I saw him talking with a man who basically grilled Dr. Connor about why he went after the City of Gold. This guy tried to make it out like Dr. Connor was a bad man."

Now Colin was more than perplexed. Mr. Tweed Jacket sought out Matthew but was associated with someone who didn't respect the guy. That wasn't reconciling.

"Thanks, again," he said to Tiffany, and she and Otto were dismissed. The former left reluctantly.

"We're going to need to speak with the staff at your gift shop," Colin said to Peterman.

"Come with me."

Twenty-Six

Frigiliana, Spain
Tuesday, 2:00 AM Local Time

Where did you learn to shoot like that?" Matthew had a million questions running through his mind, but that was the first one that came out when Angelica returned from a neighboring room, carrying five bottles of beer.

She'd excused herself not long after letting them into her house. Before that, she'd had Matthew drive around the block. She didn't say it, but he was quite certain she was looking to see if anyone was staking out the place. She must have been satisfied because she'd told him to pull into her garage.

"I don't know if that's the right question," Cal said. "I think it's *who* are you?" He leaned back in the couch and put his feet up on the coffee table in front of him.

Angelica's gaze flicked to his feet, but she said nothing. She handed Cal a bottle, then

Matthew, then went to Mel, who was sitting in an armchair and staring at the chest from the museum. Robyn was in the washroom cleaning up her arm.

"Beer?" she asked, waving the bottle in Mel's face.

"Sure." The professor grabbed it but didn't pop the top and resumed staring at the chest.

She took a seat and crossed her legs at the ankles. "My name is Angel—"

"Na-uh, not your name. We know that. Who are you really?" Cal took a long draw of his beer, smacked his lips, and wiped them with the back of his hand.

Angelica smiled, the expression just toying with her lips and disappearing quickly. "*Really.* That's my name, and I grew up in Frigiliana and returned a few years ago."

"Where were you?" Cal batted back.

"I traveled a lot."

Cal narrowed his eyes. "Sounds rather vague."

"I agree," Matthew said, leaning forward, elbows on knees, "and you never answered my question." The leniency he'd extended her was running out.

Robyn walked into the room, her arm bandaged up where the brute had clawed her.

"Beer?" Angelica offered, pointing to one that was untouched on the table beside her.

Matthew sighed and ran a hand through his hair. Poor timing on Robyn's part. If she hadn't chosen right then to return, he might have gotten an answer from Angelica.

"Ah, sure. Thanks." Robyn snapped the cap off, drank back two thirds of it, and then sat on the couch beside Matthew.

"You okay?" he asked her.

"I'll be fine." Robyn butted her head toward Angelica. "Thank you for the rubbing alcohol and antiseptic. Who knows what that creep was carrying."

"No problem."

"And I'm sorry about your friend. I really am." Robyn polished off her beer in a few chugs.

"He was more than my friend." Angelica's tongue darted out between her lips. "He was my brother. Well, half-brother, anyway."

Half-brother—and she was holding herself together so well? That, combined with her obvious skill with a gun and aversion to answering what she did for work, had the hairs going up on the back of Matthew's neck.

"People die. Sad, but it's a fact of life." Angelica sipped her beer.

"Still stinks," Cal lamented.

"I'll give you that."

So calm and composed… She could just be in shock and still processing what had happened. But it was hard to get the image of her whipping up from behind that cabinet, gun drawn, out of his mind. "We appreciate that you saved our lives," Matthew began. "We've been very open with you about why we're in Spain and who we are. I think it's time that you tell us what you do for a living."

Angelica latched eyes with him. "It's not really important."

"I'd say it is." Matthew peacocked his position. "I saved your lives."

"And I thanked you for that."

"Not in those exact words." A smirk started to form on her lips, but she must have read the room and realized it wasn't appropriate.

"Well, thank you." Matthew held eye contact with her. He wanted to trust her, he truly did, but his mind was whirling. Was she somehow connected with the thugs from Washington? And if she was, why did she kill them? But foremost was: how had these men found them? "Did you lead them to us?"

"What? Absolutely not," Angelica spat. "Do you hear what you're saying right now?"

"I do. There's no way they'd know where we were—when we'd be there—unless someone is feeding them that information. Is it you?"

Angelica's face contorted with anger. "What reason would I have? I don't even know who they are." For a second, her expression softened. "Remember it's important to me to find the treasure, too. Why would I…" Her voice petered out to nothing.

"It could be they found us some other way." Cal nudged his head toward Mel, who was still caught in rapture staring at the chest. "Earth to the professor." Cal snapped his fingers. "Where did you go the other morning, huh? I never liked you from the start. You and your stupid bag that you're hugging all the time. Are you working with the bad guys?"

Matthew relaxed his shoulders and took a deep breath. Maybe he'd been wrong in accusing Angelica.

"What?" Mel exclaimed. "Why would I? That's ludicrous. They were shooting at us."

Shooting at us... Something clicked. "But none of them hit us." Hitting a moving target would be far harder than a stationary one, but all indications pointed to the men being connected and, by extension, that would suggest they were skilled with a gun. And Cal had made for a stationary target at the chain-link fence in that alley, and they hadn't shot him.

Angelica sniffled just loud enough to gain Matthew's attention again. The thugs hadn't missed Pablo. He turned back to the professor.

"How should I know why?" Mel's voice was tight and high.

He was either a very good liar or nervous as hell. Matthew looked back at Ms. Sharpshooter.

"I'm telling you the truth," Angelica pleaded. "I'm not working with them."

There was something in the articulation of her words "not working *with them*" that told him she was working for someone. "Who are you working for?"

"I'd want to know in your position, but trust me, I can't answer that."

"Wow." Cal leaned forward. "That sounds awful cloak and dagger."

Matthew nodded at his friend.

"Call it whatever you like," Angelica stamped on Cal's comment like the banging of a judge's gavel, "but all you need to know is that I'm on your side. And we'll be safe here for a while, but if they found you at the museum, they'll find you again. You made it sound like they're organized. You told me about the SUV. That means there's at least one more vested person out there. Are they here in Spain? I would bet they are." She took a swig of her beer.

Matthew drank some of his. *Who the hell is she working for?* It was a question he batted around in his mind. The fact she just turned up "out of the blue." He was a believer in coincidence—heck, her great-great-great-grandmother was involved with Lopez—but her secrecy was almost too much to accept.

"Do you have any idea who those men are working for?" Angelica leveled her gaze on Matthew.

"If I had that answer, would I be looking at you?" he said sourly.

Angelica pressed her lips and looked over the room. "Anyone have any theories?"

"Treasure hunters." Mel took his gaze from the chest and opened his beer, though he never took a sip.

"Yes, I figured that much," Angelica said curtly and settled her gaze on Matthew. "You've been in this business a while... Make any enemies?"

"Where to start?" He sure had, but his biggest nemesis, Veronica Vincent, was facing charges for kidnapping and uttering death threats, and while she was out on bail, she would be on the no-fly list. But she had gobs of money at her disposal. Fake passports and IDs would be easy enough for her to procure. He felt sick. "I need to—" He jumped to his feet and remembered that his laptop was back at Hotel Málaga. "Do you have a computer?"

"Yes, I—"

"Good. I need to check my email." Maybe Daniel's digging had turned up the identity of who was after them. Surely if Veronica Vincent was involved, Daniel would have tried to reach out, and right now, the only way for him to do that was through email. If she was behind this, he still had to figure out how she became involved. The *why* was an easy one: she had a lust for money that could never be satisfied. "Computer?"

"This way." Angelica showed him to a small den off the dining room. "Go ahead. It should be on."

He sat in front of a desk and brought up the internet browser on a computer there, then looked at her. "Some privacy?"

"Ah, sure." She left the room.

He logged into his email, and there was a message from Daniel. As he read it, he found out more than he'd anticipated. An innocent woman had lost her life in the chase through the Washington streets. He paused there, reading the words over and over until they sunk in. There was no way, with everything going on, Matthew was going to share that with the others right now. Especially when the next paragraph confirmed his worst fears. The plate on the SUV tied back to Veronica Vincent. Now he had to understand how she'd become involved. He returned to the living room and stood in front of the professor.

"You sure you never told another person about the diary other than who you've told us about already? Just Edwin and the student?"

Mel sat back to look up at Matthew. "Not that I— Oh."

"*Oh*?"

Mel paled, and he gripped his satchel tighter. "I had a man come to the house."

"Keep talking."

"He expressed how beautiful my home was and that he ran a business in town that specialized in decorating older houses. Everything from artwork to sculptures."

That was the expertise of Vincent's business front. "And you let him in?"

"I didn't see the harm. He said he found out that I'd won the house at auction."

It shouldn't surprise Matthew that she'd have some sort of tabs in place on historical buildings, but it was still a stretch that she felt it was worth sending one of her men to the door. She was as obsessed with treasure as he was elevating legends to reality. She probably paid people to keep an ear out for any trigger words, namely anything closely resembling "priceless" or "treasure." There had to be an in-between contact. Possibly Professor Edwin or the student—or someone involved with the auctioning of the house.

"So you told this man about the diary?" Matthew asked matter-of-factly.

Mel bit his bottom lip. "Yes, I might have."

"And about the pirate treasure?"

Mel winced and trembled.

"Shit. Well, that's how we've gotten to here."

"Matt, don't tell me…" Robyn left the rest unsaid, and he faced her and nodded.

"Veronica Vincent." The name came off his lips with utter disdain, but in saying it out loud, he had an epiphany. Daniel knew about Veronica's involvement. Angelica *just* showed up, and she saved them. She was secretive about her line of work and who she worked for. The pieces were coming together. He met her gaze. "Daniel sent you."

Her brow pinched, and she shook her head. "I don't know a Daniel."

"Don't lie to me. Daniel figured out that Veronica Vincent's involved, and he reached out to you, didn't he?"

"I don't know a Daniel," she repeated.

"Stop lying," Matthew barked. "And how does he even know where I am?"

"I am telling you the truth when I say that I don't know a Daniel," she said softly, her voice barely above a whisper.

He studied her face, searching for signs of betrayal but spotted none.

Angelica licked her lips. "Listen, I'm not privy to everything."

"But someone did hire you and send you to watch over us," he accused.

"Who are Daniel and Veronica?" Mel inserted.

"Anyone want another?" Robyn got up and swayed her empty bottle. "No? Okay." She headed for the kitchen.

"Daniel's a friend," Matthew said, though he was starting to question all the man was capable of. Even if Angelica was honest when she claimed not to know, he'd bet Daniel was in the background of her employment. His privacy had been violated, but at the same time he didn't want to consider what could have happened today if Angelica hadn't been there. "And Veronica—"

"She's a murderous bitch," Cal barked. "If she crosses my path again, I'll kill her, Matt. I will, I swear to God."

Matthew believed his claim and wouldn't blame him. He wanted revenge himself. "Daniel told me that he left a message at Hotel Málaga, but I never got it," Matthew said. "So, either Veronica's men intercepted it or it got lost. Who knows?"

"My employer stressed that you could be in real danger, Matt," Angelica tiptoed. "That's why I'm here. He also filled me in on Veronica Vincent, and women like her don't give up easily. I might have gotten two of her men tonight, but there will be more. I can't stress that enough."

Robyn returned with a half-empty bottle.

Matthew sat back on the couch, picked up his bottle off the side table, and regarded Angelica. "I'm going to ask again, and I'm hoping you'll be open with me. Who are you? Really."

"Ex-military." She dropped the word like a bomb, yet without apology. "I used to be a Marine with the Spanish Armed Forces."

Her background came off her tongue easily now, making all his stubborn attempts to get her to talk earlier feel like an unnecessary obstacle course. "And now?"

"I run a security detail company for the private sector."

"You say you don't know Daniel, then who is your employer?" Matthew asked.

"As for who my contact is, that is privileged and confidential information." Her words and tone sealed the end of that topic.

"And this place?"

"One of my safe houses."

"Which is how you knew we'd be good here."

"That's right. It's a bit of a fortress. I have men on the premises—paid to remain invisible."

And they were good at that, because Matthew had yet to see one other person there.

She continued. "I still think it's best we get moving as soon as we can. Maybe we should have a look inside?" She gestured to the chest. "It might give us a clue as to the treasure's whereabouts and our next step."

"As long it's not *the* treasure." He smirked at her. The air was much lighter now with some of the larger secrets exposed.

Mel reanimated. "Does that mean we finally get to open this thing?"

"Yes, it does. Assuming…" Matthew looked around, hoping to hell someone here had the key and it hadn't been left at the El Acebuchal Museum.

Robyn pulled it out of her jeans pocket and approached the chest. "Let's have a look, shall we?"

Twenty-Seven

The Connor Residence, Toronto, Canada
Monday, 8:30 PM Local Time

Daniel had braced himself for bad news the moment he'd seen Wes's name on his caller ID, and it turned out for good reason.

"There's been a situation times three," Wes said. "Sadly, one was personal to my contact."

"Situation" coming from Wes was code for fatalities. "Sorry for your contact, but please tell me that Matthew and—"

"They're fine, and everything is under control."

Daniel sighed. That meant two of the bodies likely belonged to Vincent's men. It only brought partial relief. She wouldn't give up just because two of her men had been taken out. "Is your contact still good to proceed?" He felt for the contact's loss, but he also knew that people who played with gunfire expected loss along the way. Sounded so callous, but it was a fact.

"She is."

"She?" It was the first Daniel had heard the contact's gender.

"Yes, but I assure you that she can—"

"Oh, I have no doubt in her abilities. Is she pretty?"

"She is."

Daniel hesitated.

"Everything all right?"

"Yes, it's just that… You know what? Never mind." Daniel just hoped that the contact wouldn't prove to be a distraction for Matthew, and he'd keep his wits about him.

"Is there anything else you need from me at this time?"

Daniel had told Wes when he'd originally called for help that it was a life-or-death predicament and his friend was already in it up to his neck. "There is something else."

"Name it."

"I already filled you in about Veronica Vincent and what she's capable of."

"Why I got my best contact on the job."

"Right, well, I need you to track Veronica Vincent down. I'd bet she's in Spain, just have no way of proving it." He'd already told Wes that Veronica wasn't to leave the United States, and if she had, it would be under an assumed name and fake passport.

"I'll do what I can. No promises."

"There never are." Daniel hung up, but his phone rang immediately. "Wes?"

"No, it's Justin, Mr. Iverson."

"Well, about time." He was on edge from Wes's update more than he'd thought, and his harsh greeting netted him silence. "Sorry. Just tell me what you have," Daniel encouraged.

"I've done the digging you've asked me to. All of it," Justin said. "Where do you want me to start?"

"Is there any connection between Mel Wolf and Veronica Vincent?" He had called and added that side mission to Justin's docket—the closest he'd gotten to asking anyone to dig into her before the request he'd just made of Wes.

"Not that I could find."

Daniel deflated. Though he wasn't entirely surprised by Justin's news, he said, "You dug deep? Looked into his finances and his background?"

"Everything. He's clean. On paper, anyway. He recently bought a house on Marco Island in Florida. His bank accounts showed nothing untoward or suspicious. No large deposits."

"Lots of ways to hide money." If he was hired by Vincent to lure Matthew out for her purposes, she would have paid handsomely and maybe even taught Mel Wolf how to hide the money. Though it was unlikely, given her selfish nature. "What do you have?"

"On the professor, nothing. Now, moving on to Edwin. I did the same sort of casting of nets that I did with Mel Wolf. Edwin's not as squeaky clean. He just took out a third mortgage on his house. He has a ton of credit card debt."

Daniel had mapped out a bunch of theoretical scenarios, and one had him thinking that Edwin was somehow caught up with Veronica and her ilk. Not that he even knew what he'd based that hypothetical on. It was such a leap of logic to even go there, as he didn't really know anything about the man. But if he was involved with Veronica, he'd have money to show for it. Either that or he was extremely foolish with his finances.

"Married? Single?" Daniel asked, just for the rounded picture.

"Single. Just like Wolf."

"And the student? Brent Gibbons? How did you make out with him?"

"He was a little harder to pin down, but there's no criminal record attached to him. I got my hands on his grades, and he's at the top of his class."

"Doesn't necessarily mean he's not in on the murder of his professor." *Or leading Vincent to Mel Wolf's door...* Tuition cost a lot of money; he could have been desperate, saw a payday.

"I don't think he is. Apparently, he found the professor slumped over his desk, a gunshot to the head."

Gibbons *was* the student who found the professor, but the murder method and exact location were news to Daniel. "Lots of killers 'discover' their victims."

"According to what I found out, he was beside himself. I wish I had more for you. I did try to reach Gibbons directly. I posed as a reporter wanting his take, but his mother stonewalled me."

Daniel wasn't going to say it out loud, but he was disappointed by the little information coming from Justin. One more attempt to get something… "How did you make out with the police in Florida who are investigating the murder?"

"They are tight-lipped. Spoke with a Howard Day. He's the lead. Told him I was a private investigator hired by a company to retrieve debts owed by Edwin. I didn't figure you'd want me telling him my call had anything do with you. And I was pretty sure professional courtesy wouldn't apply. All I got was 'good luck settling from his estate' and a dial tone. Guy has a worse bedside manner than some doctors."

Justin truly had nada. Daniel took a deep, heaving breath.

"You there, Mr. Iverson?" Justin prompted.

"I am."

"Sorry I didn't really get anything helpful."

"Makes two of us, but you did what you could," was all Daniel could offer up. He bade him goodnight and ended the call. Justin might not have come through for him, but he had faith that Wes would. Although when Wes did get back to him about Veronica Vincent, it probably wasn't going to be the news he wanted to hear.

Regardless, he couldn't put off William Connor any longer. It was time to fill the man in on his son's "adventures." He'd hit the kitchen first. Best to be armed with his master's favorite brandy before he entered the lion's den.

Twenty-Eight

Before Matthew finished saying "Let's have a look, shall we?" Mel had picked up the chest and set it on his lap. For the moment, his satchel was still strapped to him, but seemed forgotten and was settled at his side.

"May I?" Mel looked from Matthew to Robyn, his palm held out.

Matthew gestured for Robyn to go ahead. She dropped the key into the professor's hand.

Mel put the key into the hole and needlessly said, "It fits," as he turned the key and opened the lid. All of it was happening far too slowly for Matthew's liking.

"Don't keep us waiting," Cal rushed out. Obviously too slow for him, too. "What do you see?"

Mel inserted his hands into the chest and came out with a leather-wrapped journal tied with a leather band. He held it in one hand and pet it with his other one. "It has to be hundreds of years old." He spoke reverently and close to an undertone.

"Don't keep us in suspense," Cal said. "Open it."

The professor shot him a glare. "You can't rush things like this."

"You can when people with guns might show up any minute." Cal gestured wildly toward the journal and the chest.

Mel held Cal's gaze for a bit then gently turned the journal in his hands. He handled it for what felt like hours, then reached inside the chest again. He came out with a few coins in his hand, and a huge smile lit up his face. He dropped them back in and pulled out two more items. "A sextant and—" he opened the lid on a small box "—a compass."

Angelica slipped off the couch and took the compass from Mel. Robyn took the sextant. Matthew watched on. Cal jumped up and went straight to Mel for the journal.

Mel pulled back, hugging it to himself. "It will be in Spanish, so unless you learned how to read it in the last couple hours, it will do you no good."

Cal snatched the chest as if it were a consolation prize and returned to his chair.

"It's beautiful and delicate," Angelica commented on the compass.

"This is incredible," Robyn said, turning the sextant over in her hands. "This is easily late eighteenth century."

"Is there anything to indicate this chest and its contents belonged to Gasparilla?" Matthew asked, his gaze on Mel.

"I'd say by deduction it would make sense. The key worked the chest's lock, and it was found in a diary written by Gaspar's son."

"That would mean Gasparilla was in the area at some point," Matthew stated, thinking it made sense if it was where his first mate lived. Maybe he'd come to visit?

"Not necessarily. Remember, legend has it that he entrusted his logbook to Lopez," Cal said. "Could that be it?"

Mel grinned, that sloth-with-fangs look again. "Could be."

Matthew nudged his head toward the professor. "What's in the journal?"

"Let's find out."

The women stopped fussing over their items, and Cal ceased studying the chest like he expected something else to pop out. Everyone's eyes were on Mel and the journal.

Mel carefully worked the leather strap and untied it. He splayed the leather cover open, and inside were loose sheets of paper. Old, browned. He flipped through a few of the pages, and as many minutes later, said, "It is Gasparilla's logbook."

Everyone laughed and hollered. When the celebration died down, Mel continued.

"From a quick glance it's an accounting of Gasparilla's quests and pillages. The names of different ships he captured and what he plundered. There's also note of how many prisoners they captured and executed."

"So…just thinking out loud here," Matthew started. "Never thought this when it was brought up before about Gasparilla handing over his logbook, but did that mean that he gave up being a pirate? Possibly even settled in Spain to live out the rest of his life?"

"There's nothing in legend to indicate that," Mel said with all seriousness.

"How does legend say he died?" Robyn asked, beating Matthew to the question.

"One version says he perished in a battle with the United States Navy, which he'd mistaken for a British merchant ship. His crew was captured and either hung or imprisoned, but Gaspar tied an anchor chain around himself and jumped into the water to his death. It's from this version that some claim John Gómez was a survivor of this battle, but there was nothing in his diary to indicate that."

"If his last battle was with the Navy, wouldn't there be a record of it?" Matthew figured he knew what Mel would say but asked anyway.

"Yes, if it had happened, but there is nothing on record." Mel's gaze dropped to the journal. "We might find out from the logbook what became of him, but it's not necessarily Gasparilla's conquests right up until his death."

"Let's get reading," Matthew said.

Robyn put the sextant back in the chest and went over to Mel. "Here, Mel, give me half."

"I'll put on the coffee." Angelica put the compass in the chest on her way to the kitchen.

Robyn and Mel headed to the dining room and sat at the table. Matthew and Cal followed. Cal had the chest, and he peered inside.

"Looking for something?" Matthew asked him.

"A treasure map." Cal smiled.

"I wish it were that easy."

"I know. Really. Why can't it be?"

Mel divvied up the journal with Robyn.

Angelica returned, and the smell of coffee wafted in with her. Matthew sniffed the air like a hound on a scent. Back home in Toronto, it was only eight thirty at night—technically yesterday. He should be wide awake. After all, they had proof that Gasparilla had indeed existed, and as Professor Wolf had put it, if his existence could be proven, it would make sense there'd be a treasure to find. Matthew just hoped he was right and that they'd get to it before Veronica Vincent.

Twenty-Nine

Robyn couldn't read fast enough to slake her curiosity, and the tightly compressed and slanted handwriting wasn't helping. It was certainly penned centuries ago, and she could credibly accept it as being Gasparilla's logbook. But to think how reluctant she had been about pirates and treasure when Mel Wolf had first shown up, spouting grand tales about both. She was typically more interested in real, tangible history than legends. Matthew was the one with his head in the clouds, entertaining myths as fact. His passion was contagious, but she still preferred quests with some grounding in reality. With Gasparilla, his existence hadn't even been proven up until this point. At least not in a quantifiable way like the logbook; she'd never put her hands on the diary Mel had found, and the scanned pages hadn't swayed her.

She lifted her head and kneaded the back of her neck. The adventures of Gasparilla would make for exciting fiction. She'd literally become absorbed in his tales of plunder and bounty.

She had been aware that Matthew, Cal, and Angelica had left the dining table in favor of the more comfortable chairs in the living room, but she'd never looked up. And that had to have been hours ago, as sunlight was pouring through the window. She'd noticed it getting brighter but still hadn't lifted her head. She'd just been so caught up in what she was reading.

Cal's snores made their way into the dining room, and she smiled. The three of them should have just turned in and gotten some sleep, but she understood why they'd want to stay nearby. Sadly, though, she hadn't encountered any clues as to the location of Gasparilla's treasure, and given the calm energy coming from the professor beside her, she'd say he hadn't either.

She had, however, read about Gaspar's battle tactics and how he treated his captives. Ruthless. He'd burn his captives' hands and let the victims bleed out. He attributed the method to a famous pirate by the name of Edward Low. He was gone by the time of Gaspar's piracy, but his legacy had lived on, and Gaspar idolized the man.

Gaspar's conquests were dated, and the inventory noted. The latter was both quantifiable in wealth and the number of captives they'd brought aboard. She wondered why Gaspar and his crew even bothered unloading them from their ships when so many of them were killed, and those who weren't—mostly women—were taken to an island by the name of Captiva. From what she could decipher, the women would serve as wives or concubines for Gaspar's crew. In other cases, if the women were of noble birth or distinguishable affluence, they'd park them on the island and hold them for ransom.

"I have something!" Mel blurted out and pointed to the page in front of him.

Cal took in one long reverberating snore and said, "What—what's going on?"

Matthew came into the dining room first, followed by Angelica, then Cal, who looked like death warmed over.

"What is it?" Robyn asked.

"The entry dates back to July 1788," Mel started. "The *Floridablanca* came upon a 'grand galleon,' as Gaspar described it. Rumored to be full of silver and gold and jewels. Upon capturing the ship, it was confirmed to belong to a viceroy of Spain. On board was his daughter."

"Josefa de Mayorga," Cal said and yawned.

"That was her name." The professor grinned. "It's right here in Gasparilla's own hand, though he spells her name as Useppa."

"What else does it say?" Robyn shimmied closer to Mel.

"Essentially that the first time he laid eyes on Josefa, he knew she was more valuable than precious jewels." Mel met Robyn's gaze, and she felt transported back in time. To think of a rugged, tyrannical pirate falling in love at first sight seemed unlikely. But matters of the heart brought down empires.

Mel went on. "He took her aboard, and his crew wanted to kill her or at least put her on Captiva Island. Remember that's what Gómez's diary said—the part about them wanting to kill her?"

"Captiva Island?" Matthew intercepted.

"I just read about it." Robyn explained the purpose of the island and its general location based on Gaspar's notes.

"It's off Florida's Gulf Coast and is north of Sanibel Island," Mel clarified, then continued. "Gaspar refused to appease his crew. He was smitten with the girl. To save her life, he sent Josefa back to Spain with his friend Lopez."

"Did he ever come to Spain for her?" Robyn asked. "After all, Gasparilla's logbook is here, and Lopez, his first mate, was here."

"I don't know." Mel seemed to ponder the question as if he could yank the answer from the ether to his consciousness.

"There's more to read," Matthew encouraged. "Maybe you'll find something to explain how it came to be here."

"Flip ahead," Cal urged.

"Do it." Matthew nodded his head at Mel and pointed to the pages in front of him. He had the back half of the logbook.

"Okay, but you realize it's like reading the ending of a book before—"

"It *is* reading the ending of the book first," Cal cut in, "but when you have more crazies with guns who could show up at any minute…it's justifiable."

Mel turned slowly from Cal to the logbook. He flipped the pages over with precise movements. The aged paper was almost brittle and certainly fragile. He arranged the sheets he hadn't read in a separate pile from the ones he had. "Ah, here we go. This looks like the last entry."

"Sitting on pins and needles." Cal smirked at Mel, and Robyn hit her friend in the arm. "Hey," Cal barked.

"Just be nice. And we know you're more excited than you ever let on." She paused and let her words sink in. "Why can't you just show it and stop pretending not to care?"

"It's my process," Cal mumbled.

Mel read the entry to himself, his lips moving as his eyes scanned left to right.

"Out loud would be nice," Cal said.

"And you understand Spanish now?" Robyn teased him.

"I meant the translation as he goes along." Cal wiped his palms down his face. "I'm just so freaking tired, and he's making this painful."

"Okay, okay…" Mel stamped out the words on a rushed breath. "His dear friend Lopez notified him that Josefa had fallen quite ill. By the time Gaspar returned to Spain, she'd died. He never got to say a final goodbye to the love of his life."

Robyn made eye contact with Angelica. Maybe it was more a girl thing, but a love story between a pirate and princess was something of fairy tales. Angelica would appreciate that even more, given that her grandmother Sanibella had been Lopez's lover. Sadly, that romance didn't have a happy ending. Maybe it wasn't so much a fairy tale as it resembled a tragic Shakespearian play. Like Romeo and Juliet fated to be kept apart in life.

"When was this?" Robyn asked Mel.

"It doesn't say, which is strange because all the other entries I've read are dated. Yours?"

"Yeah."

Mel's gaze drifted to the page again. "Oh…" Mel shifted his position in the chair. With the movement, his satchel fell from his lap to his side, though it was still suspended by the strap crossing his torso. "I may have something here." He paused, looked at Cal. "What? You're not going to say something smart, like 'spit it out'?"

"If it would make you feel better, I—" Cal's words were squashed under the professor's scowl, and Cal held up his hands.

Mel continued, a grin eating his mouth—or him eating the grin. His expression of mirth was bordering on psychotic. "Ah, yes. We might have the treasure, folks."

Robyn wasn't going to rush the man like Cal kept doing, but she wanted to. Her heart sped up anticipating what he was going to say next.

"Remember how Gaspar repeatedly told Gómez that his heart would always lie with Useppa? Well, that's how he signed off his last entry. We discussed that "heart" might represent Gaspar's treasure, and we don't think he buried the treasure on Useppa Island, as other clues led us to Spain, but what if—"

"He buried his treasure with Josefa," both Mel and Robyn said at the same time.

"Okay," Angelica started, "but Gaspar's logbook said he didn't make it back to say goodbye. So, Gaspar couldn't have buried his loved one with his treasure, *but* he could have buried his treasure with his loved one."

"He returned afterward, exhumed her body…" Cal made a show of shivers trickling down his spine and squirmed in his chair.

"I believe so." Another crazy grin from the professor.

"We have to find her grave." Matthew got up and paced. "Are there any directions, clues, landmarks?"

"He signed off with 'my heart will always lie with Useppa,' as I told you, and a bunch of scribbled numbers." Mel sat back, deflated.

"A dead end," Cal lamented.

"Not necessarily..." Matthew stopped walking. "What are the numbers?"

Mel read them off.

"Coordinates," Robyn and Matthew blurted out at the same time. They smiled at each other, and she gestured for him to go ahead.

"Latitude and longitude. It's how sailors measure their location and their destinations," he explained.

"I should have figured that out." Mel was shaking his head at himself.

"So, is it to Josefa's grave, the treasure, or both?" Matthew said.

"We need to go there and find out," Robyn said, "But the only thing with such measurements back then is it's possible they were off by hundreds of miles. They didn't know about magnetic versus true north."

"Neither do I," Cal admitted.

"Put simply, magnetic north is what is indicated on a compass, for example," Robyn explained. "True north is a fixed point that doesn't change based on where a person is in the world."

"Ah, I see."

"Sailors would use both a chronometer, which measures longitude, and a sextant to calculate latitude." Robyn rummaged in the chest and pulled out the compass and flipped the lid. "Ah. You should have taken a closer look, professor. This isn't a compass." She turned it so everyone could get a good look. "It's a chronometer."

"And what's a chronometer?" Cal asked.

"As I just said, it measures longitude," Robyn started. "Gasparilla had the best technology of his day for pinpointing latitude and longitude."

"So, the part you just mentioned about the measurements being off might not apply?" Cal asked, sounding hopeful.

"It might not." Robyn smiled.

"Great." Cal rubbed his hands together. "Let's get going."

Matthew anchored Cal to the chair with both his hands on Cal's shoulders. "Not so fast. Mel, read off those numbers?"

Mel did just that, and Matthew disappeared into a small room where Angelica kept her computer. They could hear him clicking keys on a keyboard. Less than a minute later, he was back.

"We're in the right place. The coordinates point to a spot within Almijara and Alhama Natural Park."

"We're right there." Robyn grinned. "We have to go for it."

"I agree," Matthew chimed in.

"There are gravesites along a common trek for tourists," Angelica told them. "Not sure if that's where we're being directed, but either way, it's not going to be easy to go into the park and start digging."

"We could go under the cover of night," Matthew said, his voice pulsing with excitement.

"A possibility," Angelica replied, "but regardless of when we go, we shouldn't approach the way tourists do. We'd be best to go in the back door, as it were."

"The park is watched?" Robyn asked.

"I wouldn't want to take the chance that it isn't. We'd be best to take precautions."

"If we're going in the 'back door' you mentioned," Cal began, "do we have to set out at night?"

Everyone looked at Angelica, and she smiled and shook her head. "I don't think it would be necessary. But we certainly would want to be alone when we dig. No tourists and no bad guys."

"So, we could set out any time?" Cal asked.

"We'll need to gather some supplies first," Angelica reasoned. "Hiking equipment, backpacks, shovels, etcetera. We should also prepare for the possibility of spending the night in the mountains."

"Agree wholeheartedly," Robyn said. If they were going about the discovery the legal way, they'd need to secure permits to dig and procure—a process that took months. It was part of the reason why they often worked backward. Make the find, then seek approval. Sort of like better to "beg for forgiveness than ask for permission."

"Okay, let's go shopping." Matthew took his hands off Cal, who immediately popped up. "I'll need to hit the bank for more cash first, though."

"You don't worry about it. I'll charge the purchases and add them to my employer's bill."

"Still no way you're telling me who your direct contact is?" Matthew asked.

"No, sorry."

Robyn could tell he was still suspicious of her. Leery may have been more apt. But considering she was being secretive about her employer's identity she couldn't blame him. Robyn would bet, though, that Daniel's hands were in this, and if she concluded that, it was likely Matthew had, too. And if he had, he was handling it pretty well.

Thirty

Colin was drifting in and out of sleep. The ding of his cell phone on his nightstand had him sitting up. He and James had struck some gold at the museum's gift shop when they were told that Mr. Tweed Jacket had bought a souvenir and charged it. The subpoena had been signed off on, and the process started with the credit card company. Colin had asked Officer Kennedy to notify him the second he heard anything back, regardless of the hour.

Colin fumbled with his phone. He had a text from Kennedy informing him that Mr. Tweed Jacket was Mel Wolf. Colin called Kennedy eager for more information. "What else have you got?" he pushed out when the officer answered.

Kennedy went on to tell him Wolf was an American history professor at Hodges

University in Naples, Florida. Colin wished he could figure out how that had brought Wolf to Matthew Connor.

"But there's something more important you should know, Detective." Kennedy's tone took on a dark note. "Mel Wolf is wanted in regard to questioning for the murder of a Ralph Edwin."

That had Colin sitting up even straighter. "Murder?"

"Yeah. Wolf worked with Edwin at the university. Edwin was also a professor in American history. But Edwin was shot and killed in his office just over a week ago. One bullet to the temple. No sign of an altercation."

"So Edwin had trusted his killer."

"Either that or the killer got the jump on him."

Colin's gut twisted. Were Roman Murphy and Oscar Vincent tied up with the murdered professor? Although he'd thought Veronica Vincent was the thread to follow, maybe it was Mel Wolf.

"But there's more," Kennedy went on. "Ballistics are a match between the one pulled from Judy Finch and the one from the abutment in the garage."

Colin wasn't surprised. "Fire me over the lead investigator's information. I'll take care of it."

"I'll do it right after we hang up."

"And that's now." Colin ended the call and stared across his small bedroom. It served its purpose, as did his compact studio apartment, but he was happy he wasn't there often. The space didn't feel lived in or loved, and he didn't have the time or energy to devote to making it "homey." That had been Nancy's thing. His wife had loved making things beautiful and cozy. She had a knack. She loved red wine, bubble baths, and candles, but he never would have guessed a vanilla pillar she left burning in their bedroom would have set the house ablaze and taken her out, too.

His phone pinged with another text, and it was Kennedy with the promised information. *Detective Howard Day, Naples Police Department.* Kennedy has also included his phone number, but Colin would call after he had a chance to do some looking into the Edwin murder case. But, first…coffee.

He stumbled into the kitchen, filled his jumbo mug with brew, and took it to his home office that was nothing more than a writing desk and a laptop positioned to the side of the living room. Nothing fancy, just purely functional. A word that could really sum up his life after Nancy's death. Something he made it through by pouring himself into his job.

He googled *Ralph Edwin, murdered university professor, Florida*, and the results kicked back. Edwin was found in his office at the school by a student. The student's name wasn't given, and neither were many details. Just that Edwin was shot, and foul play was suspected. Often little to no comment meant investigators were narrowing in on a suspect and didn't want to risk tipping off the killer.

Is that Mel Wolf? It could explain their interest in wanting to talk to him. What it didn't necessarily explain was why two men had chased him through the streets of Washington. Regardless, it was impossible to ignore that death followed Wolf.

Colin called the number for Day and met with voicemail. He left a vague and obscure message for the detective with his name, number, and that he was with the Metropolitan Police Department in Washington, DC. He didn't want to leave too many details so that Day could prep for the callback. It was usually best when conversations progressed organically and weren't scripted. The last thing he wanted was Day to feed him some speech to keep him at a distance.

Colin hung up and sat there, continuing to mull on Edwin's murder and his own case as he drank his coffee. His mind started to clear of sleep.

He'd watched the security videos from the Colonial Hotel enough times to know he couldn't pinpoint the shooter from them. But now he had the video from the city. It had finally come through yesterday afternoon, and he'd watched it several times. But usually *just once more* was the ticket to seeing something that was missed before. He'd emailed himself a copy of the video files and brought one up on his computer now.

He watched it play it out. The Canadian Trio and Wolf emptied onto the street from the hotel's parking garage with their two pursuers in tow. He forwarded the clips of video and watched until they made their turn down the first alley. He reversed the video and watched again.

Both Roman and Oscar had their guns out. He played it super slow. Then just a flash, easily missed—a bloom of light that ignited around the muzzle of Roman Murphy's gun. He was Judy Finch's killer. But knowing that and finding him to bring him to justice were different things.

"Son of a bitch," he mumbled and hit Play on the video.

He let it go past the point of the men going down the alley, and a few minutes later, he was leaning forward. Roman and Oscar had returned from the alley to the main street, where they got into a waiting black SUV.

The thugs had friends. Not a surprise, but if he could track the license plate, he might figure out who they were working for.

Colin sat back and sipped more coffee. Something to take seriously was Naples PD's interest in Wolf. He gave the impression of a book worm more than someone who was involved with killers. But he was hiding something—just look at how he hugged that bag of his. Before he'd let himself get carried away with fanciful tales, Colin opened his email program and drafted a new message, noting the timestamp of the SUV's appearance on the video, and sent it off to Andy in Tech to see what he could make of the image. Colin was hoping for a tag and subsequent registration information. He hit Send just as his phone rang. He answered with his official title, assuming it was the detective from Florida. He was only mildly disappointed that he'd wasted such a formal greeting on Dylan from Forensics.

"Ballistics—"

"Officer Kennedy told me," Colin cut in.

"Oh, well then." Dylan sounded miffed. "Did he also tell you the results on the blood recovered from the alley?"

"Nope."

"Just the type was O positive, but so is most of the world."

"Wow."

"Yeah, Kennedy stole my thunder."

"He never told me the type of gun. You have that?"

"A Smith & Wesson M&P 9."

"Now, that's something I might be able to use." Call waiting beeped in Colin's ear, and he let Dylan go when he consulted caller ID and it showed as *Unknown*. It was probably the Florida detective; the number blocked because bad guys wouldn't exactly answer if their screens lit up with Such-and-Such Police Department. Colin answered formally.

"Detective Doyle, this is Detective Howard Day from Naples PD. I'm returning your call." There was a marked leeriness to his voice, mixed with curiosity.

"Thank you for that. I've got some questions about a case you're working on. The murder of Professor Edwin at Hodges University."

There was a pocket of silence, then, "I'll cooperate as best I can, but I might not be at liberty to say much. The case is still open."

"But you did verify my identity."

"I verified there's a Detective Colin Doyle with the MPD in DC. Now, whether I'm actually talking to him is a little harder to confirm."

Colin smiled. He liked this guy. "Understood."

"Far as I know, you could be some PI posing as someone out to collect debts from Edwin's estate."

"That happen?"

"Yeah, some Justin Scott. So, what is it I can help you with?"

"Mel Wolf." That's all Colin said.

The other end of the line remained quiet for a few seconds, then Day said, "What about him?"

"He's a person of interest in your investigation. The one with the murdered university professor."

"He might be."

"Let's not play games. We're both adults. I assume you're a seasoned cop like I am, so let's move past the bullshit." Colin paused for impact, then continued. "Let's say I might have had the displeasure of Wolf surfacing in an investigation of my own."

"A murder investigation?"

He would rather not say, but if he wanted Day to talk… "Yes, in a roundabout way." He filled Day in on the basics of his case. "I don't want to take a leap, but Mel Wolf doesn't strike me as a killer."

"That is a leap, and one you might want to rethink. Wolf's our prime suspect. We found the gun that murdered Edwin in his bedroom."

"Son of a bitch," Colin mumbled.

"Yeah, well, I don't have to tell you, but killers come in all shapes and sizes."

Now Colin really had to unravel how Wolf factored into his own investigation. Also, who was this PI Justin Scott, and who was he working for?

"Who found Professor Edwin?"

"One of his students. A Brent Gibbons."

Add Brent Gibbons to the list of people to reach out to.

Thirty-One

Matthew couldn't get into the park and underway fast enough. Obtaining all the gear and getting organized had taken hours and was pure torture when all he wanted to do was move. He'd caught Robyn smiling at him a few times like she could read his mind and knew he was struggling with self-control. But he couldn't help it. He was ready to find that pirate treasure.

Angelica had mentioned using a "backdoor" strategy, and that's what they'd be doing. She'd studied the area of the coordinates and considered their best approach, which had them setting out into the countryside, a distance away from where the tourists typically were. One of her men was doing the driving, but he was just going to drop them off and await word from her via satellite phone for when to return and pick them up.

She was riding shotgun, and her hair was swept into a ponytail and swayed with the movement of the vehicle as it traversed bumpy terrain. Matthew was in the rear seat with everyone else and split his time between looking forward and back over a shoulder. He half-expected to see Veronica tailing them. Losing two men wouldn't even put a hitch in her plans. She'd just regroup, reorganize, and send in new recruits.

Angelica pointed for the driver to pull down a dirt path off a main road. He'd driven down about a mile when she told him to stop and let them unload.

They were surrounded by summits, and the view was specular. Just like in the villages of El Acebuchal and Frigiliana, the Mediterranean Sea sparkled in the distance. The ground here was barren and rock and dirt. Some grass and bramble and the odd pine tree, but otherwise, it appeared like forsaken land. Any ridges or cliffs in his line of sight were white-gray rock.

Angelica pulled out her GPS and smiled. "Yes. We'll set out from here. But see over there—" she pointed to a summit a fair distance away "—that's where we're headed." She directed them to look down, and there was a river cutting through the park below them. "We'll need to cut across the river and then make our way up."

They gathered their gear. Robyn, Angelica, and Matthew had hiking backpacks, while

Mel stuck solely to his satchel and Cal carried his camera equipment. The camera itself was pressed to his face now as he pivoted at the hip and snapped off shots.

They set out, careful of each step as the uneven ground threatened a twisted ankle or worse. As they trudged on, they made their way along the outer skirts of the mountain. Some of the most stunning views were potentially the most deadly.

After an hour or so, Matthew suggested they all take a short rest and drink some water before carrying on. The wind held a chill up here, but the afternoon sun was warm. A compensation that he was glad for.

"How's it looking?" Matthew asked Angelica, in reference to their current location in correlation with where they were headed.

Angelica consulted her GPS. "Looking good."

"I don't have to check your work, do I?" Matthew teased and shot a playful glance Cal's way. A jab at their time in India when Cal's directions had them meeting with a ravine, an interested third party armed with AK-47s closing in fast.

"I see we're never going to let India die." Cal drank some water and ran his arm across his mouth. "If anyone should be holding a grudge…" He raised a single brow to emphasize the point.

Matthew knew exactly what he was referring to. The choice that had been presented at the time was certain death by bullets or a possibility of survival by jumping. Matthew might have made the decision for all of them when he pushed his friends over the cliff, then took the leap himself. "Hey, we all survived."

"With a little post-traumatic stress afterward, but, yeah, we survived."

Robyn nudged Cal in the shoulder, and he smiled at her, though it seemed reluctantly.

Matthew looked over at Mel, who was standing quiet and solemn. He was glancing out over the terrain and hugging his satchel. He was dressed in beige hiking gear and boots— the personification of an adventurer—but the image fell short. The awkward professor still managed to shine through.

"How are you making out?" Matthew stepped up next to him.

"It's incredible being here." He gestured to their surroundings, and a brief smile touched his lips but never reached his eyes.

"This must be an entirely different experience to the classroom," Matthew said.

"Yeah, it is. Not actually how I saw it all playing out, though." Mel took a deep, staggering breath.

"If you would feel more comfortable back at Angelica's," Matthew started.

"No." Mel adamantly shook his head. "I want to be here. I really do." His mouth twitched like he was unsure what to do with it, what expression to make, what emotions to feel. "It's good for people to get out of their comfort zones."

"That it is. And if we put our hands on Gasparilla's treasure, trust me, my friend, this will all have been worth it." As Matthew said the words, his gaze latched with Angelica's just briefly before she turned away.

Matthew would guess there'd be no outcome that would make her feel like it had been worth her getting involved—by a long shot. But it wasn't the time to press the matter, and even if he got her aside privately, she very well might not open up to him anyway. When he lost his mother, he found it easiest not to talk about it. Saying his feelings out loud made them real, made her death real.

"We should get moving. We still have a ways to go." Matthew took the first steps away from the group.

"He's right," Angelica said, following behind him. "We have several miles to cover, and that's assuming Gasparilla's numbers are right."

"Just hope he knew his true from his magnetic north," Cal muttered. "You know, to triangulate the coordinates."

Matthew looked back at him, and he'd lowered his camera and had it dangling from his neck. He was walking in step with Mel, Robyn behind them.

Matthew angled his body toward Angelica, who was beside him. "Bet you don't do this very often, either."

"Oh, God, no. Never. Well, walking, yes." She laughed.

He wasn't going to be a pig and make some comment like it was obvious she exercised and took care of herself. "Just no treasure hunting?"

"My first."

"Glad I'm here for you." He bumped his shoulder to hers.

"Uh-huh." She smirked. "I'm sure you are. I just find it so incredible that my grandmother Sanibella is connected to this—at least in a way. It makes it that much more personal. Like I owe it to her to find the treasure."

"I can see that." Silence leveled between them, and he felt the nudge to say, "You know if you want to talk to me about what happened... with Pablo."

Several minutes passed before she responded.

"He never kept his word," she repeated what she'd said about Pablo a few times, a sad attempt to somehow lessen her grief, Matthew supposed.

He slowed his pace, but Angelica kept hers. He picked his up again.

"He was still...family," she added.

Her last word sank in Matthew's gut, and for a brief second, grief from losing his mother flooded over him. In and out like a fast-moving tide. But like water on the shoreline, it left its mark. It disheveled his emotions, upset his existence, set him off balance, if only a little. "For sure," he said.

"If it's okay with you, I'd rather focus on what we're here to do." She met his eyes, hers asking for reprieve.

"Yes, of course."

Everyone kept moving, making good time toward their destination. They had yet to see one other person, so Angelica had certainly made a wise choice in their approach. In some areas, it still seemed there were paths, sections where the plants grew apart, and the dirt and stone formed walkways. They didn't stick to those, but when they came to any, Angelica shifted their direction a bit. Sometimes it felt like they were snaking and not making much forward progress.

Eventually they came to a ridge that overlooked a rushing river about twenty-five to thirty feet beneath them. The water stretched at least fifty feet across.

Matthew looked back at Robyn, Cal, and Mel and announced the obvious. "We've reached the river. Now to get across…"

Angelica paced about twenty feet ahead, then returned, giving the impression of a caged animal assessing an escape strategy. As she'd moved, she kept her gaze on the GPS. Now she stopped and pointed across the river and ahead of where they were.

Matthew followed the direction of her finger. The summit of a mountain was visible through a thin veil of fog. It gave the appearance of an apparition, like a whisper of something that wasn't really there.

"That's where we're headed," she said. "I say we continue along the river and hope that it narrows."

"And slows," Matthew added. "Do you know of a spot like that, where we could simply walk across?"

Angelica smiled. "If I didn't know better, Dr. Connor, I'd say you were afraid of getting wet."

Matthew's mouth gaped open at her implied innuendo. "Never." He winked at her.

She bit her lip, and if it wasn't for the company, Matthew might have made a move to taste those lips…

"What do you suggest?" Robyn abruptly cut in and took position next to Matthew. "We didn't bring an inflatable boat, though we brought everything but. We could turn around and try again tomorrow."

Angelica pivoted to face Robyn. "I'd rather carry on."

"Me too," Matthew backed her up. "We're so close, I can taste it."

"You can taste it?" Robyn shot back and put her hands on her hips. "Uh-huh, I'm sure you can." She held eye contact with him and smirked.

She really did know him well—*too* well.

"Anyone against my initial suggestion?" Angelica asked, and no one raised any objections. "Great, let's hope the river presents us with a way to cross her." She started walking.

"Sure, and maybe there will be a bridge that magically appears," Cal teased and then laughed at his own joke.

"You never know, but I doubt it," Angelica said. "Now, in the more touristy parts of the park, sure, you'd find bridges. Here, I doubt it."

"Well, seeing as we're basically after a leprechaun at the end of the rainbow…" Cal was grinning. Everyone looked at him, and he waved a hand to dismiss them.

Matthew sure hoped all of this effort paid off and that Pablo's death hadn't been entirely meaningless. He'd do what he could to make sure that it counted for something.

Thirty-Two

Robyn would be happy to jump in the river right about now—even with the two-story drop and rushing currents. Angelica couldn't be any more obvious about her attraction to Matthew, and he was acting awkwardly. They'd had their long talks about moving on with other people, but come right down to it, it was still uncomfortable to have a front-row seat. She was pretty sure Matthew felt the same way when a guy showed interest in her, but they had to get to a point where it was normal for them. After all, it wasn't healthy to keep holding a flame for someone. Eventually you'd get burned. That was the thing with fire.

She watched Matthew and Angelica leading the way. Their steps falling in a regular and even stride. Their conversation seemed to come easily and naturally. She was happy for him, and she hoped he knew that, but she'd become wedged between two pairs, and it had her feeling a little alone. But Cal was in a good discussion with Mel behind her, with not much silence falling between them. It made her smile with amusement. Cal so often presented a tough front and disinterest. As he'd said before, it was just how he worked. But if only he could see the benefit of just having fun and giving in to the—

The rocks beneath her shifted and were sliding her toward the river.

"Guys!" she yelled, scrambling for solid footing, but she couldn't find any. The ground was quickly giving way.

An outreached hand shot in her face and she grabbed hold. *Cal.*

"Hold on tight," he said.

But despite his hold, she could still feel herself moving toward the cliff. She had flashbacks to India. Several stories above the water. Here it was a shorter drop, but far enough. There was no way to know how deep the water was, but it was churning, and the surface was dotted with small whitecaps. Some not so small. These observations rushed through her mind at light speed. She quickly wanted to retract her thought about jumping in the river.

Matthew and Angelica were scurrying back toward her but were cognizant of their footing. They were too far away to reach. And Cal still had a hold on her, but he was starting to slide with her. The look of pure panic gripped his features, and his eyes were nearing the size of ping-pong balls.

She closed her eyes. She didn't like how this story was going to end—and she didn't want to see it coming. Yet the instant she started free falling, her eyes shot open. Cal was tumbling above her. Then she quickly looked down as rock rained over them.

Sharp edges of stone grazed any exposed skin—her face, hands, ears, and neck. She prayed to be spared a large rock to the head. She wanted to look behind her at Cal, but she wouldn't dare. At least his screams told her he was still alive—or were they her own screams?

Above them, she heard Matthew crying out that he'd rescue them.

"Stay strong" were the last words she'd heard him say before she plunged into the river. The water was so cold it took her breath and felt like a million shards piercing her flesh. And the current was so powerful, it sucked her under, and she was completely at its mercy, being bucked this way and that like she was in a fatal washing machine.

She popped up. "Cal!" Hardly his name made it out before she was rolled back under.

She kicked her legs and moved her arms, yearning for the surface, but her efforts were getting her nowhere. She was stuck on something that was holding her under. It had to be her backpack snatched onto a piece of rock or wood. Panic seized her chest as her lungs ached for oxygen.

Just hang on! she coached herself.

She worked to get free of the bag, but the straps weren't cooperating. She was tempted to give in and accept maybe this was her time, but she found one ounce of fight. She shucked loose of the backpack and kicked like mad to reach the surface. She popped up and gulped oxygen greedily but continued being carried downriver. She searched for Cal and spotted him a few feet away, lying on his back, still.

"Cal!" she cried out, but no answer came from him.

She fought with all she had to get to him and made slow progress. When she reached Cal, he had a big gash on his forehead, and he wasn't responding to her cries.

No, this can't be!

The water continued to move them downriver, and Robyn looked up and watched in horror as Matthew, Angelica, and Mel's figures became smaller. They were of no help to them.

Defeat threatened to drown her, but her fighting instinct bubbled up from within. She'd been awarded ribbons for swimming as a child. She could surely come out the winner over some river.

But the water… It was so cold. So incredibly *freezing* cold. She couldn't feel her body anymore, and her limbs were refusing to cooperate. But she didn't want to die. Not like this. Not now. She had so much more to give.

Her eyelids started to become as heavy as her limbs, but she had to keep fighting. If not for herself, then for Cal. She had to believe he was still alive, just unconscious.

There were times she caught another look at the ridge above them and swore she saw Matthew there. Maybe it was an apparition her desperate mind created to keep her fighting. Whatever worked.

And Cal. She held on to him, feeling so responsible for his being in this predicament with her. She'd made one poor step, and all he'd tried to do was help. *Look where that got him.*

She heard her name. A faint cry at first, something she thought she'd imagined, but no, someone had said "Robyn." She willed herself to focus on the ridge again, hoping that she'd see someone there about to rescue them.

She saw Matthew just before her head went under again, and she felt like the bob on a fishing line—up, down, up, down, up, down. Through it all, she kept a firm hold on Cal. After one period beneath the surface, she came up to find Cal sputtering water.

He's alive!

"Cal..." She could hardly talk. The temperature of the water squeezed her chest.

He coughed again and seemed to come fully to. He looked around, and his eyes enlarged like they had as he'd reached for her and concluded he was going along for the ride. His head ducked under, and he came up shivering and mumbling.

"Cal...we fell in the river..." She could only serve her words in bits and pieces. "We need to..." Her body succumbed to a case of the shivers; ones so deeply embedded it was like they were a part of her. "We...need...to...get to the side."

She looked ahead, hoping that there'd be something they could grab hold of and use to bring them into shore. But there was no shore here. Just sheer rock face.

If they didn't get out of the river—and quick—they'd succumb to hypothermia. That's if they didn't drown first.

She looked up at Matthew and hoped he'd carry on and live a long, happy, fulfilling life. Because of him, she'd lived a life full of adventure and spontaneity, traits she'd learned from him.

He was pointing and yelling, but his words weren't making it to her ears. He was getting more animated, jabbing his arm toward the other side of the river. But she was feeling so cold and tired. If only she could close her eyes for a second...

Thirty-Three

Watching **Robyn fall in, then Cal,** was enough to drive Matthew mad. He paced, feeling powerless, scurrying along the ridgeline.

"Just be careful," Angelica cautioned, but he waved her off.

He should be down there helping his friends. Robyn kept going under, and Cal hadn't moved since he hit the water.

"Everyone's going to die, and this is my fault. The stupid diary. I should have left it where it was." The professor's gray hair was sticking up more than normal, and his repetitive sweeps through it didn't help. He was wearing a circular path in the dirt.

Matthew stood in front of him, stopping Mel's pacing. "I don't have time for this... your meltdown or whatever it is. You hear me? My friends are down there and—" He couldn't bring himself to finish.

The professor stared back at him, soberness settling into his eyes. "What are we going to do?"

"We're getting them out…somehow." Matthew walked along the ridge, his gaze back on Robyn and Cal. He only glanced ahead periodically to watch his next steps.

"We'll get you out of there!" he screamed to them, but he was pretty certain neither of them heard him.

At least Robyn and Cal were together now, and it appeared that Cal was conscious again.

"I don't want to be the bearer of bad news," Angelica said softly.

"What is it?" he hissed. He didn't have time for dramatics right now, only cool-headed logic. But no matter how hard he tried to grasp a sense of calm, it would slip through his thoughts and skitter to the edges of his consciousness.

"Don't you hear it?" Mel asked.

"Hear—" Matthew paused and listened. The thunder of water. "You've got to be kidding me."

"I wish it was a joke," Angelica started, "but if they go too much farther down the river, they could…"

He matched gazes with her and was relieved that she'd left the rest unsaid, the part about his best friends going over a waterfall and meeting their untimely deaths. He searched the horizon for hope, something— "There!" Matthew pointed at the branch of a pine tree that was extended over the water. It was probably low enough for Robyn and Cal to reach.

"It's going to take a wing and prayer," Angelica said.

"Then pray," Matthew kicked back.

Robyn was looking up at him, or at least it appeared that way.

"The branch!" He pointed emphatically toward the tree, hoping that somehow his message would reach Robyn or Cal. Neither gave him indication they heard him or understood him. He'd repeat himself a hundred times, a thousand times, a million times if he needed to. "The branch!"

Finally, it seemed his voice had reached them. He'd swear he made eye contact with Cal and that his words had registered. Cal even turned his head toward the direction Matthew was pointing.

Matthew let out a deep breath and a silent, quick prayer. "Keep going! You can do it!" He continued to urge them, not about to give up on getting through to them.

He resumed walking along the ridge with Angelica and Mel following close behind him. He could hear their footfalls, the scuffing of boots against rock, and small stones being kicked and tumbling, but he kept his focus on his friends. They couldn't go out this way. Not on his watch. Not on some quest he'd suckered them into. All because he wanted an excuse to get away from writing his book. A trap laid before him of procrastination and mild curiosity, and he'd taken the bait. He'd let it become personal back in Washington. His ego had become involved. He wanted to show whoever-it-was who'd shot at them that he could get the treasure out from under them. And only to find out that it was Veronica Vincent behind the entire play filled him with anger and a desire for retribution. Cal had spoken words of revenge and threatened her life, but Matthew could just as well execute her with his bare hands. Only God could help her if Robyn and Cal died today.

"Keep going!" he repeated the encouragement, and his chest lightened to see that they were making good headway across the water. "I think they'll make it."

Angelica put a hand on his shoulder and squeezed. He didn't want to dwell on the assurance and how it somehow allowed room for uncertainties to snake in.

"I'm so…cold," Robyn said through chattering teeth.

"The branch…" Cal said barely above a whisper, then repeated it louder. "Matt…he's saying *the branch*!"

She slowly turned to see a branch of an old pine tree hanging out over the water. It was about fifty feet downriver and about ten to fifteen feet across, to the opposite bank of where Matthew was. It would take a miracle and the hand of God, but they had to try. It would be far easier to give up, but she wasn't about to let the river win. She pulled from deep inside and felt a bit of calm overcome her.

"Let's…" That's all she could get out, but she and Cal moved their arms and kicked their legs, and the beast of the river fought them for every inch.

Eventually they started to make headway, but the branch was coming up fast, and they still had distance to close.

They had one shot at this. She wanted to tell Cal as much but couldn't get her mouth to speak. All her strength and adrenaline were being routed to one intent. Survival.

Mere feet away from the branch, she reached up. Her fingertips grazed the bark but danced over it.

Shit!

She tried again, reaching for a smaller piece that also jutted out. She got her hand wrapped around it and— It snapped off!

She scurried, kicking hard and fighting the current. Cal was in the same predicament, but he held out an arm and found purchase on the larger branch. He extended his other arm out to her.

He was only about six inches from the tips of her fingers, but it might as well have been several feet. She gave it one final effort and pulled on a source within she never knew existed. She latched on to Cal's hand, and he pulled her to him and the branch. The water bubbled around them, angry. It was losing. But it hadn't lost yet. Of that, Robyn was well aware.

One more tug by Cal, and she was able to grab hold of the branch. She hugged both her arms around it and dangled there, the water doing what it wanted with her legs.

"You have a firm hold?" Cal's question came out sounding like they were safe on land with no worries or cares in the world. Adrenaline was a powerful drug.

"Yes," she managed to say.

He took the arm that he'd used to pull her in and wrapped it around the branch so he was now holding on with both hands. "We need to shimmy across."

She nodded. It was about twenty feet to shore.

Cal advanced toward land one hand over the other on the branch, like a child on monkey bars.

She shadowed his lead and was doing well until she reached out her hand and it slid on wet bark. She was left hanging by one arm, her legs suspended above the water.

"Robyn!" Cal cried, aware of the situation.

"It's…okay," she said, reestablishing her hold on the branch.

They both paused there, as if contemplating what could have been, but didn't stay still for long. They got moving again, and what felt like forever later, they were over land. *About six feet* over land.

"I'll go first and catch you." Cal didn't give her a chance to respond, and he dropped down, sticking the landing like a pro gymnast. "Now it's your turn." He held up his arms to her.

She released her grip and put her faith in Cal. He had her. He'd catch her, and they'd both live another day.

Her aim had been too good. She landed on top of him, and he staggered back. His arms were around her waist, though, and he managed to keep them upright. He then set her down without a word, and she stumbled to a large rock and sat down on it to catch her breath. She rubbed her arms, freezing through her core still, and maybe that was a good thing. Just before a person dies from the cold, don't they start to feel warm? She shook aside the thought; she had no clue.

"Time to find out just how waterproof this thing is." Cal groaned as he withdrew his camera from his bag. He must have been satisfied as he put it in front of his face and pressed the shutter button a few times.

"We almost died, and your first thought is your camera?" she said through chattering teeth and then followed the direction of his camera lens.

Matthew, Angelica, and Mel were on the other side of the river, looking back at them.

"Stay there! We'll come to you!" Matthew yelled.

"Damn right you're coming to us! May I—" She started laughing so hard, it hurt everywhere. Her head, her chest, her gut. Cal lowered his camera and joined in her amusement. "*May I* suggest another way to the one we took?" She doubled over, holding a hand across her stomach. As her laughter died down, awareness of just how cold she was crept in. Slowly at first, but then with a fierce tenacity. Her body trembled, and she saw Cal's body doing the same. If only she'd been able to keep the backpack. It was waterproof, and there were blankets inside it.

"Here…" Cal sat beside her on the rock and put his arm around her. They hugged, sharing their body warmth, hungering to survive. But there was something else in his energy. Something that made Robyn both confused and uncomfortable, yet natural and completely at peace. He also made her feel secure, and as much as she wanted to retreat from his arms and the feelings stirring up in her, she couldn't move. They needed to warm each other's core temperature, but it was working faster than she would have expected. She guessed he must have felt the same way because his body molded even closer against hers.

Thirty-Four

Y ou're being serious with me right
now?"

Colin's partner sat across from him
down at the police station, seemingly amused
that Mr. Tweed Jacket, who they now knew as
Mel Wolf, was a murder suspect.

"I can't believe a guy like that—"

Colin took a deep breath. "I've told you
before, telling you again. You can't judge a book
by its cover."

"Ah, yes, you can, and it's done all the time."

"Well, it shouldn't be." With the added
emphasis, Colin felt a tad hypocritical. He was
stunned when Detective Day had told him
Wolf was their prime suspect. Based on first
impression only, the professor seemed more a
man afraid of his own shadow than one who
took the power of life and death into his hands.
At the same time, darkness seemed to surround

him.

"And his motive?" James leaned back in his chair, flung his arm over the back.

Colin had to kick aside the old-school programming that was drilled into him not to slouch or he'd ruin his back. He bit his tongue on sharing the wisdom with his partner. He wouldn't listen anyway.

"That's the thing the detective seemed to stop short on," Colin said.

"Because it's ludicrous, that's why."

"You're banking on the guy being innocent in all this?"

"I never said '*all* this.' We know he was running, so he at least has something those thugs wanted."

"And we'd do good to ask what."

James angled his head as if to say *no shit, Sherlock.*

"Let's say the professor had something the thugs wanted—the thugs whom we have names for now, as you know."

James hitched his shoulders.

"What could it be?" Colin went on.

"A clue to the whereabouts of a pirate's treasure." James kept his face straight when he said it, but once it was out, his composure quickly fell apart and he chuckled. "Listen, this entire thing is absurd."

Colin stiffened. "Obviously not to the lady lying in the morgue or her husband."

"No, I—"

"We need to figure out what brought Roman Murphy and Oscar Vincent to Washington. And if it was Wolf or something he has, is it also connected with Professor Edwin's murder?"

"I'd say it's too coincidental not to be."

"You think there's some sort of collaboration going on between this professor guy and the thugs?"

"Murphy and Vincent," James corrected. "We have their names, remember."

Colin flicked a pen toward James, and he moved out of the way just before it would have made contact with his face. James snarled but didn't say anything. Veteran cops had the luxury of getting away with things, and Colin wasn't beyond taking advantage of that perk. Might as well take what you could get.

"And to what purpose? The collaboration…" Colin studied James's face.

"There was mention of treasure."

As much as he wanted to fight the idea of treasure having anything to do with the chase through the city that resulted in Judy Finch's death, it kept coming back up. Like an old, festering wound begging for attention.

But he was at a wall for how to proceed. They had far too little information. A pirate's treasure. Mention of Spain. Nothing had come back on any of them leaving the country. Nothing had come on the SUV's license, either. They only had one string left to pull—Justin Scott. Colin would do the digging, but first, he needed more coffee. He was just about to hit the bullpen for some when the phone on his desk rang. He answered it to find Andy from Tech on the phone.

"So, I've got good news," Andy said.

"About time," Colin muttered and put the call on speaker, gesturing for James to listen in.

"And not so good news."

"Figured I should have waited for the other foot to drop."

"That SUV you were asking about. Good news is I was able to get the tag number. The not so good news is it ties back to a corporation linked to a Veronica Vincent. I'm not sure if you—"

"I know exactly who she is," Colin interrupted.

"Well, it took me a while to run this all down. The tag initially came back to a numbered corporation, but I knew you wouldn't be happy with that alone, so I kept digging."

"Good call."

"I won't bore you with a bunch of details, but I'll leave you with this: if her people are involved with your case, which it seems they are, I'm surprised there haven't been any more bodies turning up." Andy ended the call on that potent note, leaving Colin and James staring at each other.

Somehow, hearing the words drilled home

the seriousness of her involvement. Colin had more to consider than catching the man who shot Judy Finch. Matthew Connor and Veronica Vincent had a past, and maybe it wasn't pushing it to think the Canadian Trio, and possibly Wolf, were in danger.

Colin did the next thing he could think of. He searched *Justin Scott, private investigator*, and quickly found one was located in Toronto, Canada. Now that had to be more than a coincidence. Colin called and left a message but would be surprised if Justin actually called back.

Thirty-Five

Almijara and Alhama Natural Park, Spain
Tuesday, 5:00 PM Local Time

Matthew let out a deep breath when his friends made it to shore, but it wasn't time to relax just yet. They were out of the water, but they were soaking wet and would be cold. He also noticed that Robyn no longer had her backpack. Making it even more urgent to convene with them. He was pretty sure Angelica had a blanket in her bag.

"Guys!" he yelled, and both Robyn and Cal looked up. "Go back upriver following along as close to the water as you can."

"Will do." Cal was the one to call back, and for a flush of a second, Matthew worried about Robyn. A pain cinched his heart.

"Start moving as soon as you can. We have a blanket?" He glanced at Angelica, who nodded.

"Okay," Cal replied. He got to his feet and held out a hand to help Robyn up. She put her hand in his but withdrew it quickly once she was standing.

"Just follow the river," Matthew emphasized. His two friends were without any GPS or guidance system, but if they stuck near the water, they should meet up with them just fine.

It also gave Matthew a line of sight to them. He could see Robyn and Cal were moving but slowly, their bodies likely stiff from their journey down the river.

"They should be fine now," Angelica said, and he cringed at the assurance. No matter how well-meaning, it rubbed him the wrong way.

He stopped walking. "They should have been fine before. Truth is we don't know what the hell's ahead of us."

"We don't, but we keep moving forward because that's what we do." Angelica stuck out her chin and brushed past him.

She didn't want to talk about her half-brother, but it felt like she'd just made it about him. Guilt for getting involved must have been eating at her. After all, she signed up for a risky life, not Pablo. He'd simply been in the wrong place at the wrong time. But if anyone was to blame...

"You do know that what happened wasn't your fault." Matthew could feel the burden of responsibility land on his shoulders.

She stopped walking and spun around. "You sure about that?" Her deep-brown eyes peered into his. "I accepted this job, I brought him in to help me do it."

"You couldn't have known—"

"I *should* have known," she spat. "It's my job to know. It's my job to prepare." She held his gaze for a few seconds then resumed walking.

He watched after her, his heart aching for her. He could only well imagine how she felt accountable, but really all this was on him. He'd taken on this quest; he'd made the request of her to get after-hours access to the museum. As the burden of consequences settled in, a new remorse entered. His life was his to put on the line, but he repeatedly put his friends at risk, too, with his compulsion to jump into things. If they had died… He didn't even want to think about it. And in a strange way, he also felt like he should feel guilty Robyn and Cal had survived while Pablo hadn't.

He set in stride with Mel, and they followed Angelica. Matthew looked over at Robyn and Cal to make sure they were doing all right and hated the times when he lost sight of them due to trees and other obstructions.

It took them over twenty minutes to reach the area where Robyn and Cal had gone into the river. Matthew knew this because he'd also been doing a lot of staring at his watch. The sun was getting lower in the sky, and maybe once they met up, it would be best to turn around and call it a day. But they'd come this far. Guess it would depend on how Robyn and Cal were doing once they caught up with them.

Robyn and Cal stepped into a clearing. She yelled, "We there yet?" Then she laughed.

Matthew smiled. Thank God they were okay.

Another twenty minutes, and the river was a trickle by comparison to what it had been and had narrowed significantly.

"Here we go." Angelica stopped, and he caught up with her, the professor at his side. "No bridge, Cal!"

"Ah, man!" he replied.

She smiled and turned to Matthew. "I think it's passable."

He studied the river. Here the water was quite shallow and clear. Small fish swam near the bottom. Gray rock jutted out of the water here and there, making for great steppingstones.

"Not an issue," he said to her and yelled, "We'll be there in a minute!" to his friends, who were standing on the parallel riverbank.

"Just be careful," Angelica warned him as he took his first step. "The stones will be slippery."

"Yep, I got it." Matthew set out.

As he made his way across, he glanced back at Angelica and Mel. She was traversing the river like she did this every day, and Mel resembled a tightrope walker with his arms out for balance.

Each step closer, each foot, each inch, Matthew felt the urge to run to Robyn and Cal. But he paced himself and was thoughtful of the placement of each foothold.

Matthew heard the crumbling of rock and stone behind him and turned to check on Angelica and Mel again. In the process, he twisted his ankle and found himself with one leg in the water up to his knee. "Frick!"

The water was so cold it felt like it had instantly burrowed to bone. He withdrew his leg as fast as possible.

"Thought you had this," Angelica jabbed at him.

"Very funny." He proceeded to cross the river and was happy to step on solid land. He hurried to his friends and said to them, "Holy shit, that river's freezing!"

"You're telling us that?" Cal laughed heartily and pulled Matthew into a bear hug, and Robyn latched on.

The three of them stood like that for some time. Matthew didn't care that his friends were still damp; they were alive.

"Your head," Matthew said to Cal upon noticing a gash near his temple.

"Oh, it's nothing."

"Here, let me…" Angelica pulled a first-aid kit from her backpack, wiped Cal's wound, and applied a bandage.

"Thanks."

"No problem."

While they were doing that, Matthew glanced around. First to the spot where he'd slipped into the water, and second back to the shore from where they'd left. He felt like he was being watched, no matter how crazy that sounded. The shifting rock was probably just the mountain settling or something. After all, if they were being followed, he'd see whoever it was. It's not like there were many places to seek cover out here. He turned back to his friends. He was just being paranoid. All this tasting-death bit had his nerves frayed and his mind stuttering.

"If you guys want to turn back, start fresh tomorrow, I completely understand." He made the proposal and scanned their eyes.

"We're drying up. We'll be fine," Robyn said.

"It's only going to get colder as the sun goes down." They had small pop-up tents with them, but they were the backup plan—not *the* plan.

Robyn put her hand on his forearm. "We know that, but we'll be fine. I wouldn't, however, mind that blanket you mentioned."

"Oh, right." Angelica pulled out a wool blanket from her backpack and winced. "I only have the one, but it's quite large. Can you—"

"Share?" Cal cut in. "Sure...yeah, we can share. Right, Robyn?" He looked over at her, and she was nodding.

Angelica handed the blanket to Robyn. "Sorry I didn't bring anymore."

"Well, you did, but I ditched them," Robyn said off the cuff as she worked with Cal to unfold the blanket.

The two of them awkwardly tugged this way and that before Robyn finally just let go of the blanket and held up her hands to Cal. He stepped beside her and draped the blanket around himself and then her.

"Thanks," Robyn said quietly.

"So, you're sure? You want to carry on?" Matthew angled his head, studied his friends. They were fighting shivers, and he knew the feeling. He was pretty sure he'd lost feeling from his knee down on his left leg.

"Carry on, young man." Cal snickered, and Robyn followed his lead, but both stopped under his gaze.

"You two are okay?" he asked.

"Yeah, sure. Why wouldn't we be?" Cal pressed on a smile.

Robin shadowed his comment with, "Yep, we're fine."

Not really buying— Matthew heard it again: the movement of rock and stone, grating against each other, like the sound of shoes scuffing over them. "Hello? Is someone out there?" As soon as he asked the question, he realized how ridiculous he sounded. If someone was following and doing a damn good job of concealing themselves, were they really going to respond and out themselves?

"What's going on?" Mel hugged his satchel, and his eyes were darting all over the place, like he was a small little lamb in a field of wolves.

Matthew kept his gaze on the side of the river where they'd come from. He never caught any movement, and he strained to listen but didn't hear anything else. "Just thought I heard something, but it must have been nothing."

"Well, let's move, then," Angelica said. "That was the consensus, so…" She pulled out her GPS and directed them with a pointed finger where they were to go from there.

"And how far?" Cal asked.

"About ten more miles."

"Ah, easy peasy. Right, Robyn?" Cal nudged her elbow.

She shifted her body just a little farther away from him. "Let's not get too carried away."

Matthew studied his friends. They might claim to be okay, but they certainly were acting strange.

Thirty-Six

Cal felt like the worst friend in the history of the world. Not just mankind, *the entire world*, factoring in crawling beasts and slithering reptiles. Wild animals of the Serengeti and the Outback. He didn't deserve any expressions of concern for his welfare or even the blanket wrapped around him. He should probably let Robyn have it to herself. At least then they wouldn't be walking in time with each other, their hips brushing, and the sizzling chemistry between them crackling with every step.

"Here, I'll be fine." Cal smiled at Robyn as he ducked out from under the blanket.

"You sure?" she asked. He heard relief in her voice; she was feeling as awkward as he was.

For at least an hour, he'd been battling with what the hell had happened back there. He'd caught her when she'd jumped. He'd hugged a *friend* to warm her, to warm himself. It was the fact he found himself *responding* that was the problem.

Matthew was ahead of them and glanced over his shoulder for the umpteenth time. He probably saw right through Cal—or it was Cal's guilty conscience. Matthew probably had no clue what had taken place. It was likely more a matter of Matthew not wanting to let him or Robyn out of his sight.

"We're fine, Matt. We've had our dip, and we're good now," Cal said, teasing about their trip down the river as if it had been a leisurely swim. Whatever he could to divert attention away from himself and how he was feeling. The foremost was like scum. He had no right to fall for Robyn, and she was his friend. *Platonic* friend. Nothing more. And to top it off, his best friend was in love with her. The fact they'd decided not to be together was neither here nor there. Besides, he didn't really want to get involved with Robyn. She was more sister than lover—except for the way her body felt pressed against his. That hadn't felt familial; it smacked of carnal.

He was slowly going crazy—or *quickly*, depending on one's point of view. His thoughts were letting him down as they spun and weaved fabrications and fantasies, none of which he had any right to consider.

They kept on walking until the sun disappeared and Matthew and Angelica pulled out flashlights.

Angelica looked up from her GPS and stopped walking. "We're here."

"Here? Where the grave should be?" Cal looked around, and there was absolutely nothing worthy of note. Just more bramble and scraggly trees and rock, rock, and more rock. "Why do I have this sinking feeling that we might be the hundred or so miles off from our target location?"

"Because you're Cal," Robyn pushed out.

He narrowed his eyes at her. "And what's that supposed to mean?" He said it with the goal of sarcasm, but his tone didn't reach it.

"Just that. You like to see the worst in a situation before—"

"Before I see the good. Yeah, we've had variations of this conversation a few times since Washington." Again, he could hear his voice coming back to his ears. He was compliant and soft-spoken. She met his gaze, telling him she'd noticed. Cal hoped that the others didn't, especially Matthew.

"When something's fact, it tends to resurface," Robyn countered.

He turned away from her. "I know we're looking for Josefa's grave. But should there be a type of marker to watch for?"

"Given the time period, we could be looking at anything from a flat stone to a crucifix," Mel said. "It's also entirely possible there's a more elaborate marking, but if he added his treasure to her grave, I'd guess it's discreetly marked."

"Let's spread out," Matthew said.

"Here." Angelica shoved her flashlight into Cal's hand faster than he could think of refusing. "You and Robyn work together. Matthew and I will."

"And me?" Mel croaked.

"You can pick who you want to work with or just stand there." Angelica smiled at the professor, and even in the dull light, one could see his cheeks flush.

"You're welcome with us." Cal extended the invitation out of pure selfishness. He wanted to put off the conversation he and Robyn would inevitably end up having if left alone. She liked to talk about her feelings and had a strategy for pretty much anything in life. He wouldn't doubt she had planned to be a museum curator when she was in diapers and had laid out not a five-year plan, but a *twenty*-five-year plan. He certainly wasn't ready to talk about what took place earlier because he was still trying to understand it. As far as he knew, he hadn't harbored any romantic feelings for Robyn. He would have loved for her and Matthew to set their egos aside and get back together. It's not like Cal was even ready to start any sort of romantic relationship, anyhow—with anyone, let alone with Robyn. It must have just been the situation they'd survived that made them feel anything. Emotions at a high and all that.

"Thank you." Mel joined Cal and Robyn, and in the beam of their flashlights, Cal and Matthew met each other's gaze.

There was no way he could know what Matthew was thinking, but his mind fired judgment and accusations.

Get a grip, Cal told himself. Robyn might have been a planner, but he excelled at panicking and responding emotionally. He was guilty of what Robyn had accused him of, but it was part and parcel of his tendency to feel too damn much.

Matthew and Angelica went off together, far enough at a distance that their flashlight had no effect for Cal, Robyn, and Mel.

Cal moved the one he held in broad sweeps, taking in as much ground as possible. He just hoped that Robyn had been right about her suspicions that Gasparilla had measured his coordinates accurately and to within reason.

Mel lurched forward and cussed. He must have tripped on something. Cal snickered.

"You think that was funny?" Mel snapped.

"Yeah, actually."

"Did I laugh at you when you fell into the river?" Mel shot back, his eyes piercing marbles in the shadows. "I didn't. And you know why? I'm a good, decent human being."

Cal had been starting to tolerate the professor, maybe even like him, but now the guy was making it personal. "And I'm not?"

"You are sarcastic, and you complain about everything." Mel's voice got louder as he continued to speak.

"Well, you're a whiny geek who should have stayed in the library."

Mel closed the distance between them and puffed out his chest, pushing it against Cal's. Cal's hands balled into fists, and he drew back one arm—

Robyn clamped her hand around it. "Enough!"

Matthew and Angelica were coming toward them.

"Everything all right here?" Matthew asked, his gaze going from Robyn to Cal, then Mel, taking in the scene before him.

"Everything's peachy, Matt. The professor here just needs to get out of my face, though. Don't say I didn't try to be civil."

Matthew put a hand on the professor's shoulder and drew him back. The entire time Mel was watching Cal, his gaze daring him to just go ahead and throw the punch. And, oh, how Cal wanted to oblige.

"Listen, we've all had a long day. Some of us more than others." Matthew directed his words at Mel, and Cal found his shoulders squaring just a bit more.

"I tripped and what does this wise-ass do?" Mel flailed a hand toward Cal. "He laughs. That's what."

"Matt's right. We've had a long day," Angelica said, playing peacekeeper. A skill Cal imagined she pulled on from time to time in her line of work.

Matthew turned toward Angelica. "Let's just take a break, grab a snack."

Cal's stomach rumbled in response to the mere suggestion. Given his brush with death and the Robyn situation, food had been the furthest thing from his mind. And his head still hurt like a son of a bitch from where the rock had hit him. All good reasons for the professor not to press his luck with him.

"I agree," Angelica said, rooting in her backpack.

Cal listened as the two of them called the shots, but he couldn't care less right now. There was no way they'd be able to make it back to their drop-off point. Besides he was beyond ready to lay his hands on some gold coins. It was said that money didn't solve problems, but that came from the people who didn't know better.

Thirty-Seven

It was just last night that Daniel had asked Wes to look into Veronica Vincent, but the silence was deafening. If only Wes would call to say something, even if it was to provide nothing. It was twelve thirty, and he was at the kitchen table. Lauren had already served him his lunch—a simple meal of sliced turkey with cheese on rye and a garden salad. His appetite was satisfied, but his hunger for answers was another thing entirely.

His phone rang, and he answered it quickly without even looking at caller ID.

"Mr. Iverson, it's Justin."

There was a marked hesitancy in the kid's voice, like he was confused about something. "Everything all right?"

"I'm hoping you can tell me."

Daniel shifted straighter in his chair.

Justin went on. "I received a phone call from a Detective Doyle with the MPD in Washington, DC. I got the feeling it might have to do with my calling the Naples PD about Professor Edwin's murder, though I'm not sure why."

"Did he give you any details?" Daniel asked. "A reason for his calling you?"

"None. He just asked that I call him about an open investigation, but I thought I should talk to you before calling him back."

"Smart, and don't call him back."

"Don't—"

"Don't," Daniel stressed. "Let me handle him." The offer was out, and he regretted it immediately, but there was no advantage to getting Justin any more involved.

"You're sure?"

"I am. What's his number?"

Justin rattled it off, and Daniel wrote it down. "Is there anything I should know, Mr. Iverson? I didn't do anything illegal, did I?"

"You're fine, Justin. Just get back to work and don't worry about this. Pretend he never called."

"Okay."

Daniel ended the call and stared at the number. It was time to reach out to the Metropolitan Police Department in Washington. He wasn't left with a choice any longer. The detective would just keep calling Justin and would keep calling William Connor. Neither was acceptable.

Lauren came by and picked up Daniel's empty plate.

"Thank you," he told her.

"No problem."

He left the kitchen, headed for his room. He'd make the call from there. As he walked, he tried to piece things together. Justin had called the Florida detective investigating Professor Edwin's murder. Could this Detective Doyle have found out about that and seen Justin as a lead in his case? But for Doyle and this Florida detective to be talking, it meant that the connection between Edwin's murder and the one in Washington had been linked by law enforcement.

Daniel closed his door behind him and called the number with his burner. Doyle answered on the second ring.

"I'm returning your call. This is Justin Scott," Daniel said.

There were a few seconds of silence on the other end. The detective was probably trying to reconcile the voice he'd heard on the voicemail greeting with the one talking to him now.

"What can I do for you?" Daniel prompted. "You said you were calling about an open investigation."

"Yes, I was." There was a leeriness in the detective's voice. "You called a Detective Day in Naples about a murdered man by the name of Ralph Edwin."

"I did."

"Why are you interested in him? If I'm not mistaken, you're from Toronto, Canada."

"I am."

"So, your interest in that murder case…" Doyle laid the bait, but Daniel didn't bite. "Has someone hired you to look into his murder?"

"I am a private investigator."

"And of what interest is the case to your employer?"

"I'm not at liberty to say."

"Hmm."

"I'd like to know why any of this matters to a Washington, DC, detective."

There was a small pocket of silence, then, "A woman was murdered here that I believe is connected to the one of Ralph Edwin in Florida."

"Really?"

"Yes, and I get the feeling that's not a surprise to you."

Daniel's turn to stay quiet.

"I'm just trying to find a killer, Mr. Scott," Doyle said.

"I can appreciate that."

"I know that Toronto's a big city, but do you know a Matthew Connor?"

That question hit Daniel. "No, I…"

"Matthew Connor never hired you to look into the murders? We understand that he may have left the country with a man named Mel Wolf."

"Do you think this Matthew Connor is a killer?"

"I never said that."

Daniel breathed a little easier. "Who is Mel Wolf?"

"That name doesn't ring a bell?"

"Nope." Daniel was going to hell for all the lies. "You think Mel Wolf killed the professor in Florida and the woman in DC?"

"Could have."

Daniel's stomach tossed. He didn't like people just showing up in Matthew's life, and he'd been suspicious about Mel Wolf from the start, although his background hadn't raised any flags. "This Mel Wolf is a dangerous guy, then?"

"Seems so."

"There's evidence?"

"I can't say much more, as the investigations are open, but Naples PD is certainly interested in speaking with him."

Daniel felt himself go cold. Wolf could have been in on the murder of his fellow professor. At least the police seemed to think so.

"Let me know if you find yourself more open to talking." The detective disconnected.

Just when Daniel was under the impression Matthew had one enemy to worry about, he might have another one right in his midst.

His phone rang, and caller ID told him it was Wes.

"Hello," Daniel answered quickly.

"Sounding a little eager, Danny Boy."

"Not going to deny it. What have you found out?"

"Still doing what I can to run down Veronica Vincent's location, but I have the IDs on the two 'situations.' One was Roman Murphy, and the other Oscar Vincent."

"Vincent? You're sure?"

"Yes, I'm sure," Wes said drily.

"A relative of Veronica's?" Daniel didn't know she had family. He didn't think witches and devils had children or siblings.

"I'm still trying to unravel if that's the case. There are no other births registered for Veronica's biological mother, but—"

"That doesn't necessarily mean anything."

"Yeah," Wes said, deflated.

"You're not giving up on me?"

"Never, but I just wanted to let you know where things are standing."

"Thanks."

"You got it. Take care. Bye."

Veronica Vincent could have more family out there. That thought was utterly terrifying, especially if they were as evil as Veronica.

Thirty-Eight

Matthew crumpled up the wrapper from the protein bar he'd just finished and watched as the rest worked on theirs. Everyone looked whipped.

His wristwatch told him it was just after six thirty, but maybe they should make camp. He stuffed the packaging into a pocket of his backpack. "I don't think any of us have it in ourselves to walk back to the drop-off point. Maybe we should set up the tents."

"No need," Angelica said, and everyone looked at her. "Here's the thing. All I have to do is place a call—" she pulled out her satellite phone "—and we'll be picked up. Right here."

Cal was grinning. "A helicopter on speed dial."

She winked at him. "You got it. Wouldn't leave home without it."

Now she brings out a helicopter... She was full of surprises, and Matthew loved that—as well as what access to a quick getaway meant. "There's no need to rush off," he concluded.

"Hey, I'm good to resume looking." Robyn got her feet and dusted off her pants.

"Me, too," Cal chimed in, followed by Mel.

"Let's do it, then," Angelica said.

Matthew took the lead and danced the flashlight over the ground. Rock after rock after rock. If it was a stone that marked Josefa's grave, this really was the equivalent of looking for a needle in a haystack.

Mel called out again, another expletive escaping his lips and traveling through the night air like a raid siren.

"Guy's so tired he can't lift his feet." Matthew glanced over at Angelica and laughed.

"Matthew!" Robyn cried and he spun to face her. "Oh..." She held up a hand to shield her eyes. "Your light..."

"Sorry." He lowered the flashlight back toward the ground.

"I think we found something," she said.

"More like the professor stumbled onto something," Cal corrected.

Matthew gave one quick glance at Angelica, and they both set off in a fast stride toward the others.

"Look." Robyn pointed to a rock that was of a slightly different shape than the ones around it. It had edges that appeared to have been chiseled, touched by a human hand.

He bent down to his haunches, Robyn next to him.

"Do you think it's the grave we're looking for?" she asked.

He ran his fingertips over the stone. Shallow impressions. "Is that—"

Robyn put her hand next to his, and she smiled. "It's been engraved."

Angelica came up behind them and assembled the shovel she'd brought. It came in three pieces, and there was a distinctive *click* as they were snapped together.

Mel joined them at the stone. "Is there any way to make it out?"

"I don't think so." Robyn leaned in, trying to get a closer look.

Matthew gripped the edges of the stone, expecting it come free easily, but there must have been far more beneath the surface than appeared on top. "Cal, can you help me with this?"

Cal, who had been standing back a few feet, came over.

"You take that side," Matthew directed, "and I'll take…"

Both men lifted and grunted. The stone didn't budge.

"How big is this thing?" Cal straightened up.

"Let me try something." Angelica wedged the tip of the shovel into the dirt at the edge of the rock and traced around it. By the time she was finished, they were looking at roughly a two-foot diameter.

"Okay, how are we supposed to get it out?" Cal had his hands on his hips and was studying the rock.

"Pure determination, my friend. Pure determination," Matthew said.

"And teamwork," Robyn kicked out. "We all need to grab a hold on the rock as best we can and lift on the count of three."

With his friends on either side of him, Matthew flashed to the past. A time only seven months ago when they'd worked to pry the lid off a sarcophagus.

"One…two," Robyn said. "Three!"

Everyone lifted, including the professor, and the rock shifted.

"We did it. We moved it a half inch," Cal joked.

"If that." Matthew smiled, not discouraged an iota. "Let's have another go."

It took several attempts, but they eventually managed to get the rock out of its resting place. With it to the side of the divot, a good look at the rock made it clear it was more like a boulder. It was at least two feet in depth, too. *No wonder the damn thing was so hard to move.*

"Shine the light in the hole," Robyn urged Matthew.

He did so, and everyone bent over to see.

"Look at that," Cal said. "Dirt."

Robyn swatted at Cal's legs, and he moved out of her reach.

Matthew scooped dirt and let it filter through his fingers. The disappointment was crushing. Maybe it was just a boulder and not a grave marker at all. Then the beam from Cal's flashlight flicked across something. Matthew adjusted the point of his, and sure enough...

He grinned as he reached in and pulled out his finds.

He wiped them free of dirt and let out a holler. "Gold coins."

"Coins," Mel repeated and took one from him. "We're in the right place."

"I think so."

"So, is that part of the treasure? Like just a tease or the entire thing?" Cal asked. "Please don't tell me that's the entire thing."

Robyn flicked her finger at Cal's leg and made impact just above his left kneecap. He squealed and jumped back.

"Can you keep your hands to yourself, woman?"

Robyn and Cal locked eyes and seemed to dip into some sort of secret conversation. Matthew wasn't sure what that was all about and wasn't sure he wanted to know.

"Let's dig farther down and see what we find," Matthew said, holding out hope the coins were just a foregleam of what was to come. "Shovel?"

He held his hand out behind him toward Angelica and looked over a shoulder when nothing was put in his palm.

"If you don't mind…" She smirked and approached the hole, shovel in hand.

"Needed a little excitement in your life, didn't you?" he tossed out.

"Shh, don't tell anyone." Angelica jabbed the shovel into the dirt. She removed about a foot's worth, building up quite a nice dirt pile to the side of the hole, when the shovel hit something solid.

"Did you hear that?" Matthew asked.

"I heard it *and* felt it." She put her shovel on the ground and got down on all fours. She started excavating the dirt with her hands and sweeping it once she got the bulk cleared away. "It's a wooden box."

"A coffin." Cal had a self-satisfied smile on his face.

Angelica traced an outline with her shovel again and it revealed something rectangular.

They dug the ends free, and when they were finished, the five of them were looking at the lid of a wooden box.

"If anyone wants to stick a pin in this and pick up tomor—" Matthew smiled as the other four interrupted him with a resounding "No!"

The five of them lifted the box out of the hole.

"Just be careful. It's so old," Robyn said.

Once they had the box positioned on the ground, Matthew took the shovel from Angelica and pried the lid free. Robyn and Angelica shone the flashlights into the box.

The beams of light first fell on a human skull, then revealed a full skeleton from the shadows.

"Oh." Cal covered his mouth with his hand but dropped it quickly when the women looked at him.

"It's not like there's even any flesh," Robyn said to him.

"Still…"

She laughed.

Matthew put his gaze back on the contents of the box. There was more than a pile of bones. Coins were scattered within, like they'd been tossed inside after the body was laid. Whether it was Josefa, they didn't know for absolute certainty, but given they were led there from coordinates in Gaspar's logbook, it was most likely. Something in the coffin caught his eye, and he took it out, handling it delicately.

"A pirate's hat," he said.

"A tricorne," Cal tagged on. "It's the proper name for that style of hat."

Matthew studied the hat in his hands and could understand part of the name. The *tri* part. It was like three flaps were folded up to meet a rounded part that sat on the head.

"And not just any pirate's hat," the professor added. "I would bet it's none other than Gasparilla's."

"The question is, though, what is it doing in there," Robyn said. "I'm not completely up on pirates, but weren't their hats almost sacred to them?"

"Yes," Mel confirmed and pointed. "What's under the body?"

"I don't know," Matthew said.

"I can tell you what I think it is, but I'd rather see it first."

"Don't tell me we have to move it." Cal winced, and Matthew and Robyn both chuckled.

"Our friend here doesn't have much of a stomach for dead bodies," Matthew explained to Angelica and Mel.

"Can't really say as I blame him." That, surprisingly, from Angelica.

"We're going to have to move the skeleton if we want to get down there," Matthew said.

"But we do so carefully and respectfully," Robyn stressed. "Actually, let me move the bones."

"No argument here." Cal was waving his hands in front of himself and stepping back.

Robyn moved the remains from the box and set them on the lid with care and a delicate touch. Once cleared, Mel extracted what he'd seen in the coffin. It was a piece of fabric with frayed edges. Mel unfolded it and revealed that it was a pirate's flag.

"No one can argue that a pirate's been here," Matthew said, excitement rushing through him.

"No," Mel said thoughtfully, "but it just confirms something for me." He paused there as if deliberately to bait them to his hook—and it worked. "Gasparilla wouldn't have left these items behind unless he'd left his life of piracy."

"He was so heartbroken after his love's death that he decided to hang up his hat and flag?" Cal's mouth twitched, and Robyn punched him in the arm.

Everyone shared a small laugh. Even Mel.

"We know from his logbook that he didn't make it to Spain until after her death," Mel began, "so he would have come here, exhumed the coffin, and added these pieces after she was buried. A theory we'd tossed around."

"Are we to assume that what we see is what's left of the treasure?" Cal asked.

"Not sure about that part," Mel said. "Too soon to say."

Matthew was going to hold on to the hope there was much more to find, for all their sakes. How far they'd come and how much they'd lost. He glanced at Angelica, who was standing there, a resting smile on her face. All of this really must have been surreal for her, especially with her family's connection to Gaspar's first mate. He was pleased that she was extracting pleasure from this expedition, despite her personal loss. If Daniel was behind her employment, he had to wonder if the universe was actually involved.

Thirty-Nine

Matthew traced his hands over the tricorne on the outside, then he flipped it over and looked inside. Tucked into a seam was a folded piece of paper. "Look!" He carefully extracted the page and was about to start unfolding it when Robyn laid a hand over his.

"Let me," she said.

He dipped his head in agreement and let her take the paper.

"It's definitely old. Much the same as the quality of paper that was in his logbook." She unfolded it with a little difficulty as she still held a flashlight in one hand. "Someone, hold this." She shoved the flashlight to Cal's chest. "Hold it over the page." A few seconds later, she said, "It's all written in Spanish. Same styling as Gasparilla's logbook."

"Penned in his own hand," Mel said reverently.

Matthew wasn't going to correct the professor, but they wouldn't know for sure unless the two were compared by someone trained in such things.

Robyn's eyes wandered over the page, going left to right, down, left to right. She put a hand over her heart.

"What does it say?" Matthew asked.

"Well, I haven't finished it yet, but what I've read confirms that he was indeed heartbroken over the loss of Josefa."

"This was written by Gasparilla?" Mel asked.

"Yes." She smiled at the professor, then continued. "He talks of his crew wanting her dead and how her remaining on board was a threat to her life—"

"Just as Gómez's diary and the logbook told us," Mel stamped out enthusiastically.

"I have no doubt we've found Josefa's grave." Robyn grinned.

"What else does it say?" Matthew prompted.

"He wrote that he no longer had the heart for piracy and laid out a declaration that he'd live out his days in isolation. That's about as far as I've gotten so far."

"Read more." Cal nudged her arm, and she put her gaze back on the letter.

About a minute later, she looked up and smiled, her eyes wet in the light that hit them. "We've got the treasure."

"So very happy to hear that," a man said, but not a voice that belonged to Cal or the professor.

Matthew turned, and two men were coming toward them. One was clapping.

Matthew dropped the tricorne and pulled his gun, and Angelica pulled hers.

"Now, now, we don't want anyone getting hurt now, do we?" Veronica Vincent stepped into view. Her lithe frame, her long, red hair. "Matthew, we meet again."

Every part of him went cold.

Cal lunged toward her. "I'm going to kill—"

One of her men leveled his gun on Cal.

"Not so fast. We want them to cooperate with us," Veronica cooed as her guy collected Angelica's gun.

"I'll never cooperate with you." Matthew meant it, but she still sent fear hurtling through him. She was untamed and unpredictable like a wild animal or a tropical storm.

"I'm pretty sure you will." She walked toward him, slinking like a tigress circling prey.

"I will shoot you," he said through clenched teeth.

"Yeah? I very much doubt that." She reached him and put a hand on his shoulder, left it there as she walked around him. "Still looking good."

He so badly wanted to squeeze the trigger, but the men still had their weapons on Cal.

"Shouldn't you be in prison?" Matthew seethed.

"Lots of people should be, but I'm not one of them."

"Fuck that!" Cal screamed.

"Ah, ah, ah." Veronica waggled a finger in the air. "You amuse me, but not forever. Don't push your luck."

"Or what? You'll kill me?" Cal growled.

Matthew shook his head at his friend, hoping to discourage him from mouthing off. Veronica sought control in all situations, and if she felt disrespected by Cal, she'd have no problem having her goons shoot him. There really was only one thing holding her back that Matthew could figure—her desire for his cooperation.

"Why are you interested in some ancient pirate?" he asked casually, like it was ridiculous someone like her would have any interest.

She stopped walking, and with her mouth less than an inch from one of his ears, said, "I would have given you far more credit, Matthew. It has nothing to do with the pirate, rather his treasure. Thought you knew me better." She pouted.

"Don't you have enough money?"

"Sweet, silly, naive Matthew." She came around in front of him and softly tapped a hand to his cheek. "One can never have enough."

How he'd ever found her charming was beyond him. Her attractiveness ended where her personality began. He could imagine her killing her own mother if it got her closer to money. He still had the gun in his hand, but during her approach, her circling, he'd lowered it.

"Now, hand that over to me." She took the gun from him, careful in the transfer, and passed it on to one of her men. "We wouldn't want someone to get shot. Now, we understand there's some pirate booty on the line." She laughed at her own play on words, picked up the hat from the ground, and handed it to one of her men. "Looks like you're getting close to finding it. Your girlfriend there just announced to the world you found your treasure." She walked over and peeked into the coffin. "I assume it's not this measly amount of coins you were talking about." Veronica sauntered over to Robyn who was glaring at her. "So tell me, sweetie, where do we go from here?"

Robyn spat in Veronica's face, and Veronica punched Robyn's.

Angelica made a move like she was going to intervene, but Matthew shook his head for her to stay put. She was dispensable as far as Veronica would be concerned, and she didn't need to give the witch any reason to kill her.

"Leave her the fuck alone!" Matthew growled.

"I'm fine, Matthew." Robyn narrowed her eyes but rubbed at her jaw. "She hits like a little girl."

Veronica went to strike Robyn again, but Robyn juked out of the way, ducking low and going at her opponent's torso, tackling her to the ground. Robyn got in a couple blows when a gun was fired.

Matthew looked around. All of them were standing…well, except for Robyn who was now pinned to the ground by Veronica.

"That was a warning shot." The goon who'd fired, apparently into the sky, lowered his gun.

Veronica struggled to her feet, gripping Robyn's hair and pretty much dragging her up with her.

It was then Matthew noticed Gasparilla's letter was on the ground, having fallen out of Robyn's hands during her altercation.

He made a move for it, but one of Veronica's goons stepped up next to him. "I don't think so."

Veronica swooped in and snatched the letter. She dabbed the corner of her mouth with a fingertip where Robyn must have struck her and winced slightly. She took the letter to Mel. "How lovely that we meet again, Professor." She circled him much the same way she had Matthew. She turned to Matthew and said, "Your new friend here. Did he tell you he's working for me?"

Matthew's insides turned to lava. He knew he shouldn't have trusted the guy. "You son of a bitch."

Mel wouldn't look at him.

"He led me right to you." She grabbed Mel's satchel, rooted inside, and pulled out a phone. "A burner, which I've been tracking all this time."

How those men knew they were at the El Acebuchal Museum. Why Pablo was dead.

Veronica went on. "I've even been listening in on your conversations. But the good professor goes above and beyond, you see. He called me with the coordinates for here, so we knew right where to find you. Didn't know exactly when you'd get here, of course, but we kept a watch on you from a distance all afternoon."

The scuffling sound was *from the soles of boots on rock…* That meant they would have seen Robyn and Cal fall into the river and never bothered to help. But why should he be surprised by that? He clenched his fists at his sides and glared at Mel. "You were working with her."

Mel lifted his gaze to look at Matthew, but only for a brief second. "I didn't have a choice."

"'I didn't have a choice,'" Veronica parroted in a whiny sarcastic tone. "Everyone has a choice. You made one when you bought that house, found that diary, took it to Edwin. It's your fault he had to die."

Mel's gaze snapped to Veronica. Remorse or anger in his eyes…Matthew wasn't sure.

"So, go ahead, read the letter," Veronica told Mel. "Start at the good bit about the location of the treasure."

Mel glanced at Matthew as if seeking his permission.

"Don't look at him. Look at the guys with the guns, Professor. We only need one of you to read Spanish, and I know Sweet Pea over there does." She tossed a smug smirk in Robyn's direction.

Mel held out a shaky hand for the letter, and he set about reading it.

"Translate it out loud as you go," Veronica barked.

Mel jumped and proceeded to do just as she'd asked. "Basically, he left his life of piracy behind because, after he lost Josefa, he lost his passion for it. He and his crew were celebrating a recent plunder on shore. When his men fell asleep, he boarded the *Floridablanca*. After a long journey, he says, he scuttled the galleon with the bounty on board."

"You're telling me he sank his own ship?" Veronica asked, her voice full of skepticism. "With his treasure?"

"Yes…yes, ma'am. That's what the letter says."

"Where?"

"*Where*? In the let—"

Veronica looked heavenward. "I'm dealing with an idiot here. Where. Did. He. Ground. His. Ship? And don't tell me it's not in the letter." She pointed a finger at Robyn. "She announced confidently that you'd found the treasure. I'm only going to ask one more time. Where will we find the ship?"

"Off Florida's east coast," Robyn spat out.

"Nah, I don't think so. I have a feeling your story would change if we were to shoot your friend here." Veronica gestured to her goons, and both leveled their guns on Cal again.

"No, don't. I'm sorry."

"I don't like liars, Ms. Garcia."

Seconds ticked past in silence.

Eventually, Robyn said, "Professor, Gaspar wrote out the coordinates."

Mel stuck his nose back in the letter.

"I don't have all night," Veronica grumbled, and Mel rattled them off. "More like it. Now let's see where they take us, shall we?"

Matthew hated the "us" part.

Veronica pulled out her phone and pecked her fingertip to the screen. "Ah, Mexico is always a good idea. Pack your bags, kids." She made a motion with one of her hands, and one of her men made a call on a sat phone.

"We're not going anywhere with you," Matthew said firmly.

Veronica met his gaze and smiled. "But you are. You see, if you don't, I'll kill your father, then your friends, and will end with you. And I'll be sure to take my time with all of them and force you to watch."

"You fucking bitch!" he growled.

"Now, now, watch your language."

The wash of rotor blades thrummed in the distance and were making their way closer.

"It's your choice, Matthew. It's always your choice. So, what's it going to be?"

He wanted to kill her where she stood, but for now he had to comply with her wishes. "We'll cooperate."

"Very good." Veronica smiled and sauntered in the direction of the helicopter, which was coming in for a landing. Her goons stayed back, keeping their guns on them.

The first chance he had, he'd take her life— and take his time.

Forty

If that was Justin Scott who just called Colin, he was Santa Claus. Colin didn't know who it was claiming to be the private investigator, but he'd bet it was someone working for the Connors. The conversation took him nowhere, but Colin did feed "Justin" some information about the cases. Whomever it was on the phone would know that Mel Wolf was a suspect and possibly dangerous. Hopefully that would help Matthew Connor and his friends stay safe.

Colin heard back from U.S. Customs and Border Protection. The Canadian Trio and Mel Wolf had caught a charter to Málaga, Spain. There was no record of Veronica Vincent, Roman Murphy, or Oscar Vincent having left the country in recent days, not even the past month. Not that he bought that in his gut.

"Well, that's a big fat dead end," he told James.

There were still at the station. The last few hours had been pushing paperwork and making calls.

"You can't be surprised," James said. "Rich people like Veronica have money to break the rules." He bounced his pen against his desk, housing it between his index finger and thumb. "And I'm sure you thought of this, but rich people also have their own jets."

He hadn't thought of that, but he wasn't about to admit it to James.

"We just need to find out where she keeps it and see if it's in the country," James threw out nonchalantly.

Colin wasn't generous with his praise but... "You know sometimes—"

"I know. I impress even myself." James flashed a cocky grin and rubbed his chest.

"Well, Superman, make yourself busy and get on your suggestion."

"Aye-aye, captain."

"Don't you mean *argh*?" Colin asked, making a play on the pirate-and-treasure thing.

"Nope. I'm pretty sure I meant what I said." James lifted the phone receiver but didn't put it to his ear right away.

Colin said, "We just have to keep peeling back the layers if we're going to get to the bottom of this."

"Layers? Bottom? With that imagery, core

would technically work better."

"Just get on the phone." Colin smirked and looked at his computer. A lot of their day had been dedicated to talk of Mel Wolf. His means, motive, and opportunity for killing Professor Edwin. Two of the three seemed to give themselves up rather easily, but it was motive that was stumping Colin. What reason would he have for killing his colleague?

Earlier, he'd set up a conference call with the detective from Florida, and it was scheduled for fifteen minutes from now. He'd pass the time until then by calling the kid who'd found the dead professor and check something else off his list.

"Hello?" A meek-sounding woman answered the phone, and Colin wondered at first if he had the right number, but it was probably Gibbons's home where he lived with his mother.

"Mrs. Gibbons?" he took a stab.

"Who is this?"

Colin was impressed she hadn't confirmed her identity; most people did, and that made for a con man's paradise. "This is Colin Doyle. I'm looking to speak with Brent Gibbons."

"What do you want with Brent?"

"I'm afraid that's between me and him, ma'am." For the same reason he didn't give his title, he didn't want to lay out why he wanted to speak with Brent: both could scare her off the phone.

"Fine." That was followed by a soft clang as the receiver was set down on a table.

"Brent!" she screamed out in the background. "Phone!"

A few seconds later, a young man picked up. "Who is this?"

One heck of a greeting, Colin thought. "This is Detective Colin Doyle with the Metropolitan Police Department in Washington."

Time ticked off. Colin literally watched the second hand move on the wall clock.

"You there, Brent?" he prompted.

"You're from Washington?"

"Yeah, I just wanted to ask you about Professor—"

"I've been over what happened so many times... I just don't want to talk about it anymore."

"I can understand that. You were close with Professor Edwin?"

That met with a despondent, "Yeah."

"Well, I wasn't going to ask you about him."

"Okay," the student dragged out.

"I was going to ask about Professor Wolf. I expect you know him as well."

Radio silence.

"Brent, I'd just like to know—"

"It's not true what they're saying about him."

"And what's that?" Colin asked, though he

had a good idea.

"That he killed Professor Edwin. They say that's why he disappeared."

"He disappeared?" Colin would play dumb. He knew that Mel Wolf had come to Washington not long after the murder. He could admit that didn't look good, but there was still a strong niggling in his gut that pleaded the man's innocence.

"Yeah. So, did he go to Washington? Don't tell me you found him and he's—"

"No, I haven't." Colin wasn't going to make the kid say *dead*, but he was only telling it as he last knew it.

"That's good news, but why are you asking about Professor Wolf?"

"He *was* in Washington." Colin didn't want to disclose too much. "That's all I can say. But I'm hoping you have more you can tell me."

"I'll help however I can."

"Do you know why police think that Professor Wolf killed Professor Edwin?" Colin, of course, knew what the police in Florida had on him: the murder weapon. That wouldn't have necessarily reached Brent. And while theories and hypotheticals didn't always pan out, they had their place in any investigation.

"I can't think of any reason. Professor Wolf was an historian, with a quirky sense of humor, not that I found him funny. Professor Edwin seemed to get him, though. I saw them share lots of laughs."

"Did you see them together near the time of Professor Edwin's demise?" Colin thought that a friendlier word than *murder* or *death*.

"I did. That day apparently. At least that's what police tell me."

"They told you when you last saw them together?"

"No, not like they fed it to me. Just that, based on the time he died, I did see them both together earlier that day."

"Tell me about it."

Brent went on to tell him Professor Wolf came in more excited than he'd ever seen him and had beelined for Edwin.

"He found some diary," Brent began. "He was under the impression it belonged to some long-lost relative of a pirate."

"Did you catch the name?" Colin found himself asking and shook his head at the ridiculousness of the inquiry. Pirates. Treasure. Children's fairy tales.

"No, I didn't, but apparently he was mythical. Partially why Professor Wolf was so excited."

"And how did Professor Edwin react to Professor Wolf's excitement?" Colin was thinking maybe he hadn't shared the enthusiasm and that had somehow triggered Wolf into killing his colleague. But what a stretch.

"He was absorbed right into it, but Professor Wolf did something strange. He at first left the diary with Professor Edwin, asking him to date the diary. This was something Edwin loved to do, and he was good at it."

"But his job was an American history professor."

"Yes, but his passion was antique documents. Anyway, he was thrilled that Professor Wolf had entrusted the diary to him."

"He told you this?"

"Well, not in so many words, but I could tell. But Professor Wolf returned later in the day and took the diary back. He texted Professor Edwin to let him know, and he was extremely downhearted about the entire thing."

"Do you know why he took the diary back?"

"I don't.

"Well, thank you for your cooperation, Brent."

"You're welcome." Brent hung up.

An ancient diary from a pirate's long-lost relative was gelling with the overheard conversation at the diner. It also confirmed why Wolf had sought out Connor, a man who pretty much made his living discovering legends. There was another takeaway, though, and that was the kid's strong feeling that Wolf never would have killed Edwin.

Colin looked at the clock, and there was a minute until the phone conference. He nudged his head toward James, who was on the phone, and his partner held up a finger.

Seconds later, he hung up and followed Colin into a room where they'd have privacy to put Detective Howard Day on speaker. On the way, James filled him in on how he'd made out.

"I've confirmed that Veronica does indeed have her own jet. A few actually. And one of them did take off to Málaga, Spain, yesterday."

"Right on the others' tails."

"Yep."

"How many were on board?"

"Passengers? Five."

"Names?"

James smiled. "You should know better than to ask. It's a miracle I coerced what I did out of the clerk at U.S. Customs and Border Protection without a warrant."

"Then we get a warrant and get the names."

"I'll leave that to you to package for the judge to sign off on."

"You don't want to call your buddy, Judge Anderson?"

"I used up the favor he owed me."

Colin's phone rang then, and it was the Florida detective.

After brief greetings, Colin went right for it. "Not to step on any toes, Detective. You're there and I'm here, but I'm failing to see motive for Wolf to kill Edwin."

"Fail to see it or not, there's a Smith & Wesson M&P 9 recovered from his home that says he did it."

The same gun used by Roman Murphy in the fatal shooting of Judy Finch. Colin wasn't a believer in coincidence, and shooters always had a preference when it came to their weapons. "You've had it tested for prints? The casings too? Someone could have planted it at his place."

"I don't like the direction of this conversation or the implication that I'm some idiot who can't do his job."

"Not the intention."

"Sure seems like it is," Day said gruffly.

"I just want to know what makes a mild professor kill his colleague, a man he had a friendship with."

"I don't know, but as soon as I find him, you can be sure I'll be asking that question. And speaking of which, you let him slip through your fingers."

Colin took that hit on the chin. Let the Florida detective get out his frustration. "You can be certain if we get our hands on him again, you'll be the first to know."

"How kind."

"Besides the gun, what have you got against Wolf?"

"Against him personally? Nothing. Let's get that out. But there were text messages between Wolf and Edwin the day of his murder."

"And they said what?" Colin felt like he had to keep the inquiries going or the detective would just seal up altogether.

"Basically, Wolf told him he took back a diary—whatever he really meant by that, I don't know."

"Could be a literal diary."

"Yeah, or code for something."

Gibbons had probably told Day about the diary, but it seemed Day had dismissed it as inconsequential. "So, that's it? He took this diary—whatever it was—back?"

"Then Edwin responded that he was disappointed by that and could Wolf please reconsider. A few hours passed without Wolf texting anything back. Edwin messaged him again and begged him to come back with the diary. That he had some pages he'd scanned and wanted to share his thoughts. Wolf fired back immediately that he never said Edwin could copy the diary, at any time. Edwin apologized and told Wolf to meet him in his office at six o'clock. That's where the medical examiner put time of death, by the way. Between five and seven."

Then, by all means, slap on the cuffs! Day wasn't putting weight on the diary, but the texts seemed to influence him. "And who told you about the texts?"

"His phone. That was all left at the scene, as well as his ID, credit cards. The only thing that was nowhere to be found were these scans of a supposed diary. And, of course, Wolf himself."

"Brent the student...how does he fit in?"

"He found his professor, as I told you before. Tells me that Professor Wolf was always 'off' and had something against Edwin."

"Huh."

"What's that? *Huh*?"

Colin wasn't about to share the fact that he had a very different conversation with the student. "Nothing."

"Uh-huh."

"What did Brent say when you asked him about the texts and the tone of them?"

"Brent doesn't know anything about the text messages," Day said. "I wanted to approach his interview as impartially as possible. It was Brent who freaked out on scene. He pointed us in Wolf's direction right away."

"Interesting."

"Yeah. Now, if that will be all..."

"All for now."

The Florida detective disconnected.

"I'll be damned," Colin mumbled.

"What?" James asked.

"We need to look into this student more." Colin filled him in on how his call to the student went polar opposite to the conversation that Detective Day had just presented.

"And the student brought up the text messages to you," James said when Colin finished speaking. "He's playing some sort of game."

"If my years on the force tell me anything, he's guilty of far more than that." Colin met his partner's gaze. "He could be involved with the murder of his professor."

"And how does that tie in with Veronica Vincent, exactly?"

Colin let out the mother of all sighs. "I have no freaking clue."

Forty-One

It was starting to feel like they were time travelers. After all, their fourteen-hour flight left Spain about nine at night and landed in Cancun at four the next morning.

Matthew and the others caught what sleep they could, but now that they were all on the ground, if the others were like him, they were wide awake and alert. Veronica insisted on nestling as close to him as possible, and every time he shifted away from her, she managed to bridge the distance. She either didn't know just how much he despised her or didn't care; he'd guess the latter.

The group of them—him, Angelica, Cal, Robyn, Mel—and Veronica and her two goons were all loaded into a rental van and headed down the highway. Matthew was familiar with the road from Cancun to the Maya Rivera, as he'd been this way several times. Usually for fun.

He noted the fenced resorts situated like fortresses with their security towers manned by armed guards. He had no doubt marauders existed but summed it up having to do more with giving tourists the impression their resorts were safe.

The coordinates Mel had provided led them to a spot along the coast past Maya Rivera and out about twenty miles from shore.

On the plane, Matthew had listened as Veronica called ahead telling whoever was on the other end to be ready for them the minute they arrived.

Matthew watched as they passed the resort he'd stayed at the last time he was in Mexico. It didn't look like much from the road, but through the gate was a drunken tropical paradise. He could handle some of that relaxation now. Just being able to kick back, put his feet up, do a bunch of repetitive arm curls with a good, cold drink in his hand would be welcome respite.

"You must be getting excited," Veronica whispered in his ear, so close that he could feel her warm breath on his skin. They were in the back bench of the van, no doubt so she could know what was going on. Goon One drove and Goon Two sat in the first bench back from the front.

She grabbed Matthew's jaw, turned him to face her, and planted her mouth on his. She pulled back; her lips curled up in an angry rage. "Aw, why do you always fight our chemistry?"

The hairs on the back of his neck went up, and his body stiffened. There was a time he hadn't fought it, and he wished to hell he could go back and change that. He wasn't going to dignify her question with a response. All he did was blankly peer into her eyes.

"Fine. Have it your way. For now. But one day, you'll be begging for me, and I won't give you audience."

He leaned against the headrest and closed his eyes.

"Tsk. You're so mean." A definite whine to her voice. A petulant child not getting the attention she so badly craved.

He could feel her gaze on him, but he kept his eyes shut.

"Huh." She kicked back in her seat, miffed at him for ignoring her.

The rest of the drive passed in silence. As long as he pretended to ignore Veronica, she left him alone. Only when the vehicle stopped did he open his eyes, but just wide enough to make out the clock on the dash through the slits: *5:10*.

"All right. Up you get, sleeping beauty." Veronica poked his side with something sharp. His body instinctively jerked.

He opened his eyes fully to see she was smiling at him.

"At least I can get some sort of reaction from you."

He again stared at her with a blank expression. She held his gaze for a while before snuffing out, "Grr," then, "Get out!"

Robyn was the first to unload from the van, and Goon Two had her by the arm. The rest of them followed. The harbor was quiet this time of day, but a Mexican man was hurrying down the dock toward them.

"If any of you make one move to escape or do anything I don't like, I'll shoot you. If there are any eyewitnesses, I'll kill them, too. And everyone will have a burial at sea. Quite apt for our little adventure, I feel." She smirked, seemingly quite proud of herself.

"I have the ship ready for you, *Señorita*." He took his hat off and fanned himself with it.

The sun wasn't even up yet, but the air was warm.

"Very good, Jorge." Veronica gave him an alluring smile, toying with him, much the same way a cat batted around a mouse with its claws—and just as deadly.

The Mexican smiled, the balls of his cheeks round and flushed, then turned and told them to follow him. He seemed to be leading them toward a large yacht at the end slip.

"They work cheap and are so eager to please," Veronica purred, directing her words at Matthew.

He caught eyes with Angelica, and he wished she hadn't gotten roped into this. Even if that meant they never found the chest, the logbook, Josefa's grave. At least none of them would be here with Veronica and her ego. No discovery was worth that price.

They were routed onto the boat like cattle, prodded along by psychological threat, knowing that Veronica and her men were armed, and they were not. Ideally, they would have had an opening to make a move on Veronica and her men while on land, but with her threat hanging over them about more innocents being killed, it was too great a risk to take.

They watched as the ship set out, the dock getting smaller, before they were directed to the main deck where there was a grouping of chairs and an oversized couch. Matthew sat with his friends and Angelica on the latter, and Mel Wolf dropped into a chair.

Matthew found himself studying the man. His complexion was near white, and his gaze was unfixed. Either he was being forced to work with Veronica or he was stung from being exposed. Matthew wasn't sure which, but the man was avoiding eye contact.

The second he could confront the professor, he would, but now wasn't the time with Veronica's goons hanging back, guns in hand, looking for a good reason to squeeze their triggers. Veronica herself was off seeing to something. Maybe counting her riches in a stateroom somewhere or smooth-talking buyers and offering what she had yet to procure.

Another one of her character flaws. She bargained with what she didn't have.

Matthew matched his gaze with Cal's, and his friend shook his head. The situation was feeling impossible.

Veronica breezed into the area, a smile on her face, her eyes on Matthew. In her hands was the chest they'd obtained from the El Acebuchal Museum. His heart sank. They'd left it and everything else back at Angelica's house in Frigiliana.

"Where did you get that?" Angelica burst out.

"Ah, I seem to have gotten a reaction out of someone at least." Veronica walked over to Angelica. "I think you know exactly where I got it." She pierced Angelica with a glare.

"You broke into her house and stole it." Matthew tossed it out nonchalantly, as if Veronica wasn't getting to him, but his temper was boiling.

"Oh, I did better than that."

Angelica frowned.

Veronica pointed at her. "See, she knows what I'm going to say."

So did Matthew, but he sure hoped to hell he was wrong.

"I killed every single one of them."

"You bitch!" Angelica threw herself at Veronica. Her hands just brushed Veronica's neck when she fell to the deck, blood pooling from the bullet hole in the side of her head.

Matthew propelled to his feet.

"Oh," Veronica gasped then giggled. "Now I get a reaction." She caressed his cheek, and he batted her hand away. "Now, now, she didn't listen. In all fairness I said, 'nothing stupid.' Matthew, I did warn all of you."

The goon who had shot Angelica lowered his gun, a smug look of satisfaction smeared all over his face. The other goon high-fived him.

Matthew stood there, mere inches between him and the woman who had once been his lover. He couldn't feel more hate than he did right now. "She didn't deserve that," he hissed.

Veronica shrugged. "She didn't listen."

He wanted to put his hands around her neck and strangle her, watch the life fade from her eyes. His thumping heart was all he could hear, and his vision went red and pinpricked.

"Now, as I was saying before I was so rudely interrupted..." She strolled away from him.

Matthew watched after her, his mind too busy plotting her death to hear what she went on to say. He split his gaze between Veronica's back and poor, sweet Angelica. Her beautiful face now forever marred by the look of sheer terror.

"—you'll go down." Veronica snapped her fingers inches from his nose. "Did you hear me? Are you hard of hearing?"

He slowly lifted his gaze to meet hers but said nothing.

"You'll be going down, doing the scouting mission. See if the *Floridablanca* is where it's said to have come to rest."

"Whatever you want." Spoken like a robot. He refused to give her any more signs of emotion.

The rumble of the ship's engines lowered in volume, telling Matthew the captain was throttling down to a stop. Eventually, the engines were cut, and their noise disappeared altogether.

They'd made it to the destination. At least most of them had. His gaze fell to Angelica again, and a sharp pain stabbed him in the chest. His eyes filled with tears.

"Oh, please, you're acting like you were in love with the girl," Veronica said. "You only just met. There's no history like there is with you and me."

He looked her in the eye. "It's that history that will see me killing you before all is said and done."

"Ah, we'll see about that. Quite the brave words, if nothing else."

Jorge came toward Veronica. "There is something showing on the radar right under the boat about a hundred feet down."

"Marvelous. *Gracias.*" Veronica grinned at Matthew. "Come." She waved for him to follow.

One more look at Angelica's dead body and a glance at his friends told him he would be wise to comply.

The Mexican returned to the bridge, and Matthew went to the back of the boat, where two scuba suits were laid out with a pair of diving helmets.

"Put one set on," she directed him.

The asshole who had shot Angelica joined them.

"This is Hugo, one of my favorites."

Like I give a shit what his name is! Matthew got into his suit and started through the pre-diving safety checks.

"You don't trust me," she cooed.

He ignored her and carried on through the process. Checking the overinflate valve, the tank strap, the weighted belt, the tank itself, including the air valve.

"I'm ready to go," he said.

"Me too." Hugo the Asshole swapped out his gun for an underwater firearm. Since bullets didn't work in water, this invention used pressurized gas to fire spear-like bolts. Puncture the wrong spot, and a person could bleed out or, worse, become chum for sharks.

"Just in case you get out of line," Veronica said. "The suits also have markers in them, and we'll be watching from up here. So, no funny business."

"Wouldn't dream of it." The second he could make a move, he would. Without hesitation.

"You go first." Asshole motioned for Matthew to get in the water.

Matthew complied. Seconds behind him, Asshole joined him, and the two of them headed for the depth of a hundred feet. He checked the depth gauge, and they went down slowly. Each foot felt like he was getting farther away from Robyn and Cal—not just literally, but as if the situation was fast spiraling out of his control.

Matthew slowed for Asshole to come up on his right side. He wasn't comfortable with an underwater rifle on his six. There were enough potential complications with a dive in the first place.

At fifty feet down, large fish schooled in the distance, their silver scales reflecting in the beams of the light coming from his flashlight and Asshole's.

Veronica's reminder about watching them from the surface was never far from mind. Not that he could really make a move down here, anyway. Where would he go, and how would it affect his friends still on board the ship? No, he had to be smart and wait for the perfect time.

Sixty feet down.

Matthew kept kicking in an even rhythm, though his body was exhausted and begged for rest. More than just physically. Also mentally and emotionally. He'd just seen beautiful Angelica shot before his eyes. How could he ever erase that image?

Sixty-five feet.

"It should be over that way." Asshole's voice came through the speakers in Matthew's headset.

Matthew followed the direction of the man's pointing arm, and they headed farther down.

Seventy-five feet.

The deeper into the abyss they went, the darkness became suffocating. Pitch black, with nothing to see where their lights didn't touch. Not that it meant they were alone. Matthew was certain they had company, but no good would come from dwelling on that.

Ninety feet.

He perceived the hint of shadows and shapes in the space below them. Angled edges like rocks or a man-made structure.

"That's got to be it there." There was excitement in Asshole's voice, and Matthew's gaze traced to the man's hip, where his weapon was secured.

Ninety-eight feet.

Their light beams touched the surface of something. It was coated with barnacles, and crabs did their sideways dance. An eel swam through the water in a scurried attempt to get out of their way.

Ninety-nine feet.

Closer to the object now, Matthew could tell it was big, but it didn't look like a galleon.

"Boss, not sure if we have the right place," Asshole said through the comms, drawing the same conclusion.

"You're right on the mark according to radar," Veronica's voice came back.

"There's something here, but I don't think it's a ship."

"Don't think? Look closer, then talk to me."

"Yes, boss."

He and Matthew dove closer to the object. It wasn't a ship, but it was man-made.

"It's a shipping container," Asshole said.

"You're sure?"

"Yeah."

Veronica let out a string of expletives and told them to return to the surface. Going up would be more painful than it had been going down. They'd need to take it nice and slow or risk dying from the bends or decompression sickness.

Forty-Two

Robyn wished she could hear something, see something, *do* something. Anything to avoid sitting there, Angelica's dead body across from her. She squeezed away the tears that burned at the corners of her eyes, and mindlessly touched her busted lip from Veronica's blow.

Veronica stormed toward them, her heeled shoes clacking against the deck like staccato bolts of thunder. She headed straight for Mel and lifted him to his feet by the scruff of his neck.

Her gunman came closer, his gaze observant and studying the situation, poised to act.

"You gave me the wrong coordinates," Veronica slapped out like venom.

"I…I…"

Cal reached over for Robyn's hand and squeezed it. She glanced at him, but he wasn't looking at her. She just hoped he wasn't plotting something and was just simply offering his support.

"Don't lie to me. I'm not an idiot."

"I didn't." Mel gulped. "Back then…in older times, it was hard for them to triangulate latitude and longitude."

Veronica stepped aside, and her man cocked his gun in Mel's face.

"You sure you don't want to rethink that?"

"I'm telling you the truth." Mel glanced at Robyn. "The numbers could be off hundreds of miles."

"Hundreds of miles?" Veronica scoffed and turned to Robyn.

"He's right." Robyn stiffened. She hated this woman more than anything—or anyone. "We take for granted triangulating latitude and longitude, but it wasn't always easy."

Veronica slid her jaw side to side, chewing on Robyn's words.

"You believe me, or you don't," Robyn said curtly. "I don't give a shit."

"You will if I have my guy start shooting."

"I think you derive more pleasure in threatening life than taking it." Robyn jutted out her jaw, and Cal pulled back on her hand, a silent message to tone down her attitude.

"Grr," Veronica snarled and waved from her hired gun to Mel.

He roughhoused Mel, and something clattered to the deck.

Veronica picked up what had fallen and resumed full height, holding the skeleton key.

"Why do you have that?" Robyn couldn't keep the heat out of her voice. As far as she knew, they'd left it with the chest and everything else back at Angelica's safe house. The thought *safe* house ripped a hole in her heart. It hadn't proven too safe for Angelica's men.

"I found it," Mel mumbled. "I wanted to keep it. No matter what happened with the treasure. Whether we found it or not."

"Oh, we're going to find it," Veronica declared. "More like *you're* going to find it." She took the chest she'd sat on a nearby table before and shoved it toward Robyn. "I want to know everything that logbook says and that letter—it's in there, too. And don't even think about lying to me like the professor did. I won't be so understanding with you." She turned her back on Robyn, headed in the direction of the bridge, or so Robyn guessed.

She glanced from Mel to the hired gun, back to Mel. She'd been fighting her opinion of Mel from the beginning, but after Veronica said he was working with her…and the burner phone… and now the key. Any trust she'd started to feel toward the man hissed into nothingness. She'd only backed him up about the coordinates because she thought it would benefit her and her friends.

Robyn opened the chest and pulled out the sextant, chronometer, the logbook, and the letter from Josefa's grave.

She glanced up, feeling the thug's eyes on her, and confirmed the creeping sensation over her skin had happened for a reason. Another look at the hired gun, and he tossed his gaze up at the sky and all around like an idiot.

The logbook made for interesting reading, but she went to the letter. She read down until she reached the coordinates. She didn't have a perfect memory, but she could have sworn the numbers spelled out in front of her were different than the ones Mel had given Veronica.

She looked over at the professor, who was looking at her. Just when she'd written him off as more enemy than ally, he'd surprised her. His line about the coordinates being off by a hundred miles and his glancing at her had been his attempt to let her know he'd lied.

Conflicting emotions charged through her. He'd gambled with all their lives—something he had no right doing. But was it any different than what Matthew would have done if he thought it would bring him closer to discovering a legend?

Regardless, she'd keep a very close eye on the professor.

Forty-Three

Matthew watched the depth decrease on his gauge. As much as he wanted to be out of the water, his feet on solid ground, in some ways he wasn't in a hurry. He'd have to make a move once he got back on that boat if he and his friends were going to survive, and he had no idea what that move would be. He'd also have to contend with Veronica, who would be livid because things hadn't gone her way.

He glanced over at Asshole from time to time. He seemed like he was stuck in his own head. Maybe preparing for Veronica's wrath.

Only five more feet to the surface. The sunlight streamed through the water in ribbons, promising more hope than it could possibly deliver.

When they surfaced, no doubt Veronica would be there waiting, and probably the other thug, too. But if so, where would that leave Robyn, Cal, and the professor?

One more foot to go, and Matthew could feel the sun's heat reaching him through his wet suit. He still had no idea what he was going to do.

He and Asshole surfaced and took off their masks. Asshole started his climb onto the back of the ship first. Big mistake.

His underwater rifle was right in Matthew's face. Matthew yanked on it, but it didn't break free from the man's hip. Instead, it caused Asshole to lose his balance and fall backward into the water, landing on top of Matthew.

Matthew had caught a glimpse of Veronica just before going under. There hadn't been any sign of the second goon, but he'd surely come running now.

Matthew broke free and surfaced.

"Kill him!" Veronica screamed.

Matthew's entire vision became a wall of water. Asshole was holding him under. He thrashed and fought back and gained some leverage. He came up and pushed the man down. Huge bubbles surfaced, and Matthew positioned himself over the man's body, holding him under until the bubbles stopped and his body went lax.

Matthew took the firearm and pushed off from his opponent. The lifeless body rose to the surface.

Frenzied footfalls thumped across the ship's deck, and Veronica was standing there once again, this time with a pistol in hand, her arms swaying as she tried to home in on his form.

He lifted the underwater rifle, about to squeeze the trigger when he was pulled down from behind.

Asshole hadn't died. Matthew kicked fervently. His one hand was still on the weapon, but the other was free, and he was flailing it, hoping to gain some traction and to break free of the man's hold. But the goon was unworldly strong.

Matthew needed air. Now. Above him he could see the sun, appearing as a curvy yellow ball due to the ripples in the water. *Hope.* He had to carry on. The others were up there and counting on him. He had to believe that. He had to *hope*.

He stopped fighting and put his other hand on the weapon and angled it downward.

For Angelica! Matthew yelled in his head as he eased back on the trigger.

Asshole's eyes widened as the spear burrowed into his chest, but his grip tightened on Matthew's leg. It took effort to pry the man's fingers lose.

He hurried to the surface and came out gasping for air. He anticipated flying bullets. Instead, Veronica was the image of calm.

"You're going to suffer for this, Matthew, and so are your friends," she said.

She rolled a hand above her head, and the engines roared to life.

Oh shit!

"*Adiós*," he swore he heard her say over the boat's engines and the churning water in the propeller's wake.

He swam as hard as he could toward the boat, but it was pulling away from him with absolute ease. He stopped swimming and lifted the rifle. Veronica remained positioned at the back of the boat, watching and waving. Her gun now tucked away.

He pulled the trigger on the rifle, and in the next second, he heard her bone-chilling scream and watched her go down, crumpling to the deck like a marionette without a puppeteer.

"*Adiós*."

The sound of a fired gun was the last thing he heard as he surrendered to exhaustion. He could barely keep himself afloat any longer. He panted and lay on his back, still holding the rifle in one hand until his grip on it relaxed and it slowly slipped from his fingers to Davy Jones's Locker. Just before he closed his eyes, he thought he saw Robyn and Cal.

Forty-Four

Cal was shuffled with Robyn and Mel by the idiot with a gun to the stern of the boat where Veronica was screaming, "Kill him!" like some deranged lunatic. The man kept nudging Cal in the back and with every impact, Cal's temper went up a notch. Surely the hysterics were because Matthew had made a play and life wasn't going Veronica's way. And if Matthew could take a stand, so could he.

That realization ran through his head when the idiot had rounded them up. On his way, Cal had to go past the table with the chest. He didn't have time to consider what would make the best weapon but, on instinct, grabbed the sextant. He tucked the point of it into one of his pants pockets and supported the rest of it with a hand at his side.

They were almost around the main cabin of the boat and to the back when the engines started up and he heard Veronica shout out, "*Adiós.*"

He froze at the sight of Matthew in the water. His best friend wasn't in charge of the situation; he was being deserted.

"Should I shoot 'im?" the idiot asked Veronica.

"No." She smirked. "Let the sharks—"

Matthew raised his hands out of the water, a weapon in his hands.

Next thing, Veronica let out a wailing cry and hit the deck. Blood poured out around her prone form.

The man fired off a shot, and Cal watched in horror as Matthew became still—too still.

Cal pulled the sextant from his pocket and charged at the guy. He thrust the piece of metal in the back of his head, and the man howled and turned around. He put a hand to the wound, and his palm came back coated in blood. The man's eyes widened and went blank. He raised his gun on Cal.

Again, Cal lunged forward. Bringing the sextant down. This time striking the man in the forehead.

A bullet ejected from the gun. The sound of it was deafening, but in this moment, Cal felt invincible, and all he saw was the image of his friend in the water, possibly shot to death or bleeding out.

Robyn was screaming for Cal to watch himself. He pulled back his arm and brought the sextant down once more.

This time, a corner of it connected with one of the man's eyes and embedded there for a bit before falling out. The man shrieked and stopped fighting. He cupped his eye with one hand and kept touching his head with his other one. He gave one more look at Cal with his good eye and collapsed. His gun skittered across the deck.

Cal picked it up and kicked the side of the man's body with his foot. "I think he's dead." He stared at his chest and wasn't sure if he was imagining it or not, but his chest appeared to be moving. Cal lifted the gun and squeezed the trigger. There was no more movement.

He stared at the corpse, and it was like he was out-of-body, simply observing.

"Cal." Robyn's voice sounded like it was coming from the end of a long hallway.

His gaze went to Veronica. As long as she drew breath, she was a threat. She'd always be haunting them. And for all she'd put Sophie through… He felt himself going cold. Very cold. And dark.

He headed over to her. Robyn held out a hand to stay him. He took her hand and squeezed. "Get this boat turned around." His words came out calm, like he was slipping into a catatonic state.

She held his gaze and eventually nodded and headed for the bridge.

He resumed making his way to Veronica. As he closed the distance, he could hear her labored, raspy breathing and see her chest rising and falling, but in erratic movement. Blood seeped from the corners of her mouth.

The engines slowed, and the boat started turning around.

He glanced to where Matthew was still floating on the surface, and he prayed to a God he'd let go a long time ago. If only his friend could be okay… He didn't make a vow or promise in exchange for Matthew's life, but he would give anything, *do* anything.

Veronica was trying to move, her fingernails scraping the deck.

This was his chance. One bullet to end it. But it felt like an easy way out for such an evil person. She deserved to suffer, to bleed to death. It wouldn't come close to compensating for all the pain and loss she'd caused, but it would be a start.

"Karma's a real bitch," he said through clenched teeth. Karma was something Sophie had mentioned a lot. She thought he was only half listening when she'd get into that and her *feelings* or sixth sense. But he'd heard every word. He wished that he still had her around, prattling on about it.

Veronica's lips twitched, like she was trying to smile. Even dying, she was a psychopath. "You don't…" she rasped, and her voice cut out. "Have the…guts to…" She left the sentence unfinished when the boat's engines were cut. She turned her head toward the back of the boat.

Matthew was only six feet away from them, off the stern. *Good news. No sign of blood, so he has to be okay.* Has to be.

"Here," Cal said to Robyn, who had returned. He tried to hand her the gun, but she wouldn't take it. Tears beaded in her eyes, and she shook her head. He ended up tucking it into the back of his pants and jumped into the water.

"Matthew," he called out, but there was no response.

He swam out to his buddy, grabbed him under the shoulders, and hauled him toward the back of the boat where Robyn was watching on, standing over Veronica's dying form.

"Here, help me," Cal petitioned her.

Robyn reached out and grabbed onto Matthew, and between her and Cal, they got Matthew onto the back deck.

Robyn dropped beside him and pressed her fingers to his neck.

Cal watched on as she administered CPR, again feeling like he wasn't really there, like his movements and those around him were two-dimensional. He was in a self-contained universe of stillness.

Matthew coughed and spewed water. His eyes opened. Then rolled back and closed. His mouth curved into a smile.

He mumbled, "One hell of an adventure, but I want my money back."

Robyn and Cal smiled at each other and squeezed hands over Matthew's chest.

"Okay, what's going on with you two?"

Cal pulled his hand back as fast as Robyn did hers. "Nothing."

"Hmm. We'll talk later. Is she dead?" Matthew asked.

"Veronica?" Cal looked over at her and she was still hanging on. "Not yet."

Matthew struggled to turn onto his side.

"No," Robyn said, putting an arm out to discourage movement, "just rest."

"Nope." He rolled himself up to standing and went over to Veronica. "You killed innocent, beautiful people."

"No one…" Veronica coughed up blood, and it gurgled in her throat. "No…one's…innocent."

"Angelica didn't deserve to die," Matthew spat out. "But at least she took out two of your guys."

Veronica's eyes enlarged, and a tear fell down the side of her face. "She killed my—" Her hand moved at her side.

"She has a gun!" Matthew cried out.

Cal drew the gun from his waistband and pulled the trigger. The bullet found purchase between her eyes.

Everything went still. Silent.

A good while later, Matthew put his hand on Cal's shoulder. "You okay?"

"Ah, yeah." Cal licked his lips and nodded, but he wasn't able to take his eyes away from her dead form. She was gone, any threat she posed, over. In death, she was harmless. "Her *what*?" Cal croaked, keeping his eyes on Veronica's dead face. "Were one of those guys a relative or lover or—"

"Don't know."

"My God, can you imagine her having a brother or sister out there?" Cal looked at Matthew.

"Shit. I don't even want to think about it."

"Makes two of us."

"Three," Robyn interjected and stepped in front of them.

"Burial at sea," Cal said without feeling. "She seemed impressed by that idea."

"Wait. You're just going to throw them overboard?" Robyn gasped.

"We can't exactly dock in Mexico with two dead bodies on board," Matthew said. "You don't want to see the inside of a Mexican prison."

She bobbed her head side to side. "Yeah, I guess…"

"I wouldn't last in prison," Cal burst out.

"Ain't that the truth," Robyn said.

"You going to help?" Matthew asked her.

"Nope. I think you have it covered." She moved to the side.

"Okay. Have it your way." Matthew went to the top of Veronica's body and petitioned Cal. "I'll need your help."

Cal lifted her legs, and they hoisted Veronica's body over the back of the ship. It hit the water with a big splash. Next up was the hired gun's body. Two hundred twenty pounds of dead weight.

"Did you have to kill him quite so far away from the back of the ship?" Matthew shoved out through winces of effort.

"Are you being serious right now?"

Matthew was laughing, but Robyn was not. She had her arms crossed, and she was scowling.

He made a big splash, too.

When they turned around, they were facing Jorge and another Mexican man.

Oh shit. Don't tell me they're going to be a prob—

Both of them held up their arms in surrender. Their gazes cut to the water.

"We do as you tell us," Jorge's pal said in choppy English, directing his statement to Matthew.

"Just go back to the bridge. Keep us here."

"We need to talk, Matt," Robyn said.

Matthew looked around her. "Where's the professor?"

Cal looked down the ship and knew the answer. Beside a white storage container were a few life preservers. He lifted the lid on the bin. "Found him."

Mel cringed and worked to get his feet under him and out of the container.

Cal turned to walk back to where he had just been with Matthew and Robyn, and a sudden onset of nausea hit him. He bent in half, put his head between his legs.

"Cal." Robyn hurried toward him. She put a hand on his back.

"I'm fine… I'll be fin—" He burped and covered his mouth when vomit came rushing up his throat. He swallowed roughly.

"You're obviously not fine," Robyn said.

Cal struggled to straighten up. "I'm fine."

"You don't like dead bodies at the best of times," Matthew started. "You're sure you're fine?"

"I think so."

Robyn rubbed his back, and both of his friends made offers of being there for him if he needed to talk.

Cal just nodded.

"So, I guess we get them to turn the boat around and head home empty-handed." Matthew sighed.

"Well, not necessarily…" Robyn said, somehow managing to dangle promise amid their current nightmare.

"What do you mean?" Matthew asked.

"Why don't you talk to the professor here?" Robyn held a hand out toward Mel.

He was pale and kept licking his lips like he was feeling the urge to puke.

Cal barked at Mel, "Come on, what is it?"

"I gave that lady the wrong coordinates."

"You what?" Matthew gasped. "You… You… We got lucky there happened to be something down there—not the treasure—but you could have gotten us all killed."

Robyn put a hand on his arm. "But he didn't. We're all fine."

"We're not *all* fine." Matthew looked bruised by Robyn's comment.

"We're sorry about Angelica." Cal took a deep breath.

"We are," Robyn echoed. "But she didn't die because of Veronica having the wrong coordinates."

Cal shook his head. "I'm happy *that* bitch is dead."

Seconds of silence passed before Matthew said, "So, where do the correct coordinates lead?"

"I looked them up when I had them turn the boat around for you," Robyn said. "It's only about twenty-five miles from our current position."

"You miss by an inch, you miss by a mile," Matthew mumbled.

"What?" Cal asked.

"Nothing. It's a diving expression." Matthew danced his gaze over them.

Cal gave his vote. "I say, what the heck. Let's take a look."

Robyn splayed her hands open in front of herself. "We're pretty much already there."

Matthew seemed to consider their words, put his hands on his hips, and nodded. "Let's do it. We turn back now, Angelica, Pablo, her men, all their deaths would have been utterly meaningless. Let's go get that frickin' treasure and get home!"

"Argh!" Cal roared.

Forty-Five

Life looked so different to Matthew now. Somehow, there was a little light around the edges, like it glowed. He'd survived; his friends had survived. But there still was a bit of darkness that lingered on the outer ridges. More like shadows. Poor Angelica and Pablo—both of them didn't deserve to get caught up in this mess and die. Neither did Angelica's people. And they might be alive if Daniel hadn't crossed a line and had a contact employ her. On the flip of that, Matthew and his friends could have been killed in the El Acebuchal Museum—if they would have even gained access to the place.

He excused himself from his friends, found a satellite phone, and made a call that could no longer be avoided. "Daniel," he said when his call was answered.

"Matthew? Are you—"

"Angelica's not. Her brother's not. Her men aren't." There was anger in his heart toward the man he had come to consider a sort of father figure.

"I'm…" Daniel's voice disappeared.

"Don't tell me you don't know who Angelica is—*was*," he countered.

"I have a good idea, yes," Daniel stated solemnly.

"You should have left things alone. I don't need a babysitter, damn it!"

"Sir, I only did what I thought necessary—"

"No, you didn't think. And you spy on me?"

Daniel cleared his throat. "I answer first to your father, Matthew."

"That's becoming very clear. How did you find me?"

Daniel went quiet.

"Tell me," he insisted.

"Please know—"

"Yes, you answer to my father."

"After everything that took place with Veronica and—"

"Get to the point." Matthew didn't want a stream of platitudes.

"I'm sorry." Daniel sighed heavily. "I crossed a line." He paused there, and somehow it hurt Matthew too much to push him. He finally volunteered, "There's a GPS tracker in your watch."

"You… You—" He ripped the watch from his arm and threw it into the ocean.

"Your father was worried about you, and then with the police in Washington being interested in speaking with you— They reached his office, by the way. But when I found out that Veronica was behind everything, I did what I felt necessary."

"You reached out to a contact to hire Angelica."

"Yes, sir."

"Please stop calling me that." The address bristled in the vibrant light of knowing who Daniel really reported to. "And doing my father's bidding doesn't make this okay." It also hurt that not only was his privacy violated by a man he considered a friend, but by his own father. Like he wasn't capable of taking care of himself. Maybe it was time to get out from under his father's roof.

"I'm sorry that things happened the way they did with Angelica and her brother." Sincere, but the timing seemed to fill in an awkward period of silence.

"Veronica Vincent's dead," Matthew pushed out.

"Oh."

"Yeah." He wasn't about to go into detail.

"There is something you should know."

"What, Daniel?" he spat.

"It's about Mel Wolf."

"What about him?"

"He's wanted for the murder of Professor Edwin."

Matthew stared out into the distance at a seagull dancing in the air currents.

"You still there?"

"I am. Guess I can't say anything surprises me anymore." A bleak summation, but it was exactly how he felt. "I've got to go."

"Just watch your back."

Matthew ended the call and held his phone to his stomach. He loved Daniel, he loved his father, but it felt like something had broken between him and them. And now he had to handle Mel.

The boat's engines became a soft purr beneath him, and he set out to find the others where he'd left them, seated on the couch at the front of the boat.

Robyn met his gaze and blinked her eyes slowly as if she'd pieced everything together and was offering empathy.

"You killed Professor Edwin." Matthew hurled the accusation at Mel.

"I didn't," he croaked.

"That's not what the Naples police believe."

Mel trembled. "She…she…did it anyway."

"What are you talking about?" His patience was well past run out.

Mel licked his lips, briefly pinched his eyes shut. "She forced my cooperation. She said if I didn't find the treasure and get you on board, she'd have me framed for Edwin's murder." His gaze lowered to the deck. "Looks like she did that anyway."

"Her word meant shit." Matthew regarded the professor and weighed aspects of what he'd seen. Yes, the professor had deceived them at several points along the way. When it came down to it, though, he'd given Veronica the wrong coordinates.

"I'm sorry for all of it. I was a coward."

Matthew continued to think through all the steps that led to here, starting at the beginning. "If Veronica sent you to me, why the guy who grilled me at the Smithsonian?"

"I didn't want to involve any of you, but Veronica was adamant. I wanted to feel you out—your abilities, motivation, drive—for myself."

"And the chase through the streets?"

"A ruse that Veronica insisted happen. She said it would give you motivation you couldn't ignore."

That manipulative bitch!

Matthew clenched his fists. "A woman died because of that chase."

"Wh-what?" Mel stuttered.

"One of the rounds they fired went through the wall of an apartment building. Killed a woman in her bed."

Robyn gasped, causing Matthew to glance at her, but he put his gaze back on Mel. He wiped a tear from a cheek.

The engines died to nothing. One of the Mexican men hollered down that they were in position, and there was something the group might like to see on the radar.

Matthew and his friends, and Mel, wasted no time bounding up the stairs to the bridge.

Jorge was pointing at the screen. "Looks like a ship."

It most certainly did.

"We found it," Mel whispered and then grinned.

Matthew took a deep breath. "It's definitely a ship, anyway. How far down is it?" he inquired.

"Four hundred sixty-five feet."

"Far too deep to dive," Matthew said. He knew two hundred feet was the maximum for a technical diver.

"Not that you'd be in any shape, anyhow. You need some rest," Robyn said.

"I'll sleep when I'm dead."

"You *will* be dead if you don't rest." She raised her brows at him.

He didn't want to hear about limitations. He addressed Jorge. "Is there a submersible on this yacht? One that can be manned or unmanned even?" He was banking on Veronica's exuberant showiness to lend to her buying one.

"Yes, *señor*," he said. "I will show you."

"You're kidding me." Robyn followed behind Matthew and Jorge.

"There." Jorge took them to a manned submersible. It had four seats and extendible arms on the front. He'd been in one similar before, but it had been a few years. Hopefully, it would be like riding a bike.

Matthew smiled. "*Gracias.*"

Jorge dipped his head and returned to the bridge.

"This doesn't mean you can go down now," Robyn said.

"You really think you're going to stop me?" Matthew angled his head.

She scanned his eyes. "Fine, but I'm going with you."

"Me too," the professor said, apparently finding his sense of adventure.

Cal said, "I'll be here when you come back up. You know, to keep an eye on things."

"It will all be fine. Chicken." Matthew clucked and flapped his arms like they were wings, circling his friend.

"If it will shut you up."

Matthew stopped. "Worked like a charm."

"You know how to work this thing?" Robyn asked.

"Mostly. The rest I'll figure out as I go along."

"That sounds reassuring. The guy said it's four hundred sixty-five feet down. Can this thing go down that far?"

"It can probably dive over three times that. Trust me. You have nothing to worry about."

"Okay," Cal dragged out, not sounding convinced.

The four of them loaded through the top hatch, and Matthew grabbed the control tablet and put the pilot's headphones on. He sat in the front, Robyn next to him, and Cal and the professor squeezed in behind. Matthew shifted over and found himself right against the exterior wall, but something was between his thigh and the submersible. He contorted so that he could get into his pocket, had to practically lay the top part of his torso in Robyn's lap to do so, but pulled out the satellite phone.

"Didn't really need to bring this," he said as he sat it on his lap under the control tablet. He studied the display, refamiliarizing himself with the readings and controls. He powered the submersible.

"Ooh, this is getting real," Robyn hollered.

He looked over at her.

"What? I'm excited."

He laughed and started their descent. The more they went down, the more aware Matthew was of the fact the contraption was compressed and tight and… He tried to lift a hand to tug out on the scooped collar of his T-shirt but didn't have enough space to leverage the move.

His hands were sweaty on the tablet, and he could feel moisture beading on his brow.

"You okay over there?" Robyn asked.

"Nope." He licked at the top of his lip where sweat was dripping into his mouth.

She put a hand on his lap but must have sensed it was just one more infraction of his personal space he couldn't handle right now, and she withdrew it.

"Oh." This from Mel in the back seat.

Matthew looked up, and the submersible's lights were shining on what was left of a galleon, listed to her port side. Time and the elements— sea creatures and saltwater—had eaten away the masts and rusted the rigging system. Crustaceans and barnacles covered most of what was visible of the hull. The lower portion and the keel were buried in the sand.

Matthew rounded the front of the ship. The bow stem had snapped off and was no longer visible, probably also buried. As he rounded the bow, the gun ports were gaping holes with the heads of cannons poking out. They were covered in rust, and it was only from knowing what they were that they were identifiable. On the starboard were remnants of a single rowboat, but most of the wood had been eaten away.

A lone shark swam out of the inky darkness into the beams of the submersible, likely curious about them. But just as quickly as he'd appeared, he returned to the shadows.

With his eye back on the ship, Matthew marveled at the size. Even in a place such as here, where scale was hard to truly estimate, he guessed the submersible could have fit into the ship many times over.

"The *Floridablanca*," Mel said, sounding awestruck.

Matthew kept them moving forward slowly, inspecting every inch as he went along. It was truly fascinating to think of Gaspar on the seas, plundering and then celebrating with his crew. Then how he'd stolen the ship and set sail with the intention to sink her.

About two thirds down the starboard side, there was a hole in the hull that he thought they could fit through. "Should we go inside?" he asked.

"Do you need to question it?" Mel countered. "This is incredible. I can't believe we're here."

"Now that's reassuring," Cal said, but he must have inched forward more; Matthew could feel his friend's breath on the back of his neck.

Matthew swallowed roughly. Everyone was too close. It was too tight in here. Even still, he took them through the hole. There wasn't much to see but more crabs and lazy, shy eels that retreated into their homes at the intrusion.

Across from them on the port side, sand and sentiment had burst inside the hull through an opening, but it was undoubtedly a man-made hole.

"Gaspar scuttled the ship by causing an explosion on this side," the professor suggested. "Whether he set a long fuse on a drum of gunpowder or turned a cannon inward, I can't tell from this vantage point, but I'd wager on my first idea. It would give him time to get off the ship and to put space between himself and the boat as she sank."

"It must not have been too much of an explosion," Robyn said, "to leave this much ship."

"He just needed enough to make a hole so the ship would take on water," Mel said.

Matthew made the light beams brighter, and they illuminated the area that would have once been the staircase to the hold. But would they fit down the narrow passage?

He took them closer to get a better look. Time had decayed the wood and what would have likely been a rather tight walkway now yawned wide open. "Looks like we'll fit," he announced with excitement, but he was still feeling hesitant, and his claustrophobia was tightening its hold on him. He had to put out of his mind the fact that they were hundreds of feet beneath the water in what could become their tomb.

"You're taking us down there?" Cal voiced Matthew's own panic.

"Didn't come this far to turn around now." Matthew lowered them into the hold. "After all, if there's treasure to find, it will be down here."

"Oh." Robyn winced as the side of the submersible bumped against the confines of the space, but Matthew had the rig under control.

They made it down to the hold, and it was packed with items—but was it treasure?

Matthew operated the submersible's extendable arms and carefully fanned them over an area. Sediment rose and once the water cleared, chests, jewels, necklaces, chalices, coins, and kegs came into focus.

He let out a whoop, and all of them started laughing.

"We did it!" Robyn said.

Cal was shaking Matthew's shoulders.

Matthew maneuvered the submersible through the hold of the ship, and it was full of bounty. He was grinning despite his ratcheting claustrophobia and kept exploring.

"There must be millions' worth of treasure," Mel said. "In the late eighteenth century, precious jewels were often kept in kegs."

"You're telling us there's even more goodies in those?" Cal said. "I thought it was gunpowder or old rum."

"Sorry to disappoint." Mel laughed.

"No disappointment, I assure you. I'll be able to buy all the rum I want!"

There was silence for a moment as they reveled in what was before them. A dream come true, really. Finally, Mel gave voice to what they were all thinking. "This is just...*incredible.*"

"Is the entire hold full of Gaspar's plunders?" Robyn asked. "Go over there." She pointed to another section that was stacked high.

Matthew repeated the process with the arms, and more valuables were exposed.

"Yes!" Robyn cried out.

Matthew laughed with the others. All their efforts had paid off, but they couldn't make off with any of the items just yet. "I say we've seen enough for now."

The three of them let out a collective groan.

"We'll be back," Matthew said. "But we'll need to make plans to return for extraction. I need to sort out the legality of such a thing in this situation."

With the *Floridablanca* having been privately owned and it coming to rest in exclusive economic waters, Matthew thought it was most likely a case of finders keepers, but he didn't want to make a promise he couldn't keep. He'd have Daniel research that or look into it himself, which he was more inclined to do at this point.

Matthew took them up, and several minutes later, the submersible bobbed out of the water and bounced like a cork in the waves.

Matthew looked around. "Anyone see Veronica's yacht?"

"Ah…no," Robyn replied.

"Where's the ship?" The compact cabin squeezed in on him more. "Anyone see it?" But he didn't need confirmation of what his eyes and gut were telling him, and it made sense from the Mexicans' points of view. They saw them throw two bodies overboard, probably witnessed the murders. "They've abandoned us."

"I knew it," Cal kicked out. "I should have stayed on the ship."

"Who knows what would have happened then," Matthew said.

"So, what do we do now?" Cal asked. "Could we drive this thing back to land?"

Matthew considered their distance from shore. "We'd never make it. Usually these things have less than twenty hours of battery power and a top speed of three kilometers per hour."

"Or two miles," Mel said softly, stating the Imperial unit conversion.

"If you call Daniel, he'll get us out of this mess." Robyn pointed to the satellite phone in his lap.

"I'll get us out, thank you very much."

All he'd need to do was call information, get through to the Coast Guard. But he didn't exactly want to advertise their coordinates or explain why they were there or why they were in a submersible that belonged to Veronica Vincent. There'd be far more questions than he'd want to answer. "Shit," he muttered.

"Just call Daniel," Robyn pushed.

"Fine." He leaned over Robyn's lap and got the phone to his ear. The second he heard Daniel's voice, he wished to hell there was another option.

"Daniel, I know what I just told you a moment ago, but I need you to send help to my location."

Life really did have a warped sense of humor sometimes…

Forty-Six

First District Police Station, Washington, DC
Wednesday, 12:11 PM Local Time

Colin finally received news he could use, but it still left him wondering how. They'd been able to confirm that Veronica's jet had flown to Málaga, Spain, with five passengers on board. The names were fake, and nothing popped in the system. There were four men and one woman. Colin would bet his next paycheck the woman was Veronica. It was so frustrating knowing who had pulled the trigger that shot Judy and not being able to do anything about it. But maybe if he focused on things from another angle. And if he couldn't lay his hands on Roman Murphy, maybe he could get to his accomplice at the university.

"There has to be someone at Hodges in cahoots with this Veronica Vincent, someone who tipped her off about the diary and possible treasure," Colin said to his partner across from him.

James drew his feet from his desk and put them on the floor. "Someone desperate for a payday. Money is a strong motive. Want me to look into the student's finances? School can't be cheap."

"I did that already." Colin had done that not long after getting off the call with Detective Day. "Nothing indicates he had financial concerns or loans to pay off."

"Not even schooling?"

"Nope."

"Hmph." Colin sank into his chair. The word *money* repeating in his mind. It was the motive for a lot of things and most of them less than ideal. *Who has a need for money?* He concentrated on that thought, kicking it around a few times, before an idea struck him. "What about the school?"

James angled his head. "What about the school?"

"Well, universities always need money."

"Okay, what are you thinking?"

"Oh, I'm thinking so outside the box. But who else at the school could have known about this diary and Wolf's suspicions about it leading to treasure?"

"And how does Veronica Vincent get pulled into the mix?"

Colin pointed a finger at his partner. "Exactly. With a professor who's obviously interested in antique documents, I doubt his fascination stopped there, and I doubt his dabbling in antiquities was a secret from those around him. This diary probably wasn't the first thing of supposed value to pass through Edwin's hands. So, who else would know that?" Colin met his partner's gaze, and they both spoke at the same time.

"We know the student told you one thing and Detective Day another."

"Yeah, I wouldn't doubt he's in on the murder in some capacity, but I'm thinking even bigger. What about the dean of the university? He has to know what's going on in his school."

"I'll get the right to pull his financials," James offered.

"And I'll reach out to Detective Day with our suspicions. Maybe he'll pull the man in for questioning."

James nodded, and he lifted his phone receiver at the same time Colin did his.

Detective Day answered on the fourth ring, just when Colin was sure he was destined for voicemail. "Detective Doyle, to what do I owe—"

"We both have murders to solve, and connected ones at that. At least I'd stake money on it."

"Carry on."

"Have you spoken with the dean at the school?"

"Of course."

"And how did that go?"

"What do you mean, 'how did that go'? The man had lost a member of his faculty."

Colin explained to him their suspicions.

"You think the dean called in this Veronica Vincent and, as a result, Professor Edwin ate a bullet."

"Yeah." *Though I'd put it much more delicately.* "Was thinking maybe you could talk to him again, feel him out."

"I don't know why I'd do that when..." Day went silent.

"Hello? Are you still there?"

"I'm... Just a second."

Colin tapped a foot.

"I just received a message from the lab. Prints came back on the bullet casings in the gun found in Wolf's bedroom."

"And?" Colin shifted forward on his chair, and the thing clunked down.

"And it's a match in the system to a Roman Murphy."

"Ah, I see."

"I don't know why you sound like you're gloating."

"Let me tell you a little about a woman named Veronica Vincent..."

Forty-Seven

Two Weeks Later
The Connor Residence, Toronto, Canada
Wednesday, 3:15 PM Local Time

Matthew was happy to be back home, even if for now that meant being under his father's roof. But that wouldn't be for long. He'd already seen a condo in the heart of Toronto and fell in love immediately. His offer was in, but he had yet to speak with his father about it. Probably because as much as his moving out was overdue—and no matter the fact his father had been behind the violation of his privacy—he knew it would still shock and hurt him.

He and his friends returned from Mexico just under a week ago after taking a week to do "arm curls" at a resort. Research made it clear they had the full right to salvage the *Floridablanca* under the Law of Finds. This applied because, when Gasparilla had scuttled his ship, he, in effect, had abandoned it and was no longer its owner. Arrangements were underway to return, but it would take a bit to assemble a capable team together. After the treasure was recovered from Gasparilla's galleon, they'd have to appear in court to register and claim the find.

Matthew was sitting in the main living room with Robyn and Cal. The professor had flown home the day after the find, figuring it was best to face the Florida detective and clear his name. Thankfully, that wasn't hard. By the time he got there, the police had charged the dean of the university with accessory to murder times two—for Professor Edwin and the woman who had died in Washington. Matthew thought the latter charge might be harder to stick, but if it hadn't been for the dean's greed, then Veronica's men wouldn't have been chasing them through the streets and firing their weapons. It was probably bittersweet closure for the woman's husband and Edwin's family, as the man who had pulled the trigger in both cases—Roman Murphy, the giant thug—was dead.

Daniel entered the room with a tray of iced tea and distributed them. Usually food service fell to Lauren, their cook and housekeeper. "Here you go, sir," he said when he gave one to Matthew.

"Thanks." His relationship with Daniel would mend, but it would take time and reestablishment of trust.

Daniel dipped his head and went to leave the room.

Robyn took a sip of her iced tea. "I'm still working through the diary that Mel finished transcribing, but I finished reading Gaspar's logbook. Fascinating reading. But you'll never believe what I found stuck in the pages."

When they made it to Mexican shores, they found Veronica's ship abandoned, went on board, and gratefully found the chest, logbook, Gaspar's letter, his sextant, and his chronometer. They even got his tricorne and flag from her stateroom.

"At this point, I'd believe anything." Matthew put his feet up on the wood coffee table in front of him. Daniel must have heard his shoes hit from where he now was at the doorway. He shot him a correcting look—his father hated feet on the furniture. He was adamant that feet were to stay on the floor.

"What?" Cal blurted out. "Why must everything be so dramatic?"

Robyn chuckled but then in all seriousness said, "It was a letter from Lopez. He told how he'd come to find out that his friend Gaspar had been murdered."

"Murdered?" Matthew sat up straight.

"Always surrounds damn treasure, I tell you." Cal slurped his tea.

Robyn continued. "Lopez knew where Gaspar had set up his home, and when he went to visit, he found Gaspar's body. He said that Gaspar's abandoned crew had killed him."

"Well, in their defense, he did run off with the bounty they had a part in plundering." Cal lifted his glass in a toast gesture before taking another swig.

Matthew looked from him back to Robyn. "How did he know it was Gaspar's crew?"

"The manner in which Gaspar was killed." Her gaze shifted to Cal.

"What? I'm hardened now. No rookie here." He pressed his fingers to his chest.

Matthew laughed. At least Cal seemed to be doing fine, given what he'd had to do on Veronica's ship. But maybe it was too soon to tell. Traumatic things such as taking a life could come back and haunt a person later.

"His hands were burned to the bone. Gaspar would have bled out," Robyn said quickly. "It was a signature killing method for him."

"Na-huh. That's what Edward Low did to his captives," Cal corrected.

"His name was in Gasparilla's logbook."

"One of the most notorious pirates of all time."

"Gasparilla admired him."

"Well, regardless, the same thing can't be two people's signatures," Cal mumbled. "That would make Gasparilla a copycat."

Robyn shook her head. "Anyway, according to Lopez, Gaspar's body appeared to have been mutilated in various ways."

"He was tortured for information for the whereabouts of the booty," Matthew concluded.

"That's what Lopez thought," Robyn said. "Lopez said he buried Gaspar beside Josefa."

"We were right there," Matthew said.

"We were."

"Why do you guys sound so upset? We're talking about bones." Cal rolled a finger next to his ear to imply they were loco.

"There is something I'm curious about," Matthew started. "Does anything in his logbook or in the letter tell us how Gasparilla made it to shore after scuttling his ship?"

Robyn nodded. "He took one of the lifeboats and rowed into shore. From there, he bought passage across the Atlantic for Spain."

Before Matthew could say anything, his phone rang, and he cringed when he saw the caller ID. "Riley."

"Yikes," Robyn winced. "Wouldn't want to be you."

"I have a good excuse for being behind." He answered and listened as Riley set off into a small tirade, including how the police from Washington had reached out to him. *God, they were thorough.* When he stopped talking, Matthew said, "Don't worry. I'm fine."

"Then you have the chapters?"

"I don't have them."

Silence.

"I do, however, have the makings of another book."

"Can we finish this one first?"

"You have my word. It's my first priority. I'll be in touch in a couple of days with some chapters." Matthew ended the call.

"Someone sounds confident," Robyn said.

"Oh, I'm going to get it done. The world needs to know what we do, what we've done, the sacrifices we've made." His gaze went to Cal, and Cal's flicked to Robyn. Matthew dragged a pointed finger between his friends. "What's going on between you two? You've been strange since you fell in the river."

Robyn licked her lips. "It's nothing."

She and Cal fell into silent eye contact.

"It's just that…well, we almost died," Cal said. "Emotions were at a peak and—"

Matthew started laughing. "Are you serious right now? Are you trying to tell me that you two felt something for each other?"

Both of them went straight-faced.

"You—"

"Matthew." It was his father, and his voice was nothing short of a bellow.

"You guys might want to clear out."

"See you." Robyn jumped up.

Cal followed. "Call you later."

His father sat across from him. "What's this I hear about you putting in an offer on a condo?"

"I'd hoped to tell you myself." Just more evidence that his father had eyes and ears everywhere. "I think we both know it's time I move out, Dad." Not that he expected doing so would solve his father's habit of poking his nose in his business.

"You didn't even talk to me." His father stiffened.

"I don't know what you want me to say."

"This is about Daniel tracking you."

"A bit, yes." Matthew drew up and squared his shoulders.

His father seemed to consider his words. "I can't say I agree with everything that took place. Daniel did fill me in on the tracker in your watch, and I've had a talk with him." His father wrung his hands, and Matthew sat straighter.

"Are you going to fire him?" As mad as Matthew was at Daniel, he still had a soft spot for the Norwegian.

"You're not being serious," his father deadpanned. "That man is a valued employee."

Matthew was pretty sure Daniel was more than that to his father, but the man was too proud to admit it.

"Now, I guess we do both have our lives to live—and they're about as different as they can be," his father said. "I want us to still talk, though. Not all the time. I don't have time for all the chitchat, anyway. Just once in a while." His voice became gruff with emotion.

"You're my father. Of course, we'll stay in touch. We'll visit. I just can't have you worrying about me."

"I'll always worry about you, son."

The heartfelt admission tugged on Matthew's emotions and had his throat tightening. "Okay, fair enough. Maybe just hold back a bit on the surveillance."

"That's what I spoke to Daniel about, but have you stopped to consider where you might be now? If you'd even be alive if he hadn't stepped in?"

Matthew shifted his position. "You just said we both have lives to live. Now you're justifying a violation of my priv—"

"I want you to reach a ripe old age."

He wasn't sure whether to lash out at his father or not, but the smile on the man's lips stopped him from saying anything.

"A ripe old age *like me*," his father added.

He was extending an olive branch—in his own awkward way—and Matthew wanted to grab hold, but hesitated.

"Let's get some real drinks and toast to your new adventure," his father said. "Daniel!"

His father was a hard man to figure out. On one hand, he didn't love the quests Matthew went on, and on the other, he supported them.

Daniel came in with two rocks glasses, a couple fingers' worth of amber liquid in each. His father must have called ahead and requested them on his commute from the office.

When he and his father had a glass, his father raised his in a toast. "To a smoother adventure than the last one you just had."

From his lips to God's ears…

Acknowledgments

When an author gets to write a story and pretty much use full creative license, it's a fun time! The fact that there's nothing in the history books to prove the existence of the pirate Gasparilla made it more appealing to write this story. Though I must admit I wonder how a mythical person can have a named ship and a person who did exist talk about him. Maybe José Gaspar was just John Gómez's creation and the story morphed larger through people over time, but whatever the case, I hope you enjoyed my take on the pirate's life.

If you've ever traveled to El Acebuchal, you might call me out on the museum there. I didn't find any evidence that one exists but took creative license there as well. But isn't the escape into another world, imagined or partially imagined, one major appeal of fiction? I believe so.

Congratulations to Lawrence Wolf, who won the chance to name a character in this book. I hope you loved your namesake Mel Wolf.

I'd also like to make a shout-out to my amazing husband and best friend, George, who helps keep me grounded when I feel overwhelmed with edits and deadlines. I love writing and the writing process, but I've never been one to love the clock! Thank you, George!

Also, thank you to my amazing editor for helping me polish this manuscript.

Catch the next book in the Matthew Connor Adventure Series!

Sign up at the weblink listed below
to be notified when new Matthew Connor
titles are available for pre-order:

CarolynArnold.net/MCUpdates

By joining this newsletter, you will also receive
exclusive first looks at the following:

Updates pertaining to upcoming releases in the
series, such as cover reveals, book descriptions,
and firm release dates

Sneak peeks of teasers and special content

Receive insights giving you an inside look at
Carolyn's research and creative process

There is no getting around it: reviews are important and so is word of mouth.

With all the books on the market today, readers need to know what's worth their time and what's not. This is where you come into play.

If you enjoyed *The Legend of Gasparilla and His Treasure*, please help others find it by posting a brief, honest review on the retailer site where you purchased this book and recommend it to family and friends.

Also, Carolyn loves to hear from her readers, and you can reach her at Carolyn@CarolynArnold. net.

Upon receipt of your e-mail, you will be added to her newsletter mailing unless you express your desire otherwise.

Keep on reading for a sample of *Eleven*, book 1in the Brandon Fisher FBI series.

One

Nothing in the twenty weeks at Quantico had prepared me for this.

A crime scene investigator, who had identified himself as Earl Royster when we'd first arrived, addressed my boss, FBI Supervisory Special Agent Jack Harper, "All of the victims were buried—" He held up a finger, his eyes squeezed shut, and he sneezed. "Sorry 'bout that. My allergies don't like it down here. They were all buried the same way."

This was my first case with the FBI Behavioral Analysis Unit, and it had brought me and the three other members of my team to Salt Lick, Kentucky. The discovery was made this morning, and we were briefed and flown in from Quantico to the Louisville field office where we picked up a couple of SUVs. We drove from there and arrived in Salt Lick at about four in the afternoon.

We were in an underground bunker illuminated by portable lights brought in by the local investigative team. The space was eleven feet beneath the cellar of a house that was the size of a mobile trailer. We stood in a central hub from which four tunnels spread out like a root system. The space was fifteen feet by seven and a half feet and six and a half feet tall.

The walls were packed dirt, and an electrical cord ran along the ceiling and down the tunnels with pigtail light fixtures dangling every few feet. The bulbs cut into the height of the tunnels by eight inches.

I pulled on my shirt collar wishing for a smaller frame than my six foot two inches. As it was, the three of us could have reached out and touched each other if we were so inclined. The tunnels were even narrower at three feet wide.

"It's believed each victim had the same cuts inflicted," Royster began, "although most of the remains are skeletal, so it's not as easy to know for sure, but based on burial method alone, this guy obviously adhered to some sort of ritual. The most recent victim is only a few years old and was preserved by the soil. The oldest remains are estimated to date back twenty-five to thirty years. Bingham moved in twenty-six years ago."

Lance Bingham was the property owner, age sixty-two, and was currently serving three to five years in a correctional facility for killing two cows and assaulting a neighbor. If he had moved in twenty-six years ago, that would put

Bingham at thirty-six years old at the time. The statistical age for a serial killer to start out is early to mid-thirties.

The CSI continued to relay more information about how the tunnels branched out in various directions, likely extending beneath a neighboring cornfield, and the ends came to bulbous tips, like subterranean cul-de-sacs.

"There are eleven rooms and only ten bodies," Jack summarized with impatience and pulled a cigarette out of a shirt pocket. He didn't light up, but his mouth was clamped down on it as if it were a lifeline.

Royster's gaze went from the cigarette to Jack's eyes. "Yes. There's one tunnel that leads to a dead end, and there's one empty grave."

Jack turned to me. "What do you make of it?" he asked, the cigarette bobbing on his lips as he spoke.

Everyone looked at me expectantly. "Of the empty grave?" I squeaked out.

Jack squinted and removed the cigarette from his mouth. "That and the latest victim."

"Well…" My collar felt tighter, and I cleared my throat, then continued. "Bingham had been in prison for the last three years. The elaborate tunnel system he had going would have taken years to plan and dig, and it would have taken a lot of strength. My guess would be that Bingham wasn't working alone. He had help and, after he went to prison, someone followed in his footsteps."

Jack perched the unlit smoke back between his lips. "Hmm."

I wasn't sure how to read *Hmm*, but the way his gaze scrutinized me, I was thinking he wasn't necessarily impressed.

"Anyway, you'll want to see it for yourself." Royster gestured down one of the tunnels and took a step toward it. "I know I haven't seen anything like—" Royster didn't catch his sneeze in time, and snot sprayed through the air.

Ick. I stepped back.

More sniffles. "Again, sorry 'bout that. Anyway, this way."

Jack motioned for me to follow behind Royster, ahead of him.

I took a deep breath, anticipating the tight quarters of the tunnel.

Sweat dripped down my back, and I pulled on my collar again.

"Go ahead, Kid," Jack directed.

He'd adopted the pet name for me from the moment we'd met, and I wished he'd just call me by my name.

Both Jack and the CSI were watching me.

The CSI said, "We'll look at the most recent victim first. Now, as you know, the victims alternated male and female. The tenth victim was female so we believe the next is going to be—"

"Let me guess, male," Jack interrupted him.

"Yeah." Royster took off down the third tunnel that fed off from the bottom right of the hub.

I followed behind him, tracing the walls with my hands. My heart palpitated. I ducked to miss the bulbs just as I knew I'd have to and worked at focusing on the positive. Above ground, the humidity sucked air from the lungs; in the tunnels, the air was cool but still suffocating.

I counted my paces—five, six. The further we went, the heavier my chest became, making the next breath less taken for granted.

Despite my extreme discomfort, this was my first case, and I had to be strong. The rumor was you either survived Jack and the two years of probationary service and became a certified special agent or your next job would be security detail at a mall.

Five more paces and we entered an offshoot from the main tunnel. According to Royster, three burial chambers were in this tunnel. He described these as branches on a tree. Each branch came off the main trunk for the length of about ten feet and ended in a circular space of about eleven feet in diameter. The idea of more space seemed welcoming until we reached it.

A circular grave took up most of the space and was a couple of feet deep. Chicken wire rimmed the grave to help it retain its shape. With her wrists and ankles tied to metal stakes, her arms and legs formed the human equivalent of a star.

As her body had dried from decomposition, the constraints had kept her positioned in the manner the killer had intended.

"And what made them dig?" Jack asked the CSI.

Jack was searching for specifics. We knew Bingham had entrusted his financials to his sister, but when she passed away a year ago, the back taxes had built up, and the county had come to reclaim the property.

Royster answered, "X marked the spot." Neither Jack nor I displayed any amusement. The CSI continued. "He etched into the dirt, probably with a stick."

"Why assume a stick?" Jack asked the question, and it resulted in an awkward silence.

My eyes settled on the body of the female who was estimated to be in her early twenties. It's not that I had an aversion to a dead body, but looking at her made my stomach toss. She still had flesh on her bones. As the CSI had said, *Preserved by the soil.*

Her torso had eleven incisions. They were marked in the linear way to keep count. Two sets of four vertical cuts with one diagonal slash through each of them. The eleventh cut was the largest and was above the belly button.

"You realize the number eleven is believed to be a sign of purity?" Zach's voice seemed to strike me from thin air, and my chest compressed further, knowing another person was going to share the limited space.

Zachery Miles was a member of our team, but unlike Jack's reputation, Zach's hadn't preceded him. Any information I had, I'd gathered from his file that showed a flawless service record and the IQ of a genius. It also disclosed that he was thirty-seven, eight years older than I was.

Jack stuck the cigarette he had been sucking on back into his shirt pocket. "Purity, huh?"

I looked down at the body of the woman in the shallow grave beside me. Nothing seemed too pure about any of this.

"I'm going to go," Royster excused himself.

"That's if you really dig into the numerology and spiritualistic meaning of the number," Zachery said, disregarding the CSI entirely.

Jack stretched his neck side to side and looked at me. "I hate it when he gets into that shit." He pointed a bony index finger at me. "Don't let me catch you talking about it either."

I just nodded. I felt I had just been admonished as if I were his child—not that he needed to zero in on me like that. Sure, I believed in the existence of God and angels, despite the evil in the world, but I didn't have any avid interest in the unseen.

Zachery continued, "The primary understanding is the number one is that of new beginnings and purity. This is emphasized with the existence of two ones."

My eyes scanned Zachery's face. While his intelligence scoring revealed a genius, physically, he was of average looks. If anything, he was slightly taller than Jack and I, probably coming in at about six foot four. His hair was dark and trimmed short. He had a high brow line and brown eyes.

"Zachery here reads something once—" Jack tapped his head "—it's there."

JACK AND I SPENT THE **next few hours making** our way to every room where Jack insisted on standing beside all the bodies. He studied each of them carefully, even if only part of their remains had been uncovered. I'd pass him glances, but he seemed oblivious to my presence. We ended up back beside the most recent victim where we stayed for twenty minutes, not moving, not talking, just standing.

I understood what he saw. There was a different feel to this room, nothing quantifiable, but it was discernible. The killer had a lot to say. He was organized and immaculate. He was precise and disciplined. He acted with a purpose, and, like most killers, he had a message to relay. We were looking for a controlled, highly intelligent unsub.

The intestines had been removed from nine of the victims, but Harold Jones, the coroner—who also came backed with a doctorate unlike most of his profession—wouldn't conclude it as the cause of death before conducting more tests. The last victim's intestines were intact, and, even though the cause of death needed confirmation, the talk that permeated the corridors of the bunker was that the men who did this were scary sons of bitches.

Zachery entered the room. "I find it fascinating he would bury his victims in circular graves."

Fascinating?

I looked up at Jack, and he flicked his lighter.

He held out his hands as if to say he wouldn't light up inside the burial chamber. His craving was getting desperate, though, which meant he'd be getting cranky. He said, "Continue, Zachery, by all means. The kid wants to hear."

"By combining both the number eleven and the circle, it makes me think of the coinherence symbol. Even the way the victims are laid out."

"Elaborate," Jack directed.

"It's a circle which combines a total of eleven inner points to complete it. As eleven means purity, so the coinherence symbol is related to religious traditions—at minimum thirteen, but some people can discern more, and each symbol is understood in different ways. The circle itself stands for completion and can symbolize eternity."

I cocked my head to the side. Zachery noticed.

"We have a skeptic here, Jack."

Jack faced me and spoke with the unlit cigarette having resumed its perch between his lips. "What do you make of it?"

Is this a trap? "You want to know what I think?"

"By all means, Slingshot."

There it was, the other dreaded nickname, no doubt his way of reminding me that I didn't score perfectly on handguns at the academy. "Makes me think of the medical symbol. Maybe our guy has a background in medicine. It could explain the incisions being deep enough to inflict pain but not deep enough to cause them to bleed out. It would explain how he managed to take out their intestines."

Was this what I signed up for?

"Hmm," Jack mumbled. Zachery remained silent. Seconds later, Jack said, "You're assuming they didn't bleed out. Continue."

"The murders happened over a period of time. This one—" I gestured to the woman, and for a moment, realized how this job transformed the life of a person into an object "—she's recent. Bingham's been in prison for about three years now."

Jack flicked the lighter again. "So you're saying he had an apprentice?"

Zachery's lips lifted upward, and his eyes read, *Like* Star Wars.

I got it. I was the youngest on the team, twenty-nine this August, next month, and I was the new guy, but I didn't make it through four years of university studying mechanics and endure twenty weeks of the academy, coming out at the top of the class, to be treated like a child. "Not like an apprentice."

"Like what then—"

"Jack, the sheriff wants to speak with you." Paige Dawson, another member of our team, came into the burial chamber. She had come to Quantico from the New York field office claiming she wanted out of the big city. I met her when she was an instructor at the FBI Academy.

I pulled on my collar. Four of us were in here now. Dust caused me to cough and warranted a judgmental glare from Jack.

"How did you make out with the guy who discovered everything?"

"He's clean. I mean we had his background already, and he lives up to it. I really don't think he's involved at all."

Jack nodded and left the room.

I turned to Zachery. "I think he hates me."

"If he hated you, you'd know it." Zachery followed behind Jack.

Two

S alt Lick, Kentucky was right in the middle of nowhere and had a population shy of three hundred and fifty. Just as the town's name implied, underground mineral deposits were the craving of livestock, and due to this, it had originally attracted farmers to the area. I was surprised the village was large enough to boast a Journey's End Lodge and a Frosty Freeze.

I stepped into the main hub to see Jack in a heated conversation with Sheriff Harris. From an earlier meeting with him, I knew he covered all of Bath County which included three municipalities and a combined population of about twelve thousand.

"Ah, I'm doing the best I can, Agent, but, um, we've never seen the likes of this before." A born and raised Kentucky man, the sheriff was in his mid-fifties, had a bald head and carried about an extra sixty pounds that came to rest on his front. Both of his hands were braced on his hips, a stance of confidence, but the flicking up and down of his right index finger gave his insecurities away.

"It has nothing to do with what you've seen before, Sheriff. What matters is catching the unsub."

"Well, the property owner is in p-pri-prison," the Kentucky accent broke through.

"The bodies date back two to three decades with the newest one being within the last few years."

Harris's face brightened a reddish hue as he took a deep breath and exhaled loud enough to be heard.

Jack had the ability to make a lot of people nervous. His dark hair, which was dusted with silver at the sideburns, gave him a look of distinction, but deeply-etched creases in his face exposed his trying past.

Harris shook his head. "So much violence, and it's tourist season 'round here." Harris paused. His eyes said, *You city folks wouldn't understand.* "Cave Run Lake is manmade but set in the middle of nature. People love coming here to get away. Word gets out about this, there go the tourists."

"Ten people have been murdered, and you're worried about tourists?"

"Course not, but—"

"It sounds like you were."

"Then you misunderstood, Agent. Besides, the counties around here are peaceful, law-abidin' citizens."

"Churchgoers?" Zachery came up from a tunnel.

"Well, ah, I wouldn't necessarily say that. There are probably about thirty churches or so throughout the county, and right here in Salt Lick there are three."

"That's quite a few considering the population here."

"S'pose so."

"Sheriff." A deputy came up to the group of them and pulled up his pants.

"Yes, White."

The deputy's face was the shade of his name. "The in-investigators found somethin' you should see." He passed glances among all of us.

Jack held out a hand as if to say, *By all means.*

We followed the deputy up the ramp that led to the cellar. With each step taking me closer to the surface, my chest allowed for more satisfying breaths. Jack glanced over at me. I guessed he was wondering if I was going to make it.

"This way, sir."

The deputy spoke from the front of the line, as he kept moving. His boots hit the wooden stairs that joined the cellar to the first floor.

I inhaled deeply as I came through the opening into the confined space Bingham had at one time called home. Sunlight made its way through tattered sheets that served as curtains, even though the time of day was now seven, and the sun would be sinking in the sky.

The deputy led us to Bingham's bedroom where there were two CSIs. I heard footsteps behind me: Paige. She smiled at me, but it quickly faded.

"They found it in the closet," the deputy said, pointing our focus in its direction.

The investigators moved aside, exposing an empty space. A shelf that ran the width of the closet sat perched at a forty-five-degree angle. The inside had been painted white at one time but now resembled an antiqued paint pattern the modern age went for. It was what I saw when my eyes followed the walls to the floor that held more interest.

Jack stepped in front of me; Zachery came up behind him and gave me a look that said, *Pull up the rear, Pending.* Pending being the nickname Zach had saddled me with to remind me of my twenty-four-month probationary period—as if I'd forget.

"We found it when we noticed the loose floorboard," one of the CSIs said. He held a clipboard wedged between an arm and his chest. The other hand held a pen which he clicked repeatedly. Jack looked at it, and the man stopped. The CSI went on. "Really, it's what's inside that's, well, what nightmares are made of."

I didn't know the man. In fact, I had never seen him before, but the reflection in his eyes told me he had witnessed something that even paled the gruesome find in the bunkers.

"You first, Kid." Jack stepped back.

Floorboards were hinged back and exposed a hole about two and a half feet square. My stomach tossed thinking of the CSI's words, *what nightmares are made of.*

"Come on, Brandon. I'll follow behind you." Paige's soft voice of encouragement was accompanied by a strategically placed hand on my right shoulder.

I glanced at her. I could do this. *God, I hated small spaces.* But I had wanted to be an FBI special agent and, well, that wish had been granted. Maybe the saying, *Be careful what you wish for, it might come true,* held merit.

I hunched over and looked into the hole. A wooden ladder went down at least twenty feet. The space below was lit.

Maybe if I just took it one step at a time.

"What are you waiting for, Pending?" Zachery taunted me. I didn't look at him but picked up on the amusement in his voice.

I took a deep breath and lowered myself down.

Jack never said a word, but I could feel his energy. He didn't think I was ready for this, but I would prove him wrong—somehow. The claustrophobia I had experienced in the underground passageways was nothing compared to the anxiety squeezing my chest now. At least the tunnels were the width of three feet. Here, four sides of packed earth hugged me, as if a substantial inhale would expand me to the confines of the space.

"I'm coming." Again, Paige's soft voice had a way of soothing me despite the tight quarters threatening to take my last breath and smother me alive.

I looked up. Paige's face filled the opening, and her red wavy hair framed her face. The vision was replaced by the bottom of her shoes.

I continued my descent, one rung at a time, slowly, methodically. I tried to place myself somewhere else, but no images came despite my best efforts to conjure them—and what did I have waiting for me at the bottom? *What nightmares are made of.*

Minutes passed before my shoes reached the soil. I took a deep breath when I realized the height down here was about seven feet and looked around. The room was about five by five, and there was a doorway at the backside.

One pigtail fixture with a light bulb dangled from an electrical wire. It must have fed to the same circuit as the underground passageways and been connected to the power generator as it cast dim light, creating darkened shadows in the corners.

I looked up the ladder. Paige was about halfway down. There was movement behind her, and it was likely Jack and Zachery following behind her.

"You're almost there," I coached them.

By the time the rest of the team made it to the bottom, along with the deputy and a CSI, I had my breathing and my nerves under control.

Paige was the first to head around the bend in the wall.

"The sheriff is going to stay up there an' take care of things." The deputy pointed in the direction Paige went. "What they found is in here."

Jack and Zachery had already headed around the bend. I followed.

Inside the room, Paige raised her hand to cover her mouth. It dropped when she noticed us.

A stainless steel table measuring ten feet by three feet was placed against the back wall. A commercial meat grinder sat on the table. Everything was pristine, and light from a bulb reflected off the surfaces.

To the left of the table was a chest freezer, plain white, one owned by the average consumer. I had one similar, but it was the smaller version because it was only Deb and me.

My stomach tossed thinking about the contents of this one. Paige's feet were planted to where she had first entered the room. Zachery's eyes fixed on Jack, who moved toward the freezer and, with a gloved hand, opened the lid.

Paige gasped, and Jack turned to face her. Disappointment was manifested in the way his eyes narrowed. "It's empty." Jack patted his shirt pocket again.

"If you're thinking we found people's remains in there, we haven't," the CSI said, "but tests have shown positive for human blood."

"So he chopped up his victim's intestines? Put them in the freezer? But where are they?" Paige wrapped her arms around her torso and bent over to look into the opening of the grinder.

"There are many cultures, the Korowai tribe of Papua New Guinea, for example, who have been reported to practice cannibalism even in this modern day," Zachery said. "It can also be involved in religious rituals."

Maybe my eyes should have been fixed on the freezer, on the horror that transpired underground in Salt Lick of Bath County, Kentucky. Instead, I found my training allowing me to focus, analyze, and be objective. In order to benefit the investigation, it would demand these three things, and I wouldn't disappoint. My attention was on the size of the table, the size of the meat grinder, and the size of the freezer. "Anyone think to ask how this all got down here in the first place?"

All five of them faced me.

"The opening down here is only, what, two feet square at the most? Now maybe the meat grinder would fit down, hoisted on a rope, but the table and the freezer? No way."

"What are you saying, Slingshot?"

My eyes darted to Jack's. "I'm saying there has to be another way in." I addressed the CSI, "Did you look for any other hidden passageways? I mean the guy obviously had a thing for them."

"We didn't find anything."

"Well, that doesn't make sense. Where are the burial sites in relation to here?"

"It would be that way." Zachery pointed at the freezer.

We connected eyes, and both of us moved toward it. It slid easily. As we shoved it to the side, it revealed an opening behind it. I looked down into it. Another light bulb spawned eerie shadows. I rose to full height. This find should at least garner some praise from Jack Harper.

"Nothing like Hogan's Alley is it, Kid?"

Also available from
International Bestselling Author
Carolyn Arnold

ELEVEN

Book 1 in the Brandon Fisher FBI series

Eleven Rooms. Ten Bodies. One Empty Grave.

In this international bestseller, rookie FBI Agent Brandon Fisher takes on his first case with the Behavioral Analysis Unit, but will he survive long enough to catch the killer? *Eleven* is a fast-paced, spine-tingling thriller that will have you gasping for breath at every twist…

When Brandon Fisher joined the FBI Behavioral Analysis Unit, he knew he'd come up against psychopaths, sociopaths, pathological liars, and more. But when his first case takes him and the team to Salt Lick, Kentucky, to hunt down a ritualistic serial killer, he learns what nightmares are truly made of.

Beneath a residential property, local law enforcement discovered an underground bunker with circular graves that house the remains of ten victims. But that's not all: there's an empty eleventh grave, just waiting for a corpse. The killing clearly hasn't come to an end yet, and with the property owner already behind bars, Brandon is certain there's an apprentice who roams free.

As the FBI follows the evidence across the United States, Brandon starts to struggle with the deranged nature of his job description. And if the case itself isn't going to be enough to push Brandon over the edge, he's working in the shadow of Supervisory Special Agent Jack Harper, who expects nothing short of perfection from his team. To make matters even worse, it seems Brandon has become the target of a psychotic serial killer who wants to make him—or his wife—victim number eleven.

Available from popular book retailers or at CarolynArnold.net

CAROLYN ARNOLD is an international bestselling and award-winning author, as well as a speaker, teacher, and inspirational mentor. She has four continuing fiction series—Detective Madison Knight, Brandon Fisher FBI, McKinley Mysteries, and Matthew Connor Adventures—and has written nearly thirty books. Her genre diversity offers her readers everything from cozy to hard-boiled mysteries, and thrillers to action adventures.

Both her female detective and FBI profiler series have been praised by those in law enforcement as being accurate and entertaining, leading her to adopt the trademark: POLICE PROCEDURALS RESPECTED BY LAW ENFORCEMENT™.

Carolyn was born in a small town and enjoys spending time outdoors, but she also loves the lights of a big city. Grounded by her roots and lifted by her dreams, her overactive imagination insists that she tell her stories. Her intention is to touch the hearts of millions with her books, to entertain, inspire, and empower.

She currently lives near London, Ontario with her husband and beagles and is a member of Crime Writers of Canada and Sisters in Crime.

CONNECT ONLINE
CarolynArnold.net
Facebook.com/AuthorCarolynArnold
Twitter.com/Carolyn_Arnold

And don't forget to sign up for her newsletter for up-to-date information on release and special offers at
CarolynArnold.net/Newsletters.